The Life & Times of a Full Figured
Fashionista

Written by Dominique Ali

Edited by Dominique Ali & Mayra Valer

© 2015 Dominique Ali

Dedication

I dedicate this book to women, who were counted out due to their size, and who are made to feel to feel as though we are not entitled to one of life's basic wants; happiness.

I wrote this book for all the full-figured women, who are more than the curves of our hips and fullness of our lips. We are entrepreneurs, visionaries, moguls, and the shapers of industry growth. Some may say we have no place in the world, I say the world has no place without us.

Acknowledgements

This book started as an idea, it quickly morphed into characters, scenes, and situations; which I thought would be relatable. This book isn't just a work of fiction; it contains elements of real-life circumstances with a healthy dose of fashion (which is its own character) to give you a sense of each character's emotional state of mind as you follow them in their lives.

The creation of this book would not have been possible without the help, love, and support of my family and friends who encouraged me every step of the way. Especially my husband, children, mother, and brother, who passed out flyers, listened to me rant, and continued to see my potential when I was blind to it. I also want to extend a special thanks to Mayra Valer, who helped me edit, gave me expert advice, and encouraged me.

My final push to pursue my dream came from someone who asked me on a simple question from a job I had worked for years, "What are you still doing here?" Long before I knew what I was capable of they knew, but they weren't alone. On my path to becoming a writer/blogger, I've met people in the full figure/fashion industry who have continued to inspire me through their own achievements and milestones. Each piece of knowledge they've given me I held close, and to the reader; thank you for supporting my dream. Without you, I couldn't do this.

Thank You All for your support! I love and appreciate each one of you more than acknowledgements can ever express; may Gods love be with you.

Chloe

I just can't believe this! At 24 I thought I had the perfect life, or at least something that resembled one. No! Instead I'm jobless, homeless, would be fashionista/writer struggling to carry three heavy suitcases up a six story walk up, and lucky me I'm going to the top. By watching me kill myself lugging suitcases, you wouldn't think I was a college graduate from the Fashion Institute. Just last week I was living in a nice condo with my boyfriend Malik. But that too was a complete bust when last night he told me we were growing apart, he met someone, and how he noticed that I've gained some weight making him become less attracted to me. It wasn't like I was a size six when we met, but admittedly I gained some weight. I mean, I should have known something was up when he stopped coming home for nights on end, and then it got harder and harder to get him on the phone. Not too long after, the sex went from all night long to non-existent.

Last night me and my best friend Dominique went to a club opening in the East Village, everyone who was anyone was there;

which was great for me because it gave me the chance to make some industry connections, and it helps my boyfriend is a club promoter opened the door a little wider. When we got in, which wasn't a problem because we knew every bouncer in the City; we went straight to the bar.

Dominique was in her element that night. The true definition of a party girl she definitely is, Dee is a tall, slim/curvy, brown skin beauty that changed her hairstyle as often as she did men; if you knew Dee, that was often. We were at the bar all of two minutes when a guy offered to buy her a drink. Yes, buy her a drink, not me. This has happened too many times to count, but I'm not angry, I just ignore it and look the other way.

Unlike Dee, I'm short, round (more like chubby) and I've been told I have an outstanding personality. God, I hate when people say that to me. It's like gee, so there's nothing else about me that can be attractive… Thanks! So anyway, while they were talking at the bar I decided to get some breathing space, I don't enjoy being the third wheel. That's when I saw him. At first I wasn't sure it was him, then I recognized the watch he wore on his right wrist; it shown whenever the club lights hit it. It was the one I bought him for his birthday two months earlier; it was a Bellenier watch that took me months, extra writing jobs, moonlighting as a bartender in Chelsea, and borrowing money from Dee that caught my eye. I thought he was coming to my rescue, when I saw him turn the other direction. I thought he saw me but if he did why did he try to leave? I wanted to yell for him, but the music was too loud and I knew he wouldn't have heard me. So, I walked as fast as I could with six-inch heels, which were a size and a half too small, which I got from a sample sale in the Meat-Packing District.

Pushing my way through the crowd, I saw him go for the exit with some skinny girl who was wearing a long black weave, and a barely there mini dress, with last year's Prima shoes on. I couldn't make out who she was or where they were going, so I followed. When I made it outside, I saw both of them jump in a cab. I couldn't chase them in a cab, not with my feet aching from the shoes. So, I did the next best thing. I called his ass over, and over, and over again; he never answered. Then it got to the point when he shut his phone off, and I couldn't leave anymore nasty messages on his voice mail because the mailbox was full.

I left the party and told Dee that I felt like my period was coming so she wouldn't question me why I wanted to leave as soon after we got there. Truth is, I wanted to see if he would go to our (his) condo with this girl. When I got there, the place was empty. The only clothes tossed around were mine that I left when getting ready for the club. So I waited, and waited, and waited some more until I was too tired to be angry. I went through every likely scenario in my head of what happened. Maybe he didn't see me? Maybe that chick was a client? Where did they go? Is his cell back on? Damn! No, the voice mail still picks up! Maybe he can explain himself? Then I thought to myself while finishing the last glass of Vodka, "He better damn well have a reason he's not answering this phone." Then I got one.

He strolled in about a quarter to eight, with his shirt unbuttoned, with a tired look on his face like he was up all night. Right then is when I knew it was over. It suddenly made sense, the late nights, the odd behavior, everything just came together flooding my brain at once. He couldn't even look me in the face. The smell of him hit me before he could even come into the living room, the smell of cheap perfume; expensive alcohol, and the musk of sex. And as he went into why he doesn't want to be with me, all I could think is '*my god, I don't know what I'm going to do about this? Maybe if I lost some weight? Or if I tried to be more understanding to his needs.*' But it was all in vain. Through the thoughts echoing in my head, I heard him say, 'I need you to move out!' Immediately I started thinking of where I could go; back to my parents in New Jersey? Hell no! Stay with my sister China? No, she has a rotating door of men coming through her house; I can't deal with that.

Finally, I said defeated. "Can we work it out, I love you. I know we can get through this, and if you just tell me what to do, I promise I'll do it." You know all the things a woman would say to keep her man.

He said. "No, Chloe. I can't do this. This has been happening for a while. I... I... I'm sorry. Look, you don't have to leave right away. I'll give you till the end of the week to find a new place. I'll be at my friend's house till then."

"A friend's house; what friend? Larry, Rashaad, Chris, who?" I asked.

"It doesn't matter!" He said. "Just get your stuff and leave. And don't even think about trashing my stuff because I'll make you pay for every dime! I'm being generous as it is letting you stay for a week, don't push me to do something you might regret."

After that exchange, he got some clothes and left without so much as a goodbye or a look my way. I immediately dashed to the phone to call Dominique and tell her what happened. I couldn't help but let the tears flow as I told her everything. Within an hour she was at the condo helping me pack what I could to bring to her house. As I turned to leave, I couldn't help but remember the good times Malik and I had. The first time we kissed... the first time we made love. The way he made me feel while he pressed against me; all those memories we made and the future I thought we had is gone, and so was I. With a last look, and the closing of the door, it was all over.

So, here I am; at my friend's apartment, trying to figure out my next move. Dee seems excited that we were going to be living together, but I know this is not the circumstances she wanted it on. So, what's next for me? I'll tell you, having a heart attack on these stairs, that's what! As I struggled to get through the door of Dee's apartment all I could do is collapse on the floor and sob as if someone had died. The truth is someone died, me. I had put so much into the relationship I had with Malik that I left nothing left for myself. Walking through the door of yet someone else's apartment made me realize how much I didn't have. A few minutes after I had a mini breakdown as Dee came through the door with a few more bags. Seeing me like this was not a pretty sight; so like any best friend she fell to the floor, held me, and let me cry until I had no more tears left.

Hours turned into days and still I got no call from Malik, not a sorry; how are you? Nothing... For days all I could do was analyze every aspect of our relationship, just to come up with nothing. I felt so empty... Finally Dee talked me into going out to a club I use to bartend at on the lower west side; we went, and it was a lot of the same crowd that Malik hangs with. I felt like everyone was staring at me and gossiping. My insecurity couldn't take it anymore; I had to leave.

So I waited until Dominique found some dude from Brooklyn to chill with and I pulled a disappearing act on her, I didn't mean to leave my girl without telling her; but everything is too new and raw for me to just throw myself to the sharks. In the cab ride home, I looked out the window at the city and thought of the possibilities just out the door. It's time to get my life on track and figure out what business I'm going to throw myself into. What's my business? Great question, I don't exactly have one yet; but I'm working on it. In the meantime, I'm just going to enjoy my life, even with the possibility of being alone as part of the deal.

Dominique

I can't wait till tonight, me and my girl are going to kill them. I just have to stop at one more store and then get my hair done and I will be ready to get this night started; TAXI!! Walking up these stairs is a killer. One of these days I've got to move into my parent's brownstone downtown, but that would be against my principals. Just because they've got money doesn't mean that I've got to live their life, it just means I'll spend it when I want to. My apartment is small, but it's the right size for me, and it keeps me honest and low key. Oh shit! What's today? Damn! It's Friday, time for my weekly call to the folks.

"Hi mom, where's dad? At the office, I thought he was on vacation? Yes... Yes... I know. I can't this weekend mom; I have too much to do. No, I don't have a job yet... Or a fiancée. Mom, that's my other line... I got to go! Love you!"

I couldn't wait to get to this club opening tonight, I might just find the man I'm looking for or the man of the night, whichever comes first. Chloe and I walked into the club and instantly I'm home. As soon as we got to the bar, I had to order a drink.

"Chloe, do you see the men in here tonight? Oh, I think I'm going to have to get my shopping list now. Look at all the different merchandise." I said.

Chloe said, "yeah, girl. It's a lot of cuties in here."

So there we were, laughing, when this guy walked up and offered to buy us a drink; I was a game he looked like a magnificent prospect to play with later. While me and this guy talked, I found out his name was Grip, a new up-and-coming artist, and he was going to be showcasing his mix tape that night at the club; asked me to dance.

I noticed Chloe walked off into the crowd, so I assumed that she met up with some cutie. God knows that she needs to get away from Malik. I've been trying to get her to let him go for a year now. He's no good for her, he's too flirty and dismissive of her. My girl deserves so much better than a part-time man. Anyway, I'm enjoying myself with this cute Grip. He's saying all the right things to making my kitty purr, or maybe it was the alcohol, either way we are going to get it in. And the way his body is feeling, I can't wait to get out of this club. A few minutes later my girl tells me she has to leave because she feels her period coming. I began thinking, "yeah right, my homie is about to loosen up."

"Sure girl, call me in the morning." I said.

"Ok, I'll see you later." Chloe said.

Grip and I danced it up all night long, and later on we finished up at the hotel. We went to some spot close to the club; I was not about to take him to my spot; I mean, I barely knew this dude. Anyway, we were up in there and we kissing, licking, sucking, tasting; you know about to get it in real proper.

We get in the bed, and ol' boy put it down like he was about to go to jail the next day. The only thing I could hear was the grunting, panting, moaning, heavy breathing, and the cheap bed squeaking. When I woke up my hair twisted and matted to my head, that I couldn't focus on my cell phone ringing on the floor. I picked it up and looked around for Grip and he was on the floor passed out; the bed was too small for both of us to fit, so I guess he fell in the middle of the night.

I struggled out a "Hello?"

"Dee, it's me... He left me! I Can't..."

"Wait a minute!" I said. "Who is this?"

"It's Chloe... Malik left me for someone else! Dee, I don't know what I'm going to do without him! I love him! Tell me what to do!"

That's when it hit me. Now I know why she left the club early. All I could say was,

"What the hell happened? Did he hit you?"

"No," Chloe said. "He told me he's leaving, and he was going to give me a week to find somewhere to go!"

"Ok, I'm coming over right now! I'll call you when I get close!" I assured.

I put the phone down and dashed across the room, looking for my stuff. As I was putting my bra on, Grip woke up to ask me where I was going. I told him something came up, and a friend needs me. When I said something came up; he moved the sheet from his body and showed me something really came up.

As much as I hate to leave a man with a hard dick, I had to go; my girl needed me. So, I gave him my cell number and left. About 45 minutes later I got to Chloe's apartment, I didn't have to knock on the door; it was already open. When I walked in, it looked like a crime scene. I didn't know whether to leave or call the police.

I found Chloe in the living room staring out the window; no doubt blaming herself for the shit that just went down. She was that kind of person; never saw the bad in people, just the sober representative they showed her on the outside. I didn't know what to do or say, so I just hugged her as tight as I could.

Jayshawn

It's a beautiful New York morning, I can't wait to get to the office and get started on the next round of promotions. I wonder if Makayla is there; I hope so, cause I'm sick of that girl being late. Before I start a long day of phone calls, e-mails, and chasing vendors I've got to stop and get a coffee. As I walked into my favorite neighborhood café I saw someone familiar, but a little out of place. He had on club clothes at 8:30 in the morning, stunk like liquor, and look like he got in a fight. I could have kept it moving, but curiosity got the best of me; I had to see why my competition was in my part of town when he didn't live around here. As I approached him he looked like he didn't see me, so I yelled his name.

"YO! WHAT'S UP MALIK?" I said.

"Ugh... nothing man... What you doing here?" Malik said.

"Man, I live around the corner and you know my office is up the street. What, you were coming to see me for a job? I knew you were going to get tired of that nickel and dime thing, promoting small clubs and low budget rap acts, eventually. Talk to me, man." I said.

"Very funny, I'm just getting some coffee on the way home." He said.

"Oh well, ugh, tell Chloe I said hi…" and before I could finish the sentence he was out the door. I guess some people don't have any manners. That's probably why he can't step into the big time. Still, scrapping for clients and promoting would be models and rappers.

Anyway, five minutes later I was in my office ready for whatever the day would bring when I noticed Makayla wasn't at her desk. I called out to her when my phone started ringing. It was Leon Gathers, owner of Rampage, a club I am trying to promote. I would have picked it up, but it was way too early in the morning to argue with him over the DJ, music, or anything else he could come up with. If he wasn't paying me top dollar to deal with him, I would have turned him down the moment he approached me at the opening of another club. Besides, I have more pressing matters to tend to; like 1. Who am I bringing to his club opening in two weeks, 2. Make sure the talent is on time, 3. Book my trip to Atlanta, and 4. Find out where the hell Makayla is!

Oh, it's been a day too damn long. Makayla finally strolled in at 10:00 claiming she missed her train, but knowing her what she missed was her baller. When I hired her, I was under the impression that she was a hard worker, and would be a major asset to me. But what she turned out to be was a liability. Don't get me wrong, the girl does wonderful work when she works, but it's clear that she's just biding her time until she can cash in on some dude up and coming and ready to spend on her. Too bad she's a baddie.

Makayla is about 5'9', brown skin, almond-shaped eyes, long legs that lead to a plump ass, and she always has herself put together. I've never seen her without her makeup on, hair done, and clothes hugging all the right places. I would have gone there with her but; I can't sleep in her face and work with her in the morning like nothing happened. That whole scenario would not play out well, not even for me. Oh well, time to call it a day,

"Makayla, Whatever you're doing, wrap it up, I'm about to leave!" I said.

"Ok Jay," she said. "I'm sorry I was late this morning; let me make it up to you. Let's go to get a drink, my treat; you work hard enough I can pick this one up."

"No, that's ok, I need to keep my focus." I said.

"Oh, well, I can help you with that." She said, while letting her tongue linger a little longer on her lip than usual. "I've been told I'm excellent at helping someone stay focused. Do you mind if I help you, I mean that is my job as your assistant; to help you focus all your attention in the right place?" She said.

"Yeah… No, I can take it from here Makayla; thank you." I said as I turned to lock the door to my office.

The elevator ride is awkward; it was like I had an angel on one shoulder and the devil on the other. The angel was like, *'you doing the right thing don't mix business with pleasure. She's not what you're looking for.'* Then the devil made himself known.

"Stupid!" said the devil. *"You could have been tearing that hot box up right now all over your desk, floor, and bathroom. Any Which Way You Can get her! Look at her man, I bet you she waxes… probably have a butterfly tattoo on her ass, can you imagine that butterfly flapping its wings for you!"* He Stated.

I mistakenly said yeah out loud, but thankfully she didn't hear me. Then the devil went on to say, *'Look at those nice little taste me titties, I bet she got silver dollar nipples!'*

Then the angel chimed in, I guess he couldn't take the devil's comments anymore and said, *'Yeah, that ish right there looks like it might taste like strawberries.'* Then he looks at me and said as he gave the devil a pound, *'you fucked up pimp!'* and disappeared.

She was standing outside of the elevator by the time I realized we reached the lobby floor, staring at me; her face looked like she just watched some kind of psychotic episode play itself out in the elevator. I pulled myself together and stepped out like nothing happened. When we reached the sidewalk, she asked again if she could take me out for a drink; I declined her again and walked away as fast as I could before I changed my mind. I was almost sprinting home to pour myself a shot of Tequila and take an ice-cold shower.

Chloe

I've been staying at Dee's house for too long without a plan. Malik has passed through my mind these last few weeks, but I've got to be honest, it's become less and less. My primary focus is finding a steady job, it's been cool staying here with Dee; but I can't rely on her to take care of me. She doesn't really take care of herself, her parents pay her bills; my parents can barely pay their own mortgage, I know for a fact that they can't help me. So, while Dee is out, I think I should go across town to cafe Mario, grab a newspaper and an espresso, and rummage through the want ads. Something has to be in there for a fashion grad/bartender/writer, which is now recently homeless, and manless. I wonder if they have a section for that; Maybe not.

Walking down the street, there is a calm in the air. That's a rare if ever occurrence in the city. As I walked through the neighborhood and watched the people; I became bothered by the passersby. Life continued to occur even when I was so wounded by it. Birds still flew, cars still drove by, and people were still a buzz in the street. And I silently wondered to myself if I could just pick up and move on. Do I want to? I'm not the person to just lie down and die, but I am so hurt that I'm afraid if I move the pain will get worse.

Finally, I made it to the café and grabbed a table against the wall by the window where the light was good. As I unfolded my paper, the server came by and took my order. I looked out the window at the passing crowds and thought… *my god, I never thought I would be here, but I got to do what I got to do… What's first on the list?*

I know how long I was staring out that window, because by the time I looked up there was a sexy man sitting across from me, smiling in my face like he won the lotto. I was a little startled when I realized it was JayShawn. Damn, he looked good. The things we could do to each other. Oh, wait a minute, I've been single a few days and already lusting after the first dude to smile in my face. Typical Chloe, he probably just wants to make sure I didn't kill myself or something like that.

GREAT!! That's all I need; a sympathy speech from one of Malik's friends, Wonderful!! My day keeps getting better! I know what the first order of business is now; it's being single for a while until I can get my head together. No jumping into relationships, bed buddies, or internet/speed dating. It's time to concentrate on Chloe Major, and absolutely no one else! But ok, I can at least be civil to Jay, he's always been nice to me, I can't be mad at him.

"Are you going to say hi to me? Or are you just going to continue to stare at me like I'm a clown?" I said.

"Oh, well, I'm fine just staring at you. I mean, I've been doing that for a few minutes now and you didn't seem to mind. I guess whatever is out that window is more interesting than seeing an old friend." JayShawn said.

I couldn't help but smile; I always did that when JayShawn was in the room. "No, it's not; hi! How are you doing, Jay?" I said as I stood up to give him a hug.

"I'm doing good, girl! What are you doing in my area? I didn't know you came here?" Jay said.

"I just needed to get a way… I used to come here a while back when I got my first writing job, well… I thought it was a writing job, it was just getting the coffee and the bagels. But no one else really comes on this side of town much, so I knew I could breathe here and not worry about seeing Malik or any of his friends. Oops! Sorry Jay, I didn't mean you." I said.

"Hey its cool, I know you love me!" He said as he laughed. "But what do you mean, not worry about seeing Malik? Aren't the two of you living together?"

So he didn't know, I thought to myself. I didn't know whether to be relived or upset. "No, not anymore… we broke up. No, that's a lie; he broke up with me." I said. "I haven't seen or heard from him since, so I moved out and right now I'm staying with my friend Dominique. You remember her, right?"

"Yeah, I know her. That's crazy because I saw him the other morning, and he said nothing. But now I know why. I'm sorry, Chloe, I didn't know." JayShawn said.

"It's ok, I'm fine. I just need to get a job, a place to live, and stay away from men for a while, you know? Clear my head and start over." I said, only it sounded good, but it felt like a lie.

"Um hum… Well, I was on my way to my office and I always stop here for coffee, and I noticed you sitting there staring. Well, I'm sorry I disturbed you, I'll let you get back to your thoughts."

"Ok." I said. Truth was I wasn't ready for him to leave yet but I know he had a life to get back to, and I had one to start so I watched him get his coffee and turn to leave when he stopped.

"Chloe, do you want to…. uh, well have lunch with me today?"

"Yeah, that's sound good. What time should I meet you?" I asked.

"You won't have to meet me because we will already be together." Jay suggested.

"What?" I questioned.

"Let's go somewhere and talk. And then grab lunch after." He concluded.

"I thought you had to work, I don't want to keep you from your job. Look, you don't have to do this; I'm fine, I really don't want your pity." I pushed.

"What are you talking about, pity? Can't two friends catch up? It's not about Malik, I promise. And it ain't any pity either." He said.

Surprised by JayShawn's reaction, I said, "I'm sorry; it's just that… It's kind of what I expected from people. I didn't mean to offend you."

"It's cool." Jay said. "I'm sure everything is still fresh and you need to sort it out, that's why I'm here. So come on and let's go girl before you change your mind."

We left the café and walk the streets in silence. I didn't feel the need to talk right away, it just felt good to walk next to someone and not talk, but know that someone is there; I felt comfort in that. He didn't ask me questions or try to make me laugh, he just allowed me to be silent until I was ready to speak. While we were wondering, we stumbled on a small dog park, so we sat down to enjoy the scenery.

"I always wanted a Yorkie, they're so cute." I said.

"A Yorkie?" Questioned Jay, "no, I want a man's dog like a Doberman, or a Pit bull; something like that." He Chuckled. "So, do you feel like telling me what happened with Malik?" he asked.

"Truth is, I don't know what happened. I thought we were good, you know? Things weren't perfect, but I halfway expected him to be honest with me. After all this time, I was just discarded like I held no meaning or interest. I think that's what hurt the most, that I was just a placeholder for someone better." I said.

"I don't know if that is it. Maybe it's something else going on right now that you can't see because you're mad at him. But he had no right to play with your heart like that, that part is straight up, not acceptable." JayShawn said.

"Thank you Jay, it means a lot to me for you to say that. But now I have to pick up and move on, that's easier said than done; but what other choice do I have? I can't live with Dominique forever. I need a more realistic plan and going from one person's house to someone else's isn't cool; I need a game plan." I said.

"Well, I'm here for you when you need me; all you have to do is pick up the phone and call. Hey, do you want to come with me to my office? I have to make a few calls, send Makayla home since I won't be in the office for the rest of the day, then I'm all yours. What do you say?"

"Um… I don't want to take up all your time. Your work is more important, those venues will not plan their own parties and promotions. I'm ok really, I'll see you later ok." I said. As I got up to leave, I heard his voice call out for me to stop. When I turned he was hot on my heels.

"Chloe, it's really no bother; I need a break anyway. Let's just go to my office and afterwards we can do whatever you want for the rest of the day, ok?" He said.

How could I say no to him? Smiling at me like that. I was always a sucker for a good-looking man with a magnificent smile; I thought as I agreed and walked with him towards his office.

I can't believe how quickly he wore me down into saying yes. We left the park and directly across from it stood his office building. It looked like it held loft apartments, and it probably did. I knew he made good money in club promotions, but it looked as if he was defiantly branching out into unfamiliar territory. The building had a doorman, and the inside was immaculate; not a speck of dust anywhere.

We got into the elevator to the eighth floor. I noticed a strange look on his face while in the elevator, like he was remembering something he didn't want to. Maybe he had a meeting he forgot about? We got off on the eighth floor and there was nothing but rows of doors up and down the hallway; we stopped in front of a door that was wood and semi opaque glass that you could almost, but not see through. To JayShawn, a professional image was everything; and he wanted to make a good impression on clients even before the walk through his office door. Etched in gold with perfect script was the name of his company:

Euphoric Events by Jayshawn Thomas

As soon as we walked in, his assistant Makayla was up in his face trying to find out where he was. She acted more like his woman than his employee; but that's a different story all together. When she noticed me standing behind him, she almost hissed at me, and she knew what or who was holding him up. He introduced us like we never meet before and told me to sit in his small waiting area and he would be right back. I went to go sit down, but then checked out the view from the floor to ceiling windows.

Immediately, I felt something burrowing a hole in my back. When I turned around it was Makayla, looking at me crazy like she wanted to pounce on me. At that moment, I realized she had a crush bigger than what I thought on Jay. So I did what any other black woman would do. I stared right back at her with the same crazy look she gave me. She doesn't know me and I will slide her ass up and down this office and not break a sweat doing it. The way I've been feeling since the breakup with Malik, it can definitely happen. But I have to keep my cool. This is JayShawn's office and the last thing I want to do is embarrass him, especially if one of his clients pays him a last-minute visit. So I sat down and looked out the window and pictured myself somewhere else.

Before I knew, Jay was walking out of his office into the waiting area where he asked if I was ready to go. Before walking out the door, he turned to Makayla and told her to reschedule his meeting at 12:15 p.m. For the following day, call the DJ for the upcoming event, and take the rest of the day off.

As we walked out, I could hear Makayla sucking her teeth so hard you would have thought she had something stuck in them and rolling her eyes at Jay's back. I couldn't help but laugh a little at the thought of her being jealous, but quickly dismissed it. Still, it would be nice to win for once.

Malik

Last night was wild, I can't believe what happened. I never woke up with so many aches and pains before, but they all were worth it to feel what I felt last night. Baby really did her thing. Oh, let me get in the shower before she wakes up or I'll never get out of here; scorching water never felt so good on a sore body.

While in the shower, all I could do was reminisce about her body on mine all night. It all started about six months ago, Things were getting boring with Chloe, and I needed someone who is more. We were casual acquaintances and had met a few years prior. I thought she was sexy as hell, but at the time I couldn't act on getting it in with her, so I had to bide my time until the perfect moment when I could step to her the way I wanted to. I saw her at a Gentlemen's Club; I thought to myself, this is my opportunity, so I took it. And I did and I've never regretted it, Baby is amazing in bed; and her head game is out of control!

I really liked Chloe, she was amazing to me, but she was getting way too serious with me; it was like she was waiting for the ring or something. She's a great girl but I can't see myself with her anymore. Hey, I'm moving up in the world and I need a trophy on my arm to go to openings with and she just didn't fit the mold; there, I said it. I'm just trying to be honest. Why keep stringing the girl along knowing this relationship, or whatever it is, wasn't going anywhere? But with this girl; I know I'll have my clients eating out the palm of my hands. They'll look at her and say, "this guy really has it all and under control, how can I not hire him to promote my event?" yeah I can see that happening; Malik Robinson promoter to the stars!

As I stepped out of the shower, I couldn't help but admire my handiwork. Baby girl was all spread out on the bed, body one way, hair another, in the deepest sleep I've ever saw a woman in. Yeah, I tore that up real proper. When I looked at her all I could see was her riding my manhood like it was all she ever dreamed of. Her long legs wrapped around my torso, holding on, her beautiful breasts bouncing up and down with every thrust of her hips. Bouncing, grinding, slowly winding, oh! She felt amazing! I remembered seeing beads of sweat drip down from between her breast, down her stomach; I couldn't help but stop it mid journey and take it with one of her breasts in my mouth. Then I decided it was time for me to take over! I maneuvered her on her back, put her legs on my shoulders, and stroked as deep as her twat would allow, while rubbing gently on her clit; her wetness spilled on to the bed. Most chicks loved this trick! I felt her body tense up and her twat pulsate, that's when I knew right then she was about to cum.

So I pulled out quick and flipped her ass over on her stomach and buried my member deep inside her. She felt tighter in this position. If she's going to cum, it would not be without me. Shit, we were going to cum together! I felt the gentle tightening of her coochie, and the moans that escaped her were like a beautiful song, and her body went limp; she had come hard. But it wasn't over yet. It was my turn to cum. So, I continued the assault on her cooch until I felt the familiar rush enter my dick, so I pulled out and let my seeds loose on her plump, ample, ass. With that explosion went all my energy. Seeing her in this position almost reminded me of Chloe, but I quickly dismissed the thought as the calm of sleep came over me. Yeah, it was a wild night!

Now, I got to get out of here before she wakes up! I'm not helping her put her bedroom back together; I'll just call her later and see if we can repeat last night. Damn, baby is fine; but not enough to be cleaning up her spot. I'll just send her a quick text when I get downstairs. But let me take this quick picture of her spread out for memories. I'm out!

Dominique

It was around 10:30 a.m. when I got up to meet the day. Time to eat and see what Chloe wants to do; maybe I can get her out this house and into the world of the living. It's been like living with a crazy person the way she's been moping around here for the past few weeks. I know she loved ol' boy, but he did her wrong; so she just going to pull herself up by the garter belt and move on. I mean, I know it's difficult; I've been through it myself with my first love, Ramir. He was my world; I meet him in college, and we were in the same Bio class. He was gorgeous, tall, nice build, and smile. Everything about him just turned me on.

To me, he differed from the other dudes I've dated. For one, he was an Indian American, his family was from Persia and brought him up to be liberal; but expected little full-blood Indian grandchildren. So it was no surprise that his parents upset when they found out we were dating. Ramir's dad and my dad were partners on the same business venture that was supposed to bring in lots of money for their two companies; they needed each other to pull it off, that's how we met. Social functions and business dinners that our dads hosted; being in the same class just cemented the chemistry that was already there.

During large parties, we would sneak away with a bottle of Champaign we took while a waiter wasn't looking and found a quiet corner. We would just laugh and talk until the party was over. Those were some of the best memories I've had with him. It was like nothing else mattered and whatever I was feeling bad about, being with him made it all better.

I even remember the first time we had sex. It was different from what I thought it would be, but good none the less. I was so bad at bio; I was about to fail my class; I had one chance to pull a decent grade, and that was to pass the final exam. Ramir being the nerd he is became my tutor until I could pass and keep my credit cards intact.

We studied the entire time, nonstop; he was more determined than I was to pass. As long as I got at least a C, I was ok; but Ramir expected more, so he pushed me to aim higher. One late night we were studying in the library and I just couldn't cram any more information in my head, all the reading was giving me a headache; so I went for a walk through the stacks of book shelves just to clear my mind. I ended up looking at a title that caught my eye and decided to flip through a few pages. I didn't hear him creep up, and he scared the shit out of me! I dropped the book and hit my head against a shelf.

"Shit! What's your problem? You scared the hell out of me!"

"I'm sorry!" Ramir said between laughs. "I thought you heard me, but when I realized you didn't, I couldn't stop myself! You should have seen your face!"

"You should have seen your face…" I said mockingly. "No! I should've slapped you for sneaking up on me!" I said.

"Oh, really? Well, if you would've slapped me, I would have to slap you back… Right here!" He said as he slapped me right on my butt.

I didn't know whether to be mad or excited. At that point, I think he became more attractive to me. I mean, I always thought he was cute; but when he showed me he had a playful side part from the serious old man he usually is, it turned me on. His smile and lips looked so inviting and sweet that I had to lean in and taste them. Our kiss was hurried yet slow, intense yet calm. I know it sounds like a contradiction, but if you have ever been caught up in a moment of pleasure; you know exactly what I'm talking about. Up to that point, that was the most erotic moment of my life. I had never had an encounter like that before, I've been with boys before; but I never felt the way I felt when I kissed Ramir.

Before I knew it, he had me pinned against one of the bookcases with my legs gripping his waist, while his hands were holding me up by my ass. I was so glad there was no one else in the library because what came after that would've gotten us banned for life! He turned me around and started to kiss my neck, back then I wasn't wearing my hair long so pushing it out the way was no problem. I pulled my shirt over my head and stepped out of my open toe wedge shoes. Ramir seeing this, he took full advantage and slowly eased down my jeans. Every time I felt his hand on my skin, I felt myself get wetter and wetter; I know he was feeling me too; because all I could feel was his hardness against my back. Once I heard his belt buckle unloosen, I couldn't wait to feel our bodies connect. While he kissed my neck, he slid his dick inside and winded his hips. It felt so good, rolled my head back onto his shoulder and tried to stifle a moan. His hands rotated between my breast and my hips, but that wasn't enough for me, I wanted to feel every sensation; so I reach down and stroked my clit while he swiveled. As he climaxed he griped my hair and sped up, in that moment I exploded all over his dick; as I got weak, he came and quickly pulled out. He collapsed against me and we just stood there completely in awe of each other. Yeah, that was a great moment.

After that we became even more inseparable. We went out more outside of our parent's social functions and it looked as if we were going to get serious about having a relationship, but as luck would have it our dad's finished their deal and made a ton of money, so there was no reason for us to hang out anymore.

About that time, Ramir's parents noticed there was something going on between us. Whenever I called he was away, or studying; but when I called his cell, he was always waiting for my call. This confused me, because I never thought it would be an issue; though I saw what was going on. Until that point, race hadn't been an issue; me being Black, and he being Persian, who cared?

I went to my dad about it and he told me it was no problem, Ramir was a good kid; and I had his blessing; only if Ramir's parents felt the same way.

Eventually, we drifted apart; I was so hurt I hardly went out clubbing or shopping for weeks. Once the semester finished, I ended up with a B in Bio. When I went to thank him for helping me I saw he was with a chick name Kasha and they looked cozy. When he saw me approaching him his eyes lit up, but he looked at her and they sort of dimmed.

"Hi Ramir, how have you been?" I said. I hated talking to him like we were casual acquaintances.

"HI Dom! Err, Dominique. I've been ok; I haven't seen you for a while. What's up?" He said with that sexy accent I loved.

"Oh, I've been ugh… Well I just wanted to say thank you for all your help in Biology, I got a B! I… I wanted to thank you cause' without your help I would have failed, and you know my dad would have taken Kiki away (my black BMW)." I said.

He laughed loudly and said, "Yeah, I know! We can't let that happen!" He expressed, while smiling so big I thought his lips we going crack and begin to bleed; how I loved those lips. Then he caught himself because of the way Kasha was glaring at him. "You're welcome… Anytime you need help just call me, ok"

"Ok." I said, as I turned to walk away. When I got to the parking lot, I heard someone running behind me. It was Ramir, waving his arms. I didn't know what to do, I stopped and waited for him to catch up.

"Why are you running?" I said.

"Dee," he uttered while breathing heavily, "I'm sorry about my parents. I wanted to reach out to you but… Their traditional and they expect certain things from me… And I'm sorry." He said.

"Yeah… well, I figured it out. I knew this would be an issue at some point, but I wished for different. So is Kasha their choice or yours?" I said.

"Both… I didn't want to, but I'm beginning to like her. She's not you… but…" He pleaded.

"Yeah, I know. They approve, right? Was that what you were going to say?" I interrupted.

He just shook his head in agreement; I had to leave before he saw the tears start to flow; so I jumped in Kiki and sped off without so much as a goodbye. It was easier for both of us that way; I made it through my last semester of school having no other classes with him and kept my distance whenever we were in the same place. Eventually, I stopped looking for him all together.

Then one day I got a call from my mom telling me about an engagement party she was going to, one of my dad's friend's son was getting married to his college sweetheart. I didn't put two and two together until she mentioned the son's name, then she told me there was an announcement in the Newspaper. The room became twenty degrees colder as I went to my kitchen table and flipped through the pages to find the engagement/wedding section. That's when I saw their wedding announcement and looked in to the smiling faces of Ramir and Kasha.

Ganji and Qazwini

Ramir Ganji, son of

Coro and Norita Ganji

Announce

His engagement to Kasha Qazwini, Daughter of Hasam and Iman Qazwini.

On the 5th day of April

We join the two college sweethearts in love.

And adorned with blessings from their families.

The couple will celebrate their love on the 20th day of May

At The Plaza Hotel in New York.

Makayla

Call this person... Call that person. Who does he think this is? Just because I work for him doesn't mean he can talk to me the way he wants to! Humph, and the nerve of him walking in here with miss, I could stand a few hours on the treadmill. Has he lost his mind! Passing up all this for that! And to think I spend all that time working long nights for nothing. All for her to snatch him up. No! I'm not about to let all my hard work be for nothing.

The first day I walked in this office I knew he was feeling me, he could hardly keep his eyes off of my breasts as he interviewed me; and when he went to walk me out after, he held my hand and gazed into my eyes longer than a normal interviewer. I thought for sure he was going to be my new benefactor by now; little did I know that once I became an employee, I was off limits.

I did everything I could think of to get his attention, from wearing next to nothing in the office to bending down extra lower, leaning in a little further, Hell; even making suggestive comments. Nothing worked until one night we were working late on a promotion party for an upcoming rapper.

Everything that could go wrong did. The DJ got sick, the club owner upped the price of the venue, the signage had been printed with the wrong names, so the marketing for the event was in jeopardy; it was just a mess. We stayed up all night every night for a week to get things in order. The night of the event everything came together, we relaxed and let our hair down a little. It was a great night, we maintained our repetition; left the competition in the dust, got hella paid, and the featured rapper got his record deal; it was a win, win night. After the party, we caught a cab together back to the office to wrap up some loose ends.

"That was such a great turnout! I'm so glad everything came together." I said.

"Yeah, me too; it would've been a major setback for Euphoric Events. You know I couldn't have done this without you; you're my right-hand woman! Thank you Makayla." JayShawn said.

"You're welcome, Jay. That's what you pay me for, right? Do you mind if I take my shoes off? These heels are killing me; I've been on my feet all night." I said. I didn't give a chance to answer as I sat down on the white couch in his office. He watched me as I took off each shoe and massaged my foot.

"Hey, let me help you; I mean, it was my fault your corns are popping." He said as he laughed. "Do you want something to drink? I keep something in here for special occasions?" He said.

"I don't have corns! I've got beautiful feet, See!" I said as I extended my leg up so he could see how cute my feet are, and how flexible I am at

41

the same time. "Yeah, I could use a drink; what do you have?"

"Its good trust me." He said as he handed me a glass of clear liquid. I drank it and felt my chest burn, immediately after that I felt its affects.

I asked him, "what is that?"

He answered, "It's Vodka, sweetheart."

We drank and talked for what seemed like hours; as we got up to leave, I tripped and almost landed on my face until he caught me midair. As he stood me up back on my feet; I saw the look of longing in his eyes, and that's when I knew it was my chance to show him my charms. We kissed passionately while standing and slowly made our way to the floor. I arched my back and opened my legs to fit him more comfortably against me. He couldn't keep his hands off me as we melted into each other. Then suddenly he stopped. It halted so fast I didn't have time to process what went wrong. He stood up to put his shirt back on, tucked it in his pants and hurried to get away from me like I had some kind of disease; he couldn't get away from me fast enough.

"What's wrong? Did I do something?" I asked, knowing I did everything right. Well, I should have taken my shirt off; that way he would definitely not have gotten up.

"No… It's just that we can't do this and work together. I'm sorry for taking it this far. Let's just go, it's been a long night, and maybe things will look better in the morning." He said.

I just sat there dumbfounded; I couldn't believe a man, this man, and my future man turned me down! It wasn't like I'm unattractive; I know I look good. Shit! I'm in the gym three sometimes four days a week keeping my body tight. I keep my appointments at DeAngelo's Salon and Spa every week for the past three years (it's so hard to find someone who does good weaves). But I'm making a promise to myself, that man is going to be mine and no pudgy, little, nothing is going to stop destiny!

Chloe

When we got to the lobby Jay asked if there was somewhere in particular I wanted to go for lunch, I told him no. So, he told me he had somewhere very special in mind where I wouldn't have to worry about bumping into anyone that knows Malik. As we walked towards the revolving doors, he grabbed my hand and entwined them with his as we exited the building. We walked for a few blocks hand in hand; it felt weird for us to be walking down a busy city street like that. I mean, friends do it all the time. For example, if Dee and I are somewhere crowded we hold hands to weave through the crowd; but this was a different type of feeling. This felt as if he was making a claim or something like that. As we walked on, it became less and less weird and I allowed myself to enjoy walking down the street with a handsome, successful man who wanted me. I was lost in thought when we came to a stop in front of a mini market; with a strange look on my face, I turned to Jayshawn and said.

"So this is the place you had in mind?"

"Yes, and no." He said. "Were just here to pick up a few things and then we'll go and have lunch."

"Where?" I asked.

"Well, I was thinking I would make lunch for you at my house, I figure there you won't see anyone that knows Malik… Well, besides me." He laughed.

"Jay… I don't know if…" I started to say as he cut me off from my words.

"Look, were just going to sit, eat, and talk. If you're not comfortable going to my place, we can go to yours." He suggested.

"No, its fine; it's just not what I was expecting. We can go to your place, I want to see how the other half lives, anyway." I said while laughing.

"The other half," He repeated mockingly with a wide grin. "Ok, so let's grab some things and take them back to my place so I can cook for you."

"You cook? This I have to see, I never had a man cook for me; what's on the menu, Chef Jay?" I said.

"I don't know yet, you're just going to have to wait and see. But I promise you, once I give it to you, your mouth will water and you will never be able to be satisfied until you have it again. The taste of it will be on your mind until it can be quenched by me again. It will tingle and wake up every sense in your body. Believe me, no other person will appease your hunger when I'm done." He said.

As he said that all I could do was blush as a red hue covered my body. I hoped he didn't notice; but then he said, "don't turn red now, wait til I'm done first." With a wicked smile on his face, we turned to enter the mini mart. On the walk to his building, which isn't far from his office, we talked a little about Malik and how Jay and I met; we just reminisced. In no time at all, we were going into his building, where his doorman offered to help him with the bags, he declined and we continued to the elevator, and to his condo.

"You know you've arrived when you live in a place that has a doorman." I said.

He laughed then said, "I guess. This is a magnificent building and for the money I pay for it I should have someone carry me to my door, and draw me a bath. But seriously, I really love the architecture of the place. It's an old meets new world feel. The people who live here are nice, not pretentious, but down to earth. You would like it here."

"I think I could as soon as my career takes off, this is the type of place I'd like to like to live in. This is my first time in a building like this, but I feel very comfortable, like I've been here before." I said.

We got off on the sixteenth floor and started walking towards his apartment. I noticed there are only four apartments on his floor, so that meant that there are four on each floor; the space must be huge that only four can fit. He put the bags on the floor and reached for his keys. When he opened the door, I smelled the soft scent of vanilla as we walked in; a grand living room greeted us; I then followed him to the kitchen where he put down the groceries. After we took everything out of the bags, he gave me the guided tour.

"As you can see this is the kitchen, with any appliance you can store in one space, to the right is the dining room, the view is amazing at night. Follow me, this area of course is the living room; down this hall, the first door is the guest room, this door is the bathroom, that door over there is my home office, this is a closet, that door is another guest bedroom, and this door goes to my bedroom." He said.

When he opened the door, I saw in immediate view is his massive king-size bed. Upon closer inspection, I observed vast windows, plush carpet, a walk-in closet, and a bathroom with an enormous tub, with a separated shower with glass doors. This was definitely a man's room, there were no pictures on the walls and he had bottles of cologne across the ledge of the bathroom sink. Yet still it was a beautiful space. All I wanted to do was run and jump in his bed; it looked so soft and inviting.

He caught me staring at it and commented, "you want to try it out? It doesn't bite."

"What!" I said. "Oh… No, I was just thinking it needs a woman's touch, that's all."

"Yeah, you might be right. When I find the right woman, I'll have no problem letting her touch it." He laughed.

After the tour was over, he set to work cooking lunch for us. It was amazing to watch him mix all the ingredients together while carrying on a casual conversation with me like we had done that for years. He had a way of making me feel safe and comfortable, even before this. I remember when we met at the Z Lounge; I was at the bar trying to flag down the bartender when he walked up and said.

"My man, she's trying to get a drink over here." He said.

"Thanks, but I had him where I wanted him; he just didn't know it yet." I said sarcastically.

"Where is that, on the other side of the bar?" He said.

"Yes, exactly right." I laughed.

"I'm sorry, my name is Jayshawn."

"Hi my name is Chloe."

After our impromptu introductions, we found a spot in a booth and chatted. He told me he helped the owner draw in a crowd and promoted any events the owner had. We talked forever until Dee came over and told me she was going to leave with some guy named Chase. Chase was cute enough; tall, muscular guy, blonde hair, green eyes, and tanned skin, who worked as an assistant to an investment broker. So she winked at me and mouthed he's cute as she was walking away. We continued to talk for a while, and then some guy walked up and patted Jay on the shoulder and shook his hand. He congratulated him, then introduced himself as Malik. Malik bombarded his way into our conversation, then asked if he could take me home that night. I looked to Jay to see if it was ok, because I didn't know Malik and I wanted to know if it was weird or awkward since me and him were talking. He insisted I go. With him insisting, I assumed he wasn't interested in me; so I left with Malik. And that was the beginning of my courtship with Malik Jamal Robinson.

Whenever I would attend events with Malik, Jay was always there, I figure he was scoping the competition; making sure Malik didn't step on his neck, so to speak. But, no matter what was going on we always found ourselves in a corner or at a table chatting up a storm like old friends. He practically saved me from an epic fail when I had been surrounded by a cluster of high-profile trophy wives/girlfriends at a networking event in Soho. All those women could talk about was vacationing and starting families; one chick was waiting for her man to get divorced from his second wife, so they could finally get married. Also, she had a nerve to have a three-year-old daughter with him, and pregnant with their second child.

I've never seen that type of mistress before, the one with outside the hotel room benefits, and a cute party dress from Tony Murchison. As I stood there, I felt as if I was going to pass out; Jay found me and asked the ladies if he could borrow me for a minute.

As we turned to walk away, I could hear the hushed tones of gossiping women saying how handsome Jay is, and how if they weren't married or engaged they would slip him their number. As we walked, he gave me a Tequila shot and told me to down it quickly then sip some Champaign.

He asked, "Do you feel better? I saw you with the hyenas and thought you needed some air."

"I did, and this shot too! Those women are something else. See that one over there? She is having an affair with her husband's secretary, and the secretary is sleeping with the husband; she knows of course and their planning to take a vacation together. They both found out the husband is sleeping with yet another woman, but it's his partner's wife. A mess, right?" I said.

"More than… Wow, they got some girl on girl action! I think I need to be over there!" Jay said.

"Don't you dare, you better stay right here with me, and I'll kill you if you attempt to take a step in that direction!" I said.

Laughing, Jay said, "aiight killa, I'll stay here. Where is Malik? Shouldn't he be protecting you from that type of crowd? I mean, they could try to draft you into their organization."

"I don't know." I said. "He could be anywhere; last I saw him he was talking to Terrod 'TNT' Nelson about creating an underground sound for a club who's willing to showcase him."

"There he is." Jay said. "He's talking to Sienna 'Sin' Pride. She's a stripper turned model."

"Yeah, he's branching out to represent models and rappers now; trying to corner the market. Jay I need to get some air; I'll be right back." I huffed.

"I'll come with. I can't have you outside alone; something could happen to you, and I can't have that on my conscience." Jay said.

We stood outside and talked for hours, and when I checked the time, it was 2:30 a.m. the party was winding down; and Malik was coming out of building shaking hands while flashing the people with a million-dollar smile. He saw me and asked if I was ready to go; not that he had been looking for me, but if I was ready to leave. He greeted Jayshawn; we parted ways and headed for an awaiting cab. When we entered that cab I saw Jayshawn looking mad and tired at the same time. As I glanced toward the exit, Sin was standing at the top of the stairs winking at Malik; and Malik, soaking it up, was cheesing from ear to ear. Instead of being mad at Malik for flirting with Sin, I was mad at myself for leaving Jay.

Jay, proud of his culinary perfection, served; we were having turkey, ham, and cheese Panini's with corn chowder soup, and wash it down with a glass of Chardonnay.

Dominique

After I shook myself from that nightmare memory I went to see what plans me and my girl were going to make today, only to see she had already left. I must have been out of it this morning, cause I can't remember if I saw her or not. Her spot on the couch is cleaned up so she must have gone out; she could've left me a note or something. As I moved about the apartment I tried to forget the memory of Ramir, but every time I stood still long enough, the thought of him rushed into my head. I googled him last year only to find out he had become an ear, nose, and throat doctor.

Still married; he and Kasha have no children, and he has a practice on 1st Avenue. I called to make an appointment; but on the day of the appointment, I called and canceled. After I got out of the shower I went visit my parents on the Upper East Side. When I entered the brownstone home Charles my mother's cocker spaniel greeted me. The house was unusually quiet, so I looked for my dad in his office. The door is locked so at least I know he's home; maybe he was on a conference call or something. I found my mother in the sunroom surrounded by papers. Oh God! I forgot it was charity season! That time of year where wealthy people feel bad about being wealthy, so they charge thousands of dollars per plate to other wealthy people to donate it to their charity of choice for the year.

"Hi, mom," I said. "How have you been?"

"Oh, it's you Dominique! You've startled me! I am planning this year's charity benefit with Margene and Sonya. You remember them right, Hershel and Rebecca mothers?" Olivia Lawrence said to her daughter.

"I remember mom. Whatever happened to Hershel and Rebecca, any children yet?" I said.

"No, not yet; but Sonya is still holding her breath. As Am I… when are you going to settle down and get married? Your father and I are desperate for grandchildren to love. I've almost given up on you; Charles will make me a grandma before you do young lady." Olivia offered.

I knew she was going to say that; I thought. "Mom, can I be in this house ten minutes before you start calling all your friends asking about their eligible bachelor sons to marry me off to! I'm sorry I disappointed you, but Hershel and I were never going to get married; I had someone else in mind, it just didn't work out." I said.

"Oh, you mean that Indian boy you had a crush on? What was his name again?" Olivia questioned.

"It was Ramir mom. And yes, it could have been… Perfect; a perfect match." I said defeated.

"Well honey, there isn't any use living in the past; what's done is done, you and Hershel now that was a match. Tall, dark, handsome, successful Real Estate Broker. You know that girl won't make him happy; she was just runners up to you. After you broke his heart and moved to the hood; he had no choice but to marry that girl." Olivia declared.

I had to stifle a laugh. "Mom, you don't know how perfect they are together. I made the right choice by moving, and I don't live in the hood. Just because it's not Upper East Side doesn't mean it's the hood. I love it there; people are genuinely nice, they don't care about how much money anyone else has, and they're not pompous, aristocratic, arrogant, assholes!" I said.

"Hey! Watch your mouth! Is that how they teach their kids to talk to their mothers?" Olivia said.

"I'm sorry, mom. Just I hate for you to put down people who you don't know, because of their area code or account balance." I said.

"I apologize too. I didn't mean to upset you. Are you coming to the Gala? You can bring whoever you like; most of your old friends will be there." Olivia insisted.

"Ok, I'll come. I have some friends who would probably like to attend. What's the dress code?" I said as if I didn't know, I just needed an excuse to extract more money from the parental units.

"Black tie, that's the only way to throw a party." Olivia said.

"Is dad going to come out of that office, so I can say hi?" I said.

"Honey, your father is a workaholic who won't take a vacation if the world ended tomorrow; he would plan how to take over the world the day after." Olivia laughed.

"Ok mom, I'm going to head out." I said as I gave her a quick kiss on the cheek and grabbed four invitations to the Ball.

The invitation read:

Your Cardinally Invited to attend
The Race for the Cure benefit Dinner
For children battling Cancer
This event will take place on the
Evening of November 8th.
Donations for this event are
Starting at $2500;
All donations will be given to
St. Jude's Children's Hospital
This is a Black-Tie event: any person's in
any other attire will be turned away
Please bring this invitation upon arrival

A day of beauty is definitely on the agenda for this event. I wonder if Chloe wants to go; and who is going to be in attendance?

Malik

I was feeling so good about the workout I had last night; I thought I might go walk to the subway after I stop and get coffee. Damn, she must have just woken up! Because this is the third time she called me; well she's going to have to wait for daddy to give her more dick. As I was rounding the corner I saw Makayla, Jayshawn's assistant leaving his office and at this time of the morning she should come in not leaving for the day. She looked good as hell in that dress, and those shoes! Jay just didn't know what he has. If it was me, I would've hit that the minute she started filing papers. What am I saying? I did hit that! She's pretty and all, but she wants the glamorous life and my pockets are not deep enough for her… Yet. Let's find out what Jay has cooking up in the office that Makayla is out running errands.

"Hey Makayla! Slow down sweetheart, where are you running to!" I said.

"Oh. It's you, well if you must know I have a hair appointment to get to." She said.

"Hair appointment, shouldn't you be working? Where's Jay at?" I asked.

"Yeah a hair appointment, and I have the day off today Jay is off entertaining your little pudgy girlfriend." She said as she rolled her eyes at me.

"My girlfriend? Oh, she's referring to Chloe. Oh yeah, we were to have a meeting today. Where did they go again?" I asked.

"A meeting? He told me to cancel all his meetings, and you were not scheduled today. And I don't know where they went." She said.

"Ok Makayla, thanks! And I'm going to call you later about that meeting." I said as she just smiled at me while rolling her eyes, as she walked or should I say sashayed her way down the street.

I watched her walk so long I forgot what I was doing, so I started to half run half jog down the opposite end of the street hoping to catch up to Jayshawn and Chloe. I almost ran into them when I rounded the corner they were standing in front of a bodega talking and holding hands. Why were they holding hands? I stood there and watched them for a while. Twenty minutes later they came out with bags. I kept following when I realized she wasn't my girl no more; I have a new chick that is the finest piece of ass I've ever had in my corner. As I walked in the other direction, I got a text from my lady.

From: CM

Hey daddy, missed you this morning, where did you go? Not far I hope cause I need you like right now and if you don't come back, I find someone else...

To: CM

Girl u better stop playing with me! You know daddy has to work. I tell you what, I'll come by after work. I have to pick up some clothes from the house, anyway. TTYL.

From: CM

Ok, daddy but don't stay there too long I don't want you getting any second thoughts about us. I wanted this to happen for so long and I would be heartbroken if you hurt me. And if you did, I would have to leave you as my manager/promoter. It would be too awkward to keep working with you.

To: CM

Oh, no baby, there's no chance of that. Nobody can do for you what I'm about to do for u in bed or otherwise. Just keep it tight and wet for me and I promise I'll make u a star.

From: CM

Ok daddy! That's what I wanted to hear.

On my walk to meet a club owner, I thought, *'is she taking that dude back to my house? No! She wouldn't do that… would she?'* She's not that type. But I'm going to make a quick stop at my place before I meet Jojo. When I got to my apartment, I thought my heart was going to burst through my chest, but when I opened the door, there was no one there. The apartment was clean and dark, I thought for sure she was still here; it wasn't like she had anywhere to go. In the bedroom her clothing is gone, and the bed is unmade. She left a few things behind that I had bought her like perfumes and stuff. But all traces of her are gone. The bed still smelled like her though, but her side was cold and empty. As quickly as the thought passed through my head, I dismissed it. *Did I make the right decision?*

Today just wasn't my day! I was late for my appointment with Jojo, so the contract is going to remain with Jayshawn; but that's cool, I still had the event with Cyn coming up soon! It's going to be her big debut, and I can't wait for the world to see my creation. She was going to the top, and with me as her manger/man, I'm going along for the ride. Maybe if I work my connections that debut will be sooner than later, and with some rich people having a charity event coming up; that would be a good place to market her skills.

Jayshawn

I don't know what made me suggest lunch at my place, but I'm glad I did. Sitting across from Chloe was amazing. We ate and talked like we used to at parties. Malik just didn't know what he had in her. After lunch was through, we had drinks in the living room and watched some tv; it was just very comforting knowing that she was in my presence. She just stared at the tv, while I stared at her, when I realized what I was doing; excused myself to the bathroom to get my thoughts together.

Was I having another psychotic episode, like in the elevator? I don't think so; I liked her as a friend; but did I honestly think it could go further than that? She was nice and all, but not the girl I typically date; when we met at the club, I thought she was funny and told a pleasant story. Being a writer, I considered letting her handle my press releases.

Then the thought of her leaving gave me the overwhelming sense of loss. This was my rival/friend's ex-girlfriend who is also my friend. Nothing would come of this. So, why am I imagining making love to her? She smelled so good and looked so sad in that coffee shop that my heart ached for her. When I grabbed her hand it happened so fast I didn't have time to question it. We had a great afternoon I won't ruin it, but I can't help but wonder what would have happen if I had taken her home instead of Malik.

I splashed water on my face and headed back to the living room. She must have dozed off cause she was lying across the couch, and I usually have a problem with people laying on my furniture, but her I didn't mind. When I woke her up, I suggested she lie down in my bed or guest room and she looked mortified; she declined and continued to watch tv. Minutes later she dozed off again this time against my chest; it felt good to cradle her against me. She woke up and insisted she leave, but I convinced her to stay for dinner. I knew she wouldn't go out with me, so I ordered pizza and wings for a night in. As we ate, we laughed it just came so naturally, it's nice not to have to work at building rapport for once.

"So, Jay, why are you still single? I have it on good authority that Makayla will lock you down." She said.

"Maykayla, she's nice and all, but she works for me; I don't shit where I sleep. Honestly, something started with us, but I ended it immediately. She's looking for all the wrong things. I need a rider, not a woman who will leave as soon as my bank account gets low." I said.

"Yeah, but she is beautiful. You should represent her as a model or something; she has a nasty attitude for one." She said.

"Really, I thought you two were friends?" I said.

"Friends! Jay, you really don't know women do you? She practically attacked me in your office today, while giving me 'the stank face'. And a while back, when I started dating Malik; she tried to get with him until I checked her. That girl is a snake and if she could get any lower to the ground, she would be in hell." She said.

"Wow! That's some strong emotions girl! If she's like that why should I get with her? Is that the person you want to see me with? And I thought you cared about me…" I said as I pouted and gave her my best sad face.

"No, I don't want to see you with her; I just thought she was the type of female you're into. I care about you and I want to see you with someone with value; who values themselves and you. You know what I mean?" she said.

"Yeah, I do…" I confirmed.

The thought of kissing her came to my mind, and I wondered how her lips felt against mine. Later that night we caught a cab to her friend Dominique's house where she was staying. I offered to let her stay at my place, but in Chloe fashion she said 'no'. In the cab to her friend's house was the only time since I had seen her earlier that day, that we were silent. It felt good; but it left so many questions on the table. When we arrived, I told the driver to wait while I walked her to the door.

While saying goodnight, before I knew what I was doing, I had kissed her! My friend who was newly single, and clearly into the kiss herself as she kissed me back with a passion I had never seen from her. Then she suddenly pulled away from me and ran into the building, I was going to go after her but I thought it best to let her calm herself down. I knew where she was if I needed her and I knew I would need her; and she would need me.

When I returned home, I cleaned up and watched a little tv. Twenty minutes later there was a knock at my door; which was odd, because Jerry never let anyone up without calling me to ask if it was ok, especially late at night. When I opened the door, she was there!

At first she didn't say a word, she just stood in the doorway thinking of the right words to say. I was so stunned she came back, I watched her until the suspense ate away at me; then I did it! I reached out to stroke both sides of her face and with no words between us; I pulled her close to me.

As soon as my lips touched hers the intensity of our union was immediately felt through my body. All that went through my mind is to keep holding her close. Taking her clothes off came second to being locked in this position. Eventually, we made it inside the apartment and to the couch; there we slowly undressed each other. Her hands shook as she tried to remove my shirt; I grabbed her hands and removed her shirt. There they were, 'the twins' who had my attention all night as she laughed, sighed, and took deep breaths. She was not a rail thin girl, she was curvy in all the places that men loved to explore with their hands and tongues; and so I did. I explored every inch of her body and enjoyed the look of want on her face as I did. I laid her on her back and removed her jeans; her skin felt smooth and smelled delicious. Her thick, juicy thighs wrapped around my waist gave me the gentle urging to claim what I and she knew was already mine. As I reached for my zipper, I heard a ringing in the distance. The more I attempted to focus on my task; the ringing was becoming louder and more constant.

When I opened my eyes I had a pain in my neck and an ache in my jeans. I reached out for her but she wasn't there. I cannot believe I just dreamed that entire episode! I can still feel the pressure on my lips, from our kiss; It feels so real, genuine enough that my dick is still hard at the thought of it. I looked at the missed call message on my phone, decided not to look, and got to bed. Maybe if I tried hard enough, I could get my fantasy back.

Dominique

By the time I got home, Chloe was passed out. Instead of waking her up, I just went to my room and crashed. It was a sleepless night filled with tossing and turning. I couldn't do this forever. One day I was going to have to grow up and put on my big girl panties and find a job; get married and stop waiting for Ramir to rescue me. Tomorrow was going to be a new day for me and my girl.

We have to stop letting these men run our lives, even if they were probably better at doing so. This party is going to be a new start for me; maybe I'll take my mother's advice and find a husband at the charity event. I invited Chloe, but I still had two more invitations left; maybe by the time it came up we would have dates if not we could be each other's date. I might meet someone special there, who I could learn to love, and what's not to love about me.

The next day, as Chloe and I talked, she told me she was going to find a job too; and move out as soon as she saved enough money. We might have grown up differently but both of us are in the same boat the only difference is I have my parents to take care of me whereas she only has herself. I mean, her sister China was nice and all, but to me she is shifty, I wouldn't trust her as far as I could throw her; but that's my girl's family. So I kept my mouth shut. Lord knows my family ain't nothing to write home about, we just use money to hide our sins like all the other families.

I gave my mom a call to tell her I was looking for a job; she suggested I help her with the charity event like an assistant. I agreed, but that wouldn't be working; so I put my Bachelor's degree in Business to use, but with no experience it was going to prove difficult to find a job that pays over ten dollars an hour. At my mom's urging, I talked to my dad, and he found me a position in his firm. I would be the secretary to his junior VP who happened to be Hershel Elliot. Even though Hershel is an egotistical idiot, the job was from 8am-6pm Monday thru Friday. Those weren't terrible hours and for $15.00 an hour for a first job, I couldn't turn it down.

The first thing I had to do was buy a new wardrobe; I couldn't show up to work in club clothes with my tits and thighs showing. At the insistence of my mother we shopped together, she picked every outfit with matching shoes; she looked happy to see us bonding together. Admittedly, it felt good; we've never seen eye to eye, which is another reason why I left home; but to be with her like this made me appreciate the life she created for me. While I could be a spoiled princess, mom was holding the home front down; truth be told my dad hardly ever spent much time home; even to this day he puts in twelve-hour days at the firm.

Following lunch with my mom at Bethesda's; I ran into some guy that was eating a dirty water hotdog from a street vendor. As I was about to scream at him for almost getting ketchup on me he looked oddly familiar; but I couldn't place his face, or his name for that matter. He looked at me and smiled so I know he felt the same familiarity with me, but he just stood there so I took the lead.

"Well; excuse you, next time watch where you're walking!" I said with an attitude.

He said. "I'm sorry Dominique I didn't see you; how have you been you never called me after that night?"

"I'm sorry, call you? I...I... I'm sorry what's your name again," I asked.

With a laugh, he said. "Chase. Chase Greene. You don't remember me, do you?"

"No, I don't. Refresh my memory, Mr. Greene." I said.

"We met at the Z Lounge a few years ago, we... had a great night together and the next day you disappeared. Did you know I went there every weekend for two months after that just to see you again?" He said.

"I must have left an impression on you. I'm sorry I never called you Chase, life you know. Well, it was strange seeing you again." I said as I turned to walk away.

"How about we go to lunch?" He said.

"Sorry, I just had lunch. I have to go back to work, maybe some other time." I said.

"Ok, how about you give me your number this time; and this is mine. Maybe we could get together sometime." He said. As I gave him the skeptical eye he then continued, "Not like before, but a real date; you're not an easy woman to forget, or find, what do you say?"

I have no idea what made me say yes, but I did. Maybe it was out of desperation; my mom's fund raiser was coming up soon, and I needed a date. Besides, he was cute and had the most beautiful eyes I ever seen; yeah we would look good together in black tie attire. Now I would have to find a date for Chloe.

Back at work, the day just breezes by, the only problem is; I was asked to stay late. I was looking forward to movie night. It was quickly becoming a ritual with me and Chloe, but when the boss asks me to do something; I have to do it. I put in a quick call home to let Chloe know she was going to have to start without me, and I started on the next round of letters, and office memo's that had to be sent out/received by tomorrow morning.

Also, he had the nerve to ask me to put together a power point presentation to present at eight in the morning to the big wigs; including my father. What makes me angry is the fact that he knew about this meeting for a week and didn't say a word about me doing a presentation. He just dropped it in my lap and said to have it done and emailed to him by morning; I had to make thirty page handouts for twenty people. Oh, the fun I would have tonight, I never knew working girls had to work so hard to make a dollar; if I wasn't trying to change myself, I would've told him to stick those reports right up his ass and kept it cute and keep on moving.

Chloe

So much for Chinese with the bestie. Looks like I'm on my own tonight. I had some great news for her too. She had been working for her dad's firm for a few weeks now. Yet I still had no job, money and still living off of her. But today was a different day! I'd been combing through the want ads forever, searching for a job that would bring in some sort of real money. I was so desperate I even was willing to go back into retail. Anyone who worked in retail knows that it's one of the hardest hustles ever; especially if it was on commission.

After weeks of sending out my resume and writing samples, I finally got an interview at a plus size magazine called Indulgence Magazine as an assistant writer; which is more like a glorified secretary, but I still had my chance to write small puff pieces, articles, and it allowed me to take part in 'The Pit' activities. 'The Pit' was a huge writing circle that only the top writers and their assistants attend to come up with story lines, topic, ideas, seasons must haves, etc. Here I could hone my skills and move up in the ranks. I'm so exited, but I have no one to share the news with. For the first time in a few hours, I thought of Jayshawn. I was so embarrassed by how I ran away from him I couldn't call him; but he's been on my mind ever since. He's called me, but I haven't taken the calls; I don't know what to say to him. The worst part is I like him and I shouldn't feel conflicted but I do, I still have a weird loyalty to Malik.

I put in the movie Natasha Jones's Journal, when there was a soft knock at the door. I thought it might be Dee, but when I opened it; it was Mrs. Turner, Dee's resident cat lady. She wanted to know if she could borrow some milk for her cats; I obliged her by filling her container and went back to watching my movie when I heard another soft knock. This time it wasn't Mrs. Turner, it was Jayshawn. Startled and excited at the same time. All the time that had passed, I thought he would have forgotten about me.

He stood in the doorway looking good as hell, wearing dress pants, a tieless shirt, with the top buttons undone. He looked as if he was having some type of internal struggle. Finally he asked to come in; of course I let him; I mean, there is no way I'm going to push him away again. I asked what he's doing here, although I already knew.

"Why haven't you taken my calls?" He said.

"I didn't know what to say." I said flatly.

"You knew what to say." He accused sarcastically. "I knew you needed time but two weeks Chloe! Come on, I thought we were friends? If I offended you, you should've said something to me!"

"No, it's not like that!" I said.

"What's it like then? Cause you showed me something different. I like you, I wasn't expecting to but I do. So now what? You don't have anywhere to run now!" He said aggressively.

"I don't want to run from you Jay. I… I still feel like." I couldn't finish my statement because Jay interrupted.

"Cause you still love him, Right? He left you and kicked you out of his house! Baby, that's not love. Has he even called you all this time? Sent a text?" He questioned.

"No, but…" as I was about to finish my statement as Dee walked through the door, shoes in hand.

"Oh, my, my, my, what did I walk into?" Dee Said. "Hi Jayshawn, to what do we owe your visit?"

"I just wanted to clear some things up with Chloe, but I can see this is a girl's night so I'm leaving." He said.

"No, don't leave on my account. By all means continue this conversation." Dee said.

"No, I have to go anyway." He said.

"Hey Jayshawn, Chloe and I are going to my mother's charity event on November 8th. I have a date, do you mind being Chloe's?" Dee said to Jayshawn as I stood there looking mortified.

"November 8th? Yeah, I'd be happy to attend. Thanks." He said.

"Great! Here is your invitation. The party starts at 9pm so you can pick Chloe up around that time and we could all go together." She said with a bright smile.

"Ok, Chloe, I'll see you then." He said as he turned to leave.

I was about to light into Dominique when she turned to me, and with the most sincere look I've ever seen, she said. "He's good for you; give him a chance to prove it." And with that, she turned and walked to her bedroom.

The next day, I could barely look at Dee I was so mad at her. Really, I should've been singing her praises for doing something for me I didn't have the courage to do for myself. Instead of being mad at me for giving her the cold shoulder, she just smiled and said...

"Girl, why are you over there looking mad? You know good and well that you're happy Jay is going to be your date." Dee said.

I couldn't help but laugh. She knew I was faking the funk. "So..." I said. "I would have asked him myself, I was just picking my moment."

"Oh, picking your moment uh..., yeah you were picking it, as he was about to walk out of the door." Dee laughed. "Look how about we figure out what we're wearing because the Gala is going to be here quicker than you think."

"Whatever..." I said. "Who are you bringing, anyway? You didn't tell me you found a date to this little soiree, what's this guy's name?"

"Well, his name is Chase, and we sort of hooked up before, and I ran into him yesterday after lunch with my mom. He seems nice and I vaguely remember my night with him, but from what I remember it was definitely worth seeing him again." Dee said.

"Chase? Oh, I think I remember that one… What kind of name is Chase?" I said.

"It's a name of a handsome, sweet, kind, Caucasian man. He is gorgeous Chloe, I don't know what he does for a living; but he looks expensive. I think he may be the one I've been waiting for." Dee said.

"White man… yeah I remember him you met him the night I met Malik. So, you're switching over… Again. I always knew you were down with the swirl ever since you told me about that Persian guy you used to date. Well, I'm happy for you love; if you like him, I love him." I said.

"I just feel something when I think about him. And it's not the pulsating feeling between my legs either! It feels deeper somehow. Does that sound weird?" Dee said.

"No, it's not. I feel the same way about JayShawn." I said. "He is like the flame and I'm the moth, I'm just drawn to him. Everything about him turns me on. From his crooked smile when he's trying not to laugh, to how intense he can be when he wants something."

"Or someone." Dee said.

"Or someone…" I said.

"Girl, you better stop running from that man. One day he won't be there to chase you." Dee said.

"Who knows, Maybe I will." I said.

"Well you better, cause I know you need to get that kitty scratched. How long has it been? Girl you probably growing cob webs in that thing! Has Charlotte from Charlotte's Web written 'Amazing Pussy' in there yet?" Dee said.

"Oh, so now you got jokes! Ok… I got you." I said.

"I'm just saying, Jay is fine and everything so if you don't snatch him up somebody will. A man like that does not stay single for long, you keep pushing him away; he'll stay away." Dee said.

I took what she said to heart. I know I'm more than interested in being with him, but he and Malik run in the same circles and he's bound to go after the same females he does; like some kind of competition. I won't play the fool a second time around.

Jayshawn

After I left Chloe's house I caught a cab home and ran pass Jerry so fast I barely heard him say 'Good Evening Sir'. Going to this party couldn't have come at the perfect time. I was going to make her admit she wanted me. I mean, I could see it in her face, but she kept holding back. I have so much work to do before the event. I'll just send a text to Makayla and let her know that she will have to be at work early in the morning so we can get started on work business, then I can devote my time to the business of Chloe.

The next day, I got into the office at 7:00a.m., still no Makayla. I logged onto my computer and immediately checked my emails. I had a few invites to some parties, nothing out of the ordinary for me. Club owners were always inviting me to their establishments. It helps that my name is one of the biggest in the industry, and having me on the guest list is sure to bring a large, paying, liquor buying crowd. Everybody wants to be where the party is, and I definitely know which events to attend, and which ones not to.

After deleting e-mails I didn't need, I came across an invitation to a restaurant re-opening in the Bronx called Sky View. After putting the web address in the search bar, and taking the virtual tour, it seems like a nice little romantic spot, so I made a rsvp, and noted the date; yeah this could come in handy.

Makayla graced me with her presence around 10:00 a.m. I guess that was early to her. I immediately put her to work calling venues, making an appointment with my tailor, hiring a car service, calling DJ's, etc. She hadn't done this much work since she started. I know she was upset that she was ruining the polish on her nails with all the dialing, writing, and typing she was doing.

I told her to hold all my calls, accept the ones from important people. She knew who those were because she tried to hook up with more than half of them. About 3:00 p.m., she brought me a handful of messages, all from Malik. While on the phone with a client I mouthed to her 'what does he want?' she mouthed back 'a meeting' as she turned to walk out my office. As I wondered what he would want with a meeting with me for, I slowly realized, it was about the meeting he attempted to have with Jojo awhile back, but never happened.

Malik just didn't have what it took to succeed in this business; cutting a friend's throat isn't how you build a reputation. Really, Malik is too childish; trying to live the life of a baller where he doesn't pull in half the revenue. He's unprofessional, hard-headed, and to be afraid to be a man and do what he has to do; instead he's more worried about being THE MAN. That's how he lost Chloe, but that's all good cause I meant her to be mine, anyway.

By 5:00 p.m., I told Makayla to take the rest of the day off; she was only too happy to leave. A full day of actual work might have scared her for life. I stayed in the office for another hour to tie up a few things before the espresso wore off. As I locked up my office and stepped on the elevator to begin my decent to ground level, I thought about how I could work on my plan to wear Chloe down. I know she is a writer, or at least has done some writing work… Maybe I can get her to write something for me, nothing serious; maybe a press release or a blog review of some of my events. That way we would attend events together, I could show her a good time, and I could also keep my eye on her. I don't think she's found a gig yet; maybe I could help her out and myself at the same time. I pulled out my smart phone and wrote a note to myself:

Note

- Offer Chloe job to write about events my company opens
- Send Dom flowers
- Set up meeting with Malik
- Tomorrow at 11:45 see tailor for fitting

By the time I got home, I had a horrible headache from all the plotting I was doing concerning Chloe that I popped two painkillers and went to bed. As I lay there waiting for the pain to subside, I listened to the sounds of the city. I could close my eyes

78

and know what's going on in the streets below without even being there. I heard the cars passing, birds flying, bells from the bodega doors opening and closing. After a while, all the sounds became a blur as I drifted off to sleep.

Dominique

I walked excitedly into work anxiously awaiting 1:00 p.m. so that my girl and I would do a little lunch time shopping for the Gala. I knew it was going to be a long day when I saw piles of papers and folders waiting for me, I instantly deflated. As I sat down and checked Hershel's calendar I saw that he had an appointment scheduled for 11:00 and the person scheduled was Mr. Ganji. My heart immediately picked up its pace, I couldn't believe after all this time I was going to run right into Ramir's dad. That's just what I needed! For him to see me doing something as common as being an assistant instead of the Junior VP, to him I will be every bit the disappointment he and his wife thought I was all those years ago.

I tried to busy myself with all the work I had to do to prepare for the meeting; I cleared my desk of whatever clutter was around. I was so anxious that I had to go to the restroom just to gather my composure and splash water on my face. After putting some makeup back on and giving myself a little pep talk, I took my seat behind my desk and awaited the inevitable. I must have zoned out, because next thing I know someone is standing in front of my desk knocking on it. When I look up, it's not Ramir's dad; but Ramir himself.

I nervously stand, "Hello Ramir." I said.

"Hello Dominique." He returned with a sly smile. "I wasn't expecting to see you here, how have you been?"

"I... I've been fine, yourself?" I said.

"Good, very good. Should you inform Mr. Elliot of my arrival?" He said.

"Yes!" I said. I loved his accent, I thought while looking down at my phone so he wouldn't see my blushing.

"Mr. Elliot, Mr. Ganji is here." I said, trying to keep my voice from going hoarse.

"I'll be right out," Insisted Hershel.

Before I could utter the next word Hershel swung open his office door and grabbed Ramir's hand. I tried to hide my face as he interrupted the tension that was brewing between Ramir and I.

"Dr. Ganji, how are you?" asked Hershel.

"I'm just fine. As long as the pollen count stays high; I will continue to have lots of patients in and out of my office. How is your family?" asked Ramir.

"The wife is going on and on about moving out of the city; so we're going to look for some properties in New Jersey. Hey, let's step into my office to see if we can find a property for you and your lovely wife," Responded Hershel.

And just like that Hershel whisked him into his office and shut the door, leaving murmurs of voices as the door clicked closed.

Malik

I've been calling Jayshawn's office nonstop today, though I don't know why. If he answered; what would I say to him? Leave my ex alone? That would make me look bad; like I cared what she did or what they did together. What I really need to be concentrating on is getting into that party. There's no way in hell I going to pay $2,500.00 per plate to get some contacts. Maybe my homie Chris can hook me up; he works for a caterer that does most of the upscale events around the city. Maybe my new money maker and I can get in on their tab.

After I put in a call to my man, I had a way into the party. We would meet with Chris as the party starts by the service entrance, while everyone is running around trying to get everything in place we can just slip in among the guests; no one will keep tabs on that entrance, so we could get in unnoticed.

But first we have to look the part, so that means I have to see what Cynsation has to wear. Matter of fact, I think I'll just head over to her spot anyway so she can thank me for granting her an audience with such an elite crowd.

Damn, going to this chick apartment was a mission! I thought as I walked passed burned down buildings, kids running in the street, and several types of music from apartments with thin sheetrock for walls, for what seemed like hours. She lives so far I thought I was going to end up in Canada or some shit. I got to get her to move closer to Manhattan. Wait, Wait, that's it! As the idea formed in my mind, I'll convince her to move in with me. Chloe isn't there, and what better way to keep my bootie and my money flow coming in. And I know she won't say no, what chick in the right mind wouldn't want to live in a condo.

When I reached her building, I couldn't believe this is where I spent the night. Maybe I was still in a drunken haze from having good sex that I didn't notice the filthy floors, graffiti on the walls, and the familiar smell of dry piss that radiated from what seemed like every part of the building. I ran up four flights as quick as I could, touching nothing to her studio apartment and banged on the door so hard it might have come off if she hadn't had opened it so quick.

"Damn!" She said, as she pulled open the door. "Why are you banging on my door like that?"

"Oh, I'm sorry, sweetheart." I proclaimed with a slow, sly grin. "I just couldn't wait for you to open the door." I said, as I scooped her up in my arms and placed slow kisses all over her lips, neck, and chest. "I have some fantastic news for us baby…"

"Really..." She said, "What kind of news?" She moaned as my kisses were having the desired effect on her.

"I got us into a charity ball, where all the who's who of entrepreneurs, business owners, ballers, and music industry people are gathering to help the less fortunate." I said.

"How did you get us in? I heard parties like that cost a lot of money; did you talk to one of your industry friends to get us in?" Cyn said.

"Yeah baby, you know it." I said, as my mind raced to find another excuse, but her excuse was good enough. "So, babe, this is a black-tie event, do you have something you can wear?"

She lazily let me go and walked over to a closet on the far side of the room. She pulled out a short, red, sequined dress that looked to be so thin it would show every part of her magnificent body for all the rich elite to see. She held it up for me to inspect.

"What about this? I think this would be nice. What do you think?" Cyn said.

"Nah, nah, nah," I said as I held up the dress to her. I took her by the hand, closed the closet door to show the floor-length mirror. While we stood in front of it, I ran my hands up and down the curves on her body.

"The dress you wear has to be sexy yet tasteful, flatter your shape and the curves of your body without giving too much away." I uttered, as I pressed my lips to her neck, slowly licking it and gliding my hands down the length of her body, starting at her breasts and ending at her hips. "It has to be a dress suitable for a star, because that's what you are, baby; a beautiful, sexy, talented star; every man in that room will want you, while every woman will want to be you. But you have to have the right presentation to get their response. And once you have their attention, we will get all the backing we need to get into the studio and record your album. This dress will get their attention, but the dress I'm going to get you will make you famous. Do you like the sound of that?"

With moans escaping her throat, she said yes. I knew this was my moment to satisfy the craving I've had since the last time I saw her. I slid her tee shirt above her head, exposing her beautiful breasts, and then easing down her boy shorts with a fluidity that is undeniable. Pushing her now naked body against the wall, I removed my clothes.

Caressing her inner thighs I dropped to my knees, anchoring her to the wall, I put her legs on my shoulders. Facing the object of my desire, I couldn't help but admire her handy work. Getting regular waxes sure kept her cookie looking as good as the rest of her. Salivating like a starving man, I dove into her warm core; immediately she flooded my mouth with molten nectar. Drinking it all up, I could have kept my lips there longer; but my dick pulsated with the pounding of a jackhammer just as I felt her tremble.

Feeling her weaken; I eased down her legs and walked her over to the bed. Laying her down as if she was the most precious of objects, I fucked her as if any minute someone was going to walk in on us. She lay on her back, body bouncing relentlessly and in perfect sync with my movements. The more I pounded into her body, the louder and more reckless her moans became. Taking her left breast into my mouth, I played with her nipple with my tongue. Biting and sucking it as I felt her body arch beneath me, aching for release.

Upon gaining apex into her body, the tightness of her almost made me cum right then; but I slowed my rhythm until I could get control of my body. Then, just to play with her clit a little, I removed my dick and stroked it gently on the engorged clit. Doing that made her cry out louder, arch her back, and lifting her legs that begged to be penetrated once more.

Getting enough of my game, I re-entered her hot, moist body. Making slow, deliberated circles inside her; her body began to flush, and I knew she was about to cum again. I know I was at my peak when my mouth began to get dry and I felt a familiar tingle at the base of my spine threatening to travel up and then back down. Feeling myself about to cum, I pumped faster, then I pulled out of her body and came on her stomach with a force that could have made it all the way to her face; she was lucky this time. Usually I would have grabbed her head to thrust her lips to my dick and came all over her face and mouth. But hey, the night is still young. Maybe I could leave that for round two. As she drifted off to sleep, I brought up the subject of her moving in with me for tomorrow while she's making me breakfast.

Chloe

As much as I don't want to admit it, Dominique did me a favor by inviting Jayshawn to the Gala. Now only if she wasn't running late so she could help me find a dress. I've never been to a party like this before, and Dee being from that world knows the dress code. But then again, I don't know if she knows how to shop with a big girl. I mean, we've shopped together before but only at places that sell straight sizes and plus sizes; never a place like the Sweet Spot Boutique that only caters to a more curvaceous woman, I thought as I aimlessly browsed through the racks. Shaking my mind out of a self-inflicted funk, I remembered how much I loved this store. It was perfect! It caters to women between 18 and 40, carries an array of beautiful clothes for all plus sizes; which is rare because most places stop at a certain size. They also make custom pieces and alter whatever they sell. Yeah, this was a fat girl's dream store. The owner/designer Tasheema 'Tash' Wilcox has been on the cover and interviewed countless times by Indulgence Magazine, and other magazines and bloggers.

While thumbing through the racks I found a gorgeous floor-length gown. It is all black, leather busts, strapless gown, with a sweetheart neckline with satin and tulle skirt. Holding it up to get a better view of its details, I wondered if Jayshawn would like it on me. I quickly snatched it and ran into the dressing room before anyone else could grab it.

While undressing I could see that the dress would fit snug around my breasts and torso; but the fabric felt good on my skin, as if it was made just for me. The reflection staring back at me through the mirror has me in complete awe. Suddenly a wave came over me, and I felt a feeling of change in the air, like I was changing before my own eyes in a boutique dressing room.

As I stood there, I heard a knock at the door. I quickly yelled out that someone is in here, not sure if I remembered to lock the door. The voice speaking back at me was Dee; ready to yell at her for being so damn late, I pulled back the door so hard my hair went flying. I stood in the door and watched her expression change from looking a little sad to surprise when she saw me.

She pushed the door opened a little more and gazed at me as if she was taking in the beauty of the gown. She took a step back and a smile slowly crept across her face.

She said, "That's it! That's the dress you're wearing. Now we have to find you some shoes!"

"Shoes... What the hell did Hershel have you doing that took so long?" I asked.

With her face and body visibly strained she said, "He was meeting with a new client and wanted me to make sure everything was in order; real estate buyers want to make sure they're getting the value of their money."

I wasn't convinced, there was more to the story, and she didn't want to spill. Whatever it was I wasn't going to beat it out of her, when she's ready she'll let me know. In the meantime, I agreed to go shoe shopping after leaving the boutique with the sexiest dress about to be worn by a big girl. Leaving the store, my money was low. I haven't been working in a while, and my assistant gig wasn't starting until the next week. I'm basically living off of my savings and Dee; thank god she had rich parents!

After browsing in a couple of stores and finding nothing in my budget, we found a Consignments shop called Trixie's Tradable Couture. I remember seeing a blog about it once, but never thought to track it down. Instead of looking for shoes, I found myself looking through the accessories station wondering who had once worn some of these pieces, and what circumstances had led them to bring them to a consignment shop. Not paying any attention, Dee snuck up behind me startling me for a second. She was holding a pair of Stewart Weltzer strappy open-toed shoes.

"These would look great with your dress, Try them on!" She said.

"These shoes are over three hundred dollars; even used I can't afford those!" I said as I was starting to lose patience with my frugality.

"STOP IT! You're trying these shoes on, and whatever money you can put on the shoes, put on them; and I'll pay the rest. That's it not another word about it!" Dee scoffed with finality.

"Ok, fine. I'll try them on; and if my toe goes over the tip by a hair I'm not buying them!" I said with my own false sense of finality.

I sat a chair and attempted to fasten the ankle strap. After several attempts, I finally got them on and stood in front of the mirror trying to imagine them with the dress. I hate to admit it, but my girl has taste; she was right they were perfect.

As I clutched the shoes tightly in my hand so to not give any other shopper the indication that I wasn't going to purchase them, I followed Dee to a rack that had some of the most beautiful gowns I've ever seen. She seemed to be enthralled with a very sexy red gown. It's spaghetti strapped with an embroidered jewel bust and flowing taffeta skirt. It is beautiful, and it suited her personality. It gave a sexy, flirty, feel with a hint of sophistication.

Purchasing her dress, and my shoes we made our way out of the store towards the first food vender we could find. Shortly after eating, Dee went back to work, and I headed off back to our apartment to inspect the day's purchases, and ensure I made the right choice in attire. I knew there was still something on her mind that she didn't want to discuss, but I couldn't force it. I think what really bugged me about it was the fact that she was never a person to bite her tongue, or beat around the bush. Whatever was on her mind she said regardless of the consequences, and the fact that she didn't tell me what was going on made me worry for my friend; whatever it was it's major. Unbeknownst to me was how major it was going to be.

Ramir

I walked out of Mr. Elliot's office
expecting to see Dominique attentively waiting for
us to emerge; instead I was greeted by the
emptiness of a vacant seat. Trying to hide the
disappointment of not seeing her, I turned to Mr.
Elliot and shook his hand before taking my leave.
Making my way to the elevator then to the lobby I
thought it would be a good thing that I didn't see
Dominique. What would I even say to her after all
these years? Would I inquire of her marital status?
Or if she was in good health; of course she was in
good health, she looked better than she did when
we were in school together.

Returning my visitors badge with security,
I exited the building. As I did, I felt the sting of
regret wash over me. No sooner did I look up, I
found myself chest to chest with the person who at
that very moment consumed my thoughts.
Obviously surprised to have walked into someone,
she apologized profusely before realizing it was
me. After a wave of recognition came over her,
she tried to straighten herself. Leaving a ketchup
stain on her face where her hot dog had landed I

pulled my handkerchief from my breast pocket and gently cleaned away the smudge.

Grabbing my hand to remove the handkerchief she stuttered "thank you, I... I can do it."

"Sorry," I said. Standing in awkward silence I asked her how she was doing. Stammering for a moment she got out her answer. Returning the question, I also gave a brief answer. Turning on her heels, she quickly said her goodbyes heading into the building, unable to let her leave like that, I grabbed her arm and looked deeply into her eyes and told her it was fantastic to see her again; she smiled that beautiful smile I remember, nodded and entered the building.

Still gazing at the revolving door she disappeared into, I didn't hear my driver ask if I had any other appointments for the afternoon. Replying then instructing him to return me to my home, I gave him the rest of the afternoon off. On the ride through the city, my thoughts were filled with her. I found myself eager to see her face, but how? I never entertained the idea of leaving my family, but Dominique was my first love that I never got the chance to develop before it ended; one never gets over their first actual love, or lover.

Before the car came to a full stop, I somehow conceived in my mind that I could have both. With Kasha and myself searching for a home upstate, and keeping our apartment in the city; it would be possible. The only question left is, could I actually go through with it? One thing I know for sure was that I had to see her again, even if it was only one more time.

Chloe

This morning was colder than the previous few days, making transitioning fall to the brisk air of winter will do that. I stepped into the crisp morning air with an intended target, a destination if you will. As I walked to the subway, I reminded myself to use perfect or at least close to perfect diction when addressing my new boss for the first time. Working in bars and hanging out it clubs and lounges sort of made me a little lax in vocabulary.

Hell, it was a miracle I even landed this job; if I hadn't had ran into an old Fashion Institute friend, I wouldn't have known to apply to Indulgence Magazine. I was so nervous I shook as I searched for a seat on the train. If I didn't find one soon, there was going to be a problem! I can only do a few hours at a time in these shoes, and I know when I get to this job they are going to have me walking all over the place to get familiar with the office. After standing for ten minutes the train cleared out, most of the riders were getting off in the financial district so I could snag a seat. I laughed to myself at how I acted last night. I made my best friend hide from me because my emotions ran so high. I made her help me find the right first

day of work outfit and talked her ear off with all
the background research I did on the magazine.

Indulgence Magazine: The Magazine for
the Curvaceous Woman is owned and operated by
Hennison James Black. He was given the task of
CEO of the magazine from his now late father
Paul Black. The late Paul Black had to give his
playboy son a pet project to keep him busy. With
Mr. Black having to save his son from himself, he
thought to manage a business would well use him.
Also, the slew of false paternity suits that were
being thrown at Hennison; Mr. Black had to find
something to sate his son's appetite for beautiful
women.

Editor and chief of Indulgence or as she's
known to the staff as the real boss is Clair
Winters; ex-full figured model, accomplished
business woman, impeccable dresser, and rumored
mistress of Paul Black; though that was never
proven to be true. My role at Indulgence is to be
an assistant to Clair's assistant. That spoke
volumes to how busy, and popularity of the
magazine. I wouldn't have much interaction with
Clair, but whenever I was going to be in her
presence, I was going to leave an impression on
her.

The only thing left to add to what I knew
about the Black family dynasty was to mention
Annette Black, Paul Black's widow, and Laura
Black his daughter, and Hennison's sister. There's
not much mention of them outside of Mr. Black's
obituary, they must have taken his passing hard.
Then again it must have been difficult for
Hennison to fill his father's shoes. Paul Black was
a revolutionary man, who had vision and saw the

value in things that others didn't. I mean, why else would a rich white man invest in the plus size market? Perhaps he could see that the plus size industry is a very valuable, untapped or should I say LARGELY untouched market in mainstream fashion, either way I'm excited that someone had taken an interest, and therefore made it possible for me to produce income.

Nearly missing the stop, I scrambled to get off the train. Only walking a few not so short New York blocks I stood in front of my future. I stood and watched the revolving doors of The Black Building wondering if I had what it took to be a writer. It was all well, and good to be self-proclaimed, and to get notice once in a while, but this is a whole new ball game. I was stepping into the big leagues! From here on out, it would be fly or die for me, and there was no way I was going to let Malik think he took the best of me when he left. I guess subconsciously I was putting on all this pressure just to prove that I could make it and be somebody outside of what he thought I was. Truthfully, he never knew who I was. But that's not here or there I have to focus and get through my first day.

Walking into The Black Building, one would think it was a well-oiled machine. Upon entering a person had their choice of two large garnet desks that housed security personnel busy signing visitors in and out, while simultaneously protecting the buildings inhabitants. Between the two desks was a large walkway that led to two elevators bound for the other publications in the building. Oh, did I forget to mention that The Black Building not only housed Indulgence

Magazine but also Rouge Magazine; which is geared towards straight size (more socially acceptable) women, Arsenal; a men's magazine, Black Events and Catering, The studio; where all the visual elements were born, a café, and finally Human Resources offices whose job it is to supply each of these places with employees. Vince from HR told me to meet with Cassidy Martin on the fourth floor, and she would give me direction from there. I began to become anxiety ridden once again as the elevator slowed then stopped on the fourth floor; I wondered if I had made the right outfit choice. Wearing a black leather front panel pencil skirt with white wrap top, and black and gold pumps; I hope I wasn't over doing it.

Standing in front of me as the doors opened was a gorgeous blonde, with legs and curves for days! She looked straight at me as I exited; she introduced herself as Cassidy Martin and began to lead me on a very hasty tour through Indulgence. She escorted me to a large wall-less space that looked like a miniature maze of cubicles. Dropping off my belongings quickly, we made all the usual rounds through the office. She showed me the conference rooms; the duplicity room (which is a fancy word for copy room), the advertisement team's office, the office where the editors and executive editors sit, the media room, and she introduced me to Vivian the front desk receptionist for Indulgence; by the end of the tour my head was spinning.

Each floor housed a magazine or office, complete with their own receptionist to route calls and such. On this floor was also Clair's office which sat towards the back. Though she didn't take me to meet Clair, she pointed out where her office is located. Cassidy seemed nice enough, as she spoke to me you could tell she's done this tour so many times she could probably do it in her sleep. Though tedious, there was no trace of strain, or discomfort in her voice as she spoke. I really appreciated that about her.

Other assistants I've met in the past seemed to have a rather large stick stuck firmly in their ass, like it was some sort of competition; maybe it was, but Cassidy didn't project that image. She informed me of a meeting that was going to take place in the next five minutes; which now makes sense as to why we toured so quickly. Stopping back at my cubical office, I grabbed a pen and small notepad from my purse, and followed Cassidy into conference room A.

This was a small room with large uncovered windows, and a large rectangular table with faux leather chairs. Lined against the walls were faux leather ottomans matching the chairs at the table, I assumed this area was for the assistants to sit. Walking into the room all eyes were on me, probably wondering who the hell I was. Taking a seat on an ottoman, I watched as the office inhabitants began to fill the small space. The more important people sat at the large table, as the assistants lined the walls; notepads and tablets in hand. The last person in the room to make an appearance was Clair Winters and her top assistant Cassidy.

Taking her seat at the table's head, and Cassidy to her right she began the meeting. Seeing Clair in publications didn't do her any justice. Stunning is the first word that came to mind when describing her. A chocolate beauty, she stood at about 5ft 9in, with an hourglass shape, long chestnut hair (obviously Brazilian Wavy), wearing a red Margaret Chapman pants suit, and black Tobias Forge stilettos. Her face not revealing her age, she began to speak with an air of authority that made all sit up and take notice. First attacking the editorial team she began to relentlessly drill them for better material.

Mentioning that circulation was up 20% for this month from the previous year, she wanted to make a statement with the next issue. Next, was media team who were in charge of the photo shoots and layouts. Actually managing to squeak out an accepting nod they were now off her radar. Whispering slightly to Cassidy, she returned her attention to the staff and briefly announced that they had new staffers and to show them the ropes, make them feel at home, and catch them up on the subject of the upcoming issue and familiarize them with the new ad campaigns. Calling out my name, she asked me to stand so everyone would see me, and then she called another name. She announced Kellendra Boaden who would also be an assistant to Cassidy. With introductions made and delegations given she dismissed the staff, and they went scurrying off to their various departments not wanting to linger and get another tongue lashing.

Cassidy asked Kellendra and I to stay. Trying to introduce myself properly to Kellendra, I was met with a barely touching hand shake and a slight eye roll. Oh yeah, I can tell this was going to be a walk in the park working with her; I secretly wondered if she was related to Makayla.

Following Cassidy out into her small office that adjoined with Clair's, Cassidy handed us files containing everything we need to know for the upcoming weeks. And I do mean everything; from editorial deadlines, events, ad's calendar, company history, and what we are expected to have completed by the end of the week. I don't know about Kellendra, but my load was extensive for a first day.

My first task was to secure a meeting with Margaret Chapman and her team, order three dozen roses for a celebrity dressing room who is also having a photo shoot the next week, as well as setting up her dressing room to her exact specifications. I was also in charge of scouting fresh ideas for future features, I'm sure that was a general task just to keep the flow of great ideas coming in; but in any event I felt important. Returning to my mini office, I took a deep breath and prepared to get started on the rest of my life. I was taking the first steps to my independence and honestly it felt great!

Dominique

I can't believe how shook I was to see Ramir after all these years. I went to work every day after that scared he might call to make another appointment with Hershel. The thought of being in his presence sent my body quivering, I don't know if it was out of fear, or anticipation; either way I had to prepare myself by dressing to the nines. I mean, I always look good, but my goal was to be irresistible. I had to show him what he's been missing. Was that childish? Maybe it was. But would it be satisfying to show the man that broke my heart that I had moved on and became a huge success without him being in my life? HELL YES!

He had no idea what would greet him next time he entered this office. Unfortunately, I would have to wait to have satisfaction. Hershel would be out of the office in the coming weeks in preparations of showing new properties, acquiring properties, and all around not getting on my nerves; which was the best part. I know we used to date, but that was a million years ago!

He would just have to get over the fact that he just couldn't do it for me. I mean, he really couldn't do it for me. In our two month courtship I slept with him three times, and every time was like I was giving to charity. You know... Something you really don't want to do, but you do it to make the other person feel good about themselves, and in turn you feel good too, but minus the fact that I felt good after; or during for that matter.

I think in some ways he was punishing me for the break up. He couldn't be too heart broken over it, because a few short weeks later he started dating Rebecca Denis, after a year of dating and at his parents urging he married her. I almost laughed to myself thinking about all the bad sex she was condemned to.

Poor woman; she's in her prime and struck down by the high demands of society living. But I guess it was worth it to have vacations twice a year, an unlimited Black Card, and access to exclusive parties. In any case, I shouldn't be too hard on him, after all he didn't choose me to be his assistant, my father chose for him, so I guess he's just as stuck with me, as I am with him. Still, every once in a while I see the look of want in his eyes; which I ignore and keep going like I saw nothing, but one day we would have to address it if it becomes an issue.

Sitting at my desk preparing the expense report for my dad, I got a call on my cell. Usually I would ignore a call from a number I didn't know, but curiosity and boredom got the best of me; I said to myself 'what the hell, I can always hang up.'

Saying 'Hello?' with a question in my voice I heard a slight laugh, then a smooth voice drifted into my ears.

"Hello Dominique." The mysterious voice said. "I was wondering if we could go out tonight if you're not busy, or do I get to see you again at the Gala?"

As he said that, I knew exactly who it was. "Chase!" I said. "I'm surprised you called, I wasn't expecting you to... How are you?"

"I'm well, but I can be better if I saw you tonight. So, what do you think about it? Me and You dinner, you can pick the place?" He said.

After taking a second, I agreed to dinner with Chase. Honestly, it would take my mind off of Ramir; and I never turn down a free meal or a good looking man. We made plans to meet at 8p.m. at Jupiter Restaurant in Manhattan. I figured he would be more comfortable in a place closer to what he's used to. I could only imagine how he reacted if I took him to a soul food spot.

Stepping out of the cab, I was surprised to see him standing outside of the restaurant. Greeting me with a smile and hug we entered Jupiter's arm and arm. Walking straight in and escorted to the best table, I didn't know if he frequented this place often or if he gave the guy at the door a huge tip, either way I was impressed. Despite its cosmic name, Jupiter's was a very classy place, renovated from what used to be a Sushi Bar, it had certainly morphed into an up and coming hot spot among the rich, young, elite.

It was surprising how easy it was to talk to him. We didn't have any of those first date awkward questions like, where do you work? Or what is your life's greatest goal? Really, we're passed that since we already know each other intimately. Yet the conversation wasn't uncomfortable, we talked as if old friends catching up; I never had that before and it felt comforting. We laughed whole heartedly, ordered Champagne, and sampled food off of each other's plates. To the casual observer we must have looked like a couple in love; I let myself feel that for just a moment. Feel how good it would be to have not just a lover; I had plenty of those to last me the next several lifetimes. But to have the love of a person who deserved to have mine in return. That's what I thought I would have with Ramir; I wonder if he has that with his wife.

After dinner we walked a bit to burn off all the food and wine we drank. Walking down the street the comedy didn't stop! He had me laughing so hard my stomach was threating to touch my back. Stopping only to catch my breath, I turned to find him looking in the direction of a small club tucked in an ally on the side of a building.

Gesturing me to follow, we approached the door to find a small bar with a great house band. Taking seats in a booth close to the stage, we ordered yet another round of drinks; sat and enjoyed the music. Exiting the stage the band took a break before the next set and the bar had R&B playing in the background to entertain the crowd between sets.

Softly caressing my hand Chase guided me to the dance floor joining other dancers. Holding me firmly in his arms we began to rock slowly, easily catching the beat. Swaying in time with each other, I felt the softness of his skin against my cheek, and I was immediately transported back to the night we shared together.

How could I have been so stupid as to not have pursued him? Well, I can't worry about that now; what's done is done and I'm enjoying myself with him now. We were so close I could smell the Tobias Forge cologne he wore. Inhaling his scent deeply, I made a memory of tonight. I was so lost in the atmosphere I didn't notice that music had stopped, and the band began to play once again.

Whispering in my ear that the music had stopped, I pulled away from him returning to the booth where we sat. Cradling my hand in his hands, he stared in my eyes and asked if I was ok. Replying yes, I made an excuse about being tired and having to work the next day. Giving me an understanding look, he grabbed our jackets, and we took our leave. Disappearing into the ladies room to get myself together he insisted on waiting for me in the bar. At my urging he agreed to meet me at the entrance.

Walking out the door of the club, the cold air hit me instantly that it almost took my breath away. Joining Chase, we walked towards the street, pulling up in front of us as we emerged was a jet black town car with tinted windows. Opening the door for me, he informed me of calling the car to make sure I got home safely. Insisting it dropped me off first I gave the driver my address, and then Chase gave his. The car was cozy with warm air coming forcefully through the vents, I had to unbutton my jacket exposing the low cut top, and skirt that stopped above the knee; that I selected this morning in anticipation of Ramir showing up unannounced in the office.

The entire ride was in silence; which was the most awkward part of the night. Through it all

Chase reminded me of his presence by caressing the inside of my palm. He slowly led a trail starting from my palm to my arm and settling on my face. I didn't know if it was the liquid courage we consumed throughout the evening or the want we both were feeling; but we leaned into each other and kissed. We embraced each other so deeply that we nearly forgot the driver had a full view of the show. Stopping as to not be a part of Taxi Car Chronicles that came on cable television, he asked if I wanted to go back to his place; agreeing he informed the driver that there would be one stop.

Arriving at his apartment, we tried to be casual entering the building. We contained ourselves until we got to his door. He had a spectacular place, with a magnificent view. It was open and airy, yet it had a feel of hominess; he had one hell of a decorator. Taking my jacket, he led me to the living room, and asked if I wanted a drink. Declining I sat in front of his fireplace he switched on with a remote. Getting himself a beer, he took a seat next to me and removed my shoes. Taking my left foot into his hands he rubbed all the parts that ached.

"Chase, how did you know I needed a foot rub?" I asked.

Not even looked up; he smiled and replied, "any woman who worked all day in 6 inch heels, goes out on a date, then out dancing deserves a good rub; don't you think?"

Hitting the right spot at the right time I answered "YES! I never knew a man could be this considerate."

"I'm not other men you've ever dated Dominique." He said as if he wanted to make it clear to me that no one would ever measure up to him.

Silenced, I snuggled into his couch and enjoyed my message. Feeling his hand glide slowly and intently up my legs, I opened my eyes and saw him gazing at me. Leaning forward I took his face in my hands and kissed him with intention. Following my lead he stroked my neck and shoulders before settling himself on top of me. Still clothed we kissed wrapped in each other's arms until we were left breathless. Feeling the discomfort of the couch we continued the assault on each other in his bedroom.

Undressing me down to my bra and panties then we laid on his king bed and slowly caressed each other. Between kisses and intimate touches I thought maybe I didn't want him to be a notch on my bedpost but something real. I immediately stopped him, and the alertness made him pause. Asking if I was alright, and if he'd done something wrong, he backed off slowly. I told him I liked him and didn't want to repeat the mistakes we had done before. Looking disappointed he nodded in agreement and laid flat on the bed. I stood to put my clothes back on when he grabbed me and pulled me close.

"Now, where do you think you're going?" He asked.

"Home," I replied. "Since we're not doing this, I figured I would go."

"I don't want you to go; we can stay the night together and not have sex. I mean, if you can't contain yourself I understand." He said with a sly smile.

"Really? Oh, I can contain myself buddy." I said as evenly as I could.

With that I climbed into bed beside him and we spooned under the covers. This was the first time in a long time I slept with a guy and didn't really sleep with him. Either I'm growing as a person; or Chase Greene is the guy I've been looking for, then lost, and he found me again. I don't know what this was, but it felt damn good to have it. With a quick text to Chloe to let her know that I wasn't coming home, I wrapped myself in the warmth of Chase's body and drifted off to sleep with the night sounds of the city fading into the background.

Jayshawn

Giving direction to outside contractors is a nightmare! To cut expenses, the venue used its own people to assist with the set up. I need this venue transformed before the club owners walk through the doors and see the lack of progression. Tonight Club Mayhem is debuting new artist Cynsation; she was a stripper turned singer overnight courtesy of Malik. I hear through mutual friends that he's branched out into managing to corner the entertainment market.

Though the artist is his; the club owners refused to let him handle the showcase due to his lack of vision. Malik is a man who is about immediate satisfaction, but not perfection. With that, the contract went to me, in the PR world I'm known for creating amazing experiences and making things that don't fit work in cohesion. Focusing my attention on the lighting at the moment, I had to alert the tech to the lighting cues. Believe me 'Cynsation' was going to need all the help she could get, listening to the tracks she would perform, and all the auto tune used to cover up a barely audible voice, I have to amp up party-goers by creating a specific feel. I also had to get a feel for her sound so that the theme would match her performance which helped me to design the right atmosphere.

Everything was coming together with not a moment to spare! Doing my last checks of the sound and lighting the only thing left to do was get this girl on stage, it was almost time to open, and she was nowhere to be found. At a quarter to 10:00 Liam the owner asked if everything was ready because a line formed leading down the block. I know he knew better than to ask me that; so I let it slide.

Informing him that everything was good to go, he asked where Malik was; I guess he was unaware that Malik and his artist were running late. 10:15 the doors opened, the drinks started flowing, and I brought in a local band to warm up the crowd. Everything looked great, despite the lack of expert workers; they executed my vision for this event, and the only thing missing was an artist to perform.

Most of the audiences were regular party-goers with a mix of talent scouts, bloggers, and amateur song writers and producers looking for the next money maker. Running out time, and sensing the restlessness of the crowd, Liam paced the dance floor. He knew that if he didn't deliver what he promised; that he would have to refund everyone, and he was not about to give none of them their money back. Shit, if he had to put on a wig, and lip sync he would do it.

After about an hour of stalling the twosome graced us with their presence. Bypassing hair and makeup, Cynsation went straight to the stage, without a sound check it was no telling what was about to happen. Malik blew a kiss to Cyn and turned to Liam and whispered something to him, no doubt trying to smooth things over and defended their disheveled looks. On perfect cue the lights dimmed on the dance floor and brightened on the stage alerting the audience to the beginning of the performance.

Staggering to the stage was a disheveled looking woman with shiny leggings and a green sequin top. Pausing to say something quickly to the band, they put down their instruments and left the stage. Immediately I got the DJ's attention and gave him the cue to play the track, with no sound check it was going to take a miracle for her to pull off three songs. Catching the eye of the in house lighting tech, I signaled for the countdown to lower the lights. Taking the stage for her introduction, Malik went to center stage and with a practiced smile he introduced Cyn to the audience.

"Good evening everyone, thanks for coming out." He said with a smooth voice. "The talent you're about to witness tonight is a young lady by the name of Cynsation! Being a model she brings a regality and remarkable poise to her art. As an R&B singer she brings the sexy and lyrical complexity. Ladies and gentlemen, give a round of applause to CYNSAAATION!" He yelled.

As rehearsed, the lights dimmed to give a sensual vibe with the spot light slowly approaching center stage. The music began to play and Cynsation sauntered her way to the mic. Beginning to sing she cupped the mic and began to move rhythmically with the slow melody. I was surprised to see that she could actually sing. With her green sequin top glittering as she moved, she looked like she was singing to someone in the audience. Following the trail she led with her eyes, I found the object that was holding her attention. Tucked in the back of the crowd, sitting at one of the few small tables was Malik. Now it all made sense! This was the chick Malik left Chloe for! Wow, I knew he was dirty motherfucker but to leave her in order to control a client and play mind games with both is low even for him. But still if he hadn't I wouldn't be in the running to take his place.

Finishing up her first song, the second was a faster paced pop song. As the tempo picked, you could tell this wannabe diva was completely inebriated. She tried to cover up her drunkenness by attempting to keep up with the beat, but it was obvious that her attempts failed. Watching her crash on stage and taking the clubs good name with her, I tried to think of how I could salvage this situation. Looking through the crowd, I could find Malik nowhere. So, I did the only thing I could think of doing; I ran to the lighting director and told him to watch me for instructions.

Giving the band the sign to re-take the stage, I met Cynsation's gaze in an attempt to get her to follow my lead. Knowing she was bombing on stage by the sudden shift in the crowd she gave a slight nod. Switching quickly to the next song, she began to speak to the crowd; this time sounding alert. Giving the audience the title and date of her debut album's release, she engaged the crowd once again with a heartfelt ballot.

Finishing her set I ushered her quickly off the stage and instructed the band to play the house music. Taking her into a small dressing room, I could see the embarrassment in her face. Not realizing I was staring at her it took me a second to realize she was talking to me.

"I can't believe that just happened." She said through weepy eyes. "I thought they were going to love me, I did nothing but make a fool of myself! I should've never listened to Malik... He told me that a few drinks would take the edge off! And when I looked for him in the crowd he was gone! Can you find him for me... PLEASE?"

Never the one to make an upset woman more so, I went to find Malik. Finding him at the bar smiling a shark like grin in the direction of female company, I quickly whispered the situation to him. Shooting me a dirty look he excused himself to check on his girl/artist. That lack of care for business and the mixing of it with personal entanglements is a bad look, but as long as he's ok wearing it, I'm good.

Later that night as I walked across the empty dance floor, I stared into the emptiness of the club making mental notes of all that occurred as to not have something like this catch me off guard again, in this business you have to measure, and re-measure all angles and if something doesn't work, you have to make it work; tonight was a prime example of that.

After Malik consoled his half hysterical artist, he quickly exited the club only stopping to get a few dollars for their take of the night; getting my final payment, I too left. Arriving home after 3 a.m., I took a quick shower to wash off the night and dove into my bed. Before nodding out I checked my phone to see if I'd had any missed calls from Chloe. I've been tempted to call her for days, but I really didn't want to push her too far too fast and end up pushing her away. Looking at my phone I saw I in fact had a missed call, but it wasn't from Chloe. I can't believe Tarin had the gull to call me after all this time!

"Fuck her!" I said out loud as I slammed the phone down and switched off the light.

Chloe

My first work week was a complete disaster! Being new in any company is hard, but add in the fact that I worked with high powered, fast paced, models and wannabe's who survived on water, lattes, and wheat crackers; and that intensifies the madness by thousands! Seriously, I've got to learn to bring flats with me in my purse; I thought as I started to climb the first flight of stairs. Working in heels all day then taking the train home and walking up six floors can really wear a girl's feet out.

Reaching my apartment I couldn't wait to take off my shoes and tell Dee about all the craziness of the day; then I realized the apartment was dark. Knowing this meant Dee was with her new boo Chase; I felt a small twinge of disappointment. She's been spending so much of her time with Chase that I don't get to see her anymore. Don't get me wrong! I'm happy for her, but really I just miss my friend. I only see her in the mornings before she leaves for work, nowadays I don't see her then since she's been taking some of her clothes over to Chase's.

Throwing my stuff on the couch, I went to the kitchen to pour myself some wine to ease off some tension. Deciding that wasn't enough, I put on some music and began to remove my clothes. Only wearing my bra, and work pants; I peered at the files that needed my immediate attention and said 'fuck it' out loud and walked towards the bathroom for a hot shower.

While letting the hot water run over the sore parts of my body, I thought about what it would be like if I lived alone. Would I night after night come home to any empty apartment with stacks of work to do? Can I break myself out of this funk and find a man to spend my nights with? Not realizing I was talking out loud I asked, *'When was the last time I spoke to Jay?'* not remembering, I got out the shower, quickly dried off, and grabbed my phone to call him. Stopping short of the call button I decided to text him instead. If I talked to him on the phone, he might hear the want in my voice, and either come over or send a driver to come get me; I don't know if I'm ready to take it there yet.

Opening the message tab, I began to write… "Hi Jay, I miss you!" Then quickly deleted it; it sounded too desperate. Then I wrote, "Hey, long time no hear from," And that looked ok to send so I hit the button and waited for him to reply. Trying to get dressed, I looked at my phone every few seconds, and also checked to make sure the ringer was on so I didn't miss the message alert when he texted back. Sitting idle for a while I started on the paper work I brought home. Looking at the heavily detailed form marked 'Coco's Dressing Room Requirements' I dreaded having to pull items from the appropriately named 'Warehouse'.

The Warehouse is the area below the Black Building and also at another off site location where the company keeps different types of furniture, costumes, clothes, sets, props, and all kinds of fun stuff when they're having photo shoots or have clients who require special accommodations, and Coco Caliente was one of those clients. Coco is a girl out of New Jersey who used to be a waitress in one of the hotel/casinos in Atlantic City. So the story goes, she was serving drinks to this guy who just so happened to be a famous boxer who fell in love with her; so when he left A.C. she did too.

Being bored and having her new man traveling a lot she begged him to finance her singing career and being that he knew of some heavy hitters at the magazine, he pulled some strings and got her an interview and a cover shot on Indulgence. She wasn't what I consider being a plus size girl, but she was thick in all the right places, so I guess that qualified her without taking away the credibility of the magazine. It was my job to cater to her every whim while she was shooting the cover photo starting with her dressing room. The list is as follows:

Coco Caliente's Dressing Room

1. The room must be ALL WHITE:
>Chairs
>Walls
>Pillows
>Rugs

Table
Lamps/w shades
Mirror (floor length)

2. Flat Screen TV (Only plays Coco's music)

3. Guest area

4. Tall crystal vases with 2 dozen long steam red and yellow roses

5. Crystal vase filled with white, red, and yellow candies

6. White sheer curtains covering the entry way to the dressing room

7. Photos of Coco (so she could get inspired)

8. Personal stylist

9. Changing area

10. Personal Masseuse

11. Yoga instructor

12. Personal stylist

13. Water, Wines, and assorted cheeses

And the list goes on and on… I can't believe someone would request all of this for a two hour photo shoot. I mean, she only had a few crappy videos, a few decent songs, and an album that barely put a blip on the radar of the music world; she couldn't possibly go all diva with just that under her belt! But I guess when you have people to feed your ego anything is possible. After looking through as much as I could before my eyes got droopy, I checked my phone one more time and decided to go to bed.

Lying in Dee's vacant bed, I stared at the ceiling and watched as the lights from the cars as they danced on it. I lay there wondering what Jay was doing, what Malik was doing and finally about the day ahead tomorrow. In the dark I imagined the feel of Jayshawn's lips on mine and wanted that to happen again. Is it weird that I remember every detail of our embrace? His breath inhaling me deeply, the pressure of his lips, the warmth of his arms as they cradled my body, and finally the beating of his heart on my chest; I remembered it all and the memories of it came flooding back as if it was happening now. Now trying desperately to sleep, I put in my ear buds and listened to some R&B to lull myself to sleep.

Waking from a restless sleep, I threw myself in the shower and got ready for another day at Indulgence. I loved working there, but when I get the picture in my mind; I see something different from the reality I was living. In my mind's eye, I was climbing the ladder and graduating to Associate Editor. Recognizing my talent, Clair took me under her wing, and taught me all about the business. Together we traveled the fashion world from the stages of Milan to the catwalks of NYC and we reveled in the attention.

And the men! The men fell at our feet and prayed for us to step on them just to say they got within sniffing distance. In reality, I was still an assistant, Clair Winters did not understand who I was, and men… yeah right, I couldn't pay them to forget my name. Walking into the Black Building, I strolled mindlessly to the elevator. Deep in my thoughts I barely heard a voice yell to hold the elevator.

Snapping out of my temporary stupor, I reached to stop the doors from closing. Stepping onto the elevator was the 'big man' himself, Hennison Black. Feeling the temperature drop 10 degrees I tried not to stare at him, he was gorgeous in pictures; but in person they didn't do him any justice. Standing so close to me I could smell every sensuous inch of his cologne; Hennison was the type of man that made you drool when he entered the room. Grabbing the attention from every person man/woman alike; he oozed sexuality.

According to Power Players Business Magazine (which he owns shares in) who did a story on him last year; he stood about 6ft 4in tall, and a chiseled 230 pounds of exquisite man muscle. Educated in the finest higher education institutions of the world the man boasted a business mind unmatched by his peers. Paul Black wasn't grooming his only son to take over the publishing world, but the world. Yeah, Hennison Black was a catch for any women; and he caught most of them and then threw them back in the water like a fisher that caught a guppy instead of a prized Marlin. Deep in a world of my creating, I heard him say good morning to me.

"Oh, I'm sorry. Good Morning." I said, trying to keep from rushing the words out of my mouth.

Surprisingly keeping conversation with me, he continued by saying, "You must be new to the building; I haven't seen you here before. Do you need help find Human Resources?"

"No, I don't. I mean, I am new to the building, but I don't need Human Resources. I work for Indulgence Magazine on the fourth floor." As soon as the words left my mouth, I kicked myself! Of course he knew where Indulgence is, this was his company! Idiot!

Smiling a brilliant smile he said, "Oh, Indulgence; I hope Clair is treating you well there."

"Yes!" I said hurriedly. "She's been good, and her assistant Cassidy are amazing, they've made me feel welcome (everyone except Kellendra, but that's a different story)."

"Pardon my rudeness," he said as he reached his hand out to me. "I'm Hennison Black and I want to welcome you to The Black Building. I hope every experience you have here will make you feel welcome and part of the team."

Trying to hide my blushing, I reached back and introduced myself. "Hello Hennison; I'm Chloe Major. It's nice to meet you."

The ding of the elevator bell signaling my stop interrupted our exchange, and I excused myself. As I turned to exit Hennison said 'I'll see you around.' Returning his ever so slight flirtation I responded with one of my own, 'I hope you do.' And I turned on my heels and sauntered out of the elevator.

The rest of the day went by in a blur. I don't know if I was still riding high from my brief exchange this morning, or I loved my job; I was starting to feel like I was going somewhere. After so many years of working dead-end jobs, and freebee writing gigs I was starting to think I had chosen the wrong career path; but by a chance meeting with an old friend I was able to find the career I wanted (God, is always on time isn't he?).

Stealing a glance I realized that I had to get to Cassidy's office so we could take a trip to 'The Warehouse' and get what they needed for Coco Caliente's dressing room. Heading towards her office, she was already coming towards me. Matching her strides, we went straight to the elevators and to the basement. Quickly telling me about the items in The Warehouse, she explained that whenever I needed to get something for a client, I had to fill out a form and have her or Clair, and the secretary in charge of The Warehouse sign off on it; it's how they are able to keep track of the comings and goings of company property.

Handing me the form I scanned it and nodded in understanding. When the doors opened, I expected to see a dark, dusty, slightly mildewed basement full of junk.

Instead I was greeted by a carpeted seating area, and small wooden desk. Sitting with authority behind it was Grace; who was in charge of The Warehouse. Hugging Cassidy, Grace asked if we needed the movers this time. Responding yes, Grace quickly called for them and told them to bring the hand trucks. Grabbing keys from her desk drawer, Grace unlocked a large wooden door that sat to the left of her desk.

Upon entering a large, brightly lit, floor to ceiling white room with clean tiled floors, I was in awe of how organized it is. It wasn't like walking

123

into a basement at all, but an actual furniture store complete with everything that a person would need to furnish thirty homes. It also has racks of odds and ends, which add perfect little touches and give a space a homey personality. Realizing I was being left behind I sped walked to catch up to the ladies.

Each one of us grabbing a shopping cart, Cassidy asked me to read out loud the items we needed. One by one we went from section to section picking up any and everything that fit the theme of the dressing room; all that was heard echoing through the corridors of The Warehouse were the clicks of heels on the tiled floors, shuffling of fixtures, and laughter of three women.

With Cassidy and Grace telling stories about past projects, and all the things that can might go wrong, I listened intently trying to make mental notes of those situations just in case I need to refer to them if I had the same issues. I couldn't believe how much I was learning from a simple shopping excursion. Finishing up and paperwork signed, Cassidy and I headed to Black Building Studios to set up Coco's dressing room. By the time we reach the studio on the sixth floor, the movers were already moving in furniture pieces from the freight elevator.

Trying desperately to follow Coco's specifications to the letter, Cassidy and I finished forty-five minutes before she strolled into the building. Introducing ourselves briefly we left to allow the studio team to do their thing. Back in my cubical, I collapsed in my chair. Going over files and schedules, I glanced at the calendar and realized the Gala was only two weeks away! I had so much work to do between now and then, not to mention that I hadn't heard from Jayshawn. Picking up my phone I sent him a quick text.

To Jayshawn Thomas:

Hi Jay, I haven't heard from you. The Gala is a couple of weeks away and I wanted to make sure you were still going... Dominique asked and I didn't know what to tell her.

Not one minute later I got a reply.

From: Jayshawn Thomas:

Sorry doll. I had a lot of business to take care of this week. It's funny because I was waiting to get a text from you. Yes, I still plan to be your date. Don't tell me you're missing me? How's your day going?

Chloe:

It's going well. The job is fast paced, but I love it! I always wanted to work in publishing, we haven't had an idea session yet; but I ready when we do. Missing you? Whatever... Just checking in that's all.

Jayshawn Thomas:

Checking in are you, if you say so. Oh, and I'm aware of how far away the Gala is; and I'm looking forward to it. This will be our first time on a date and I intend to make a good impression on you. Can I see you tonight?

Chloe:

Tonight... I don't know, I have a lot of work here... Can I let you know later?

125

Jayshawn Thomas:

Of course doll. I'll be waiting for that call. I have to let you go I have a meeting in a few. Call me later.

I couldn't help but smile at the phone as I put it down. Spinning around in my chair, I was startled to see that Hennison was standing in my cubical!

"OH MY GOD!" I screamed, as I saw him standing there.

"I didn't mean to scare you, you just look so happy on your phone that I couldn't help but watch you. Who were you talking to, anyway?" He said with inquiry in his voice.

"No one, just a friend I haven't heard from in a while. What can I do for you?" I asked.

"Nothing," He replied. I was here to see Clair and thought I would stop to see how we're treating you here. I was told that you set up Coco's dressing room; good work she was very happy with it."

"Thank you. I had help and direction from Cassidy." I said.

As I finished my statement Kellendra came around the corner with a stack of files in hand. Coming into my cubical and interrupting our exchange she informed me of a meeting that was going to take place tonight as she threw files on my desk and quickly turning on her heels walking out. Explaining that I had to get back to work; Hennison left me to work on the load that Kellendra left. Poring over file after file I felt like my brain was going to explode. Taking a break, I

126

walked to Cassidy's office. She looked like she had just as much work as I did.

Looking up she said "Hey, what's up?"

"Nothing, I just need a break." I replied.

Smiling and shaking her head she said "The first few weeks are always the roughest. Soon you will be able to do this stuff in your sleep. It was a lot for me to take in to when I started here, but you adapt to the life and roll with it. Is this what you always wanted to do?"

"Yeah, I've always wanted to be in publishing; just more on the writing side." I responded.

"Everyone who comes here has an assumption of going on to be something, but they all forget that you have to start from somewhere else. If that's what you want to do then do it. Wait for your opportunity and go for it. Me, I've seen and done it all." Cassidy held.

"Why are you Clair's assistant Cassidy? I mean no disrespect but I know that you've had opportunities offered to you, especially from working with Clair; you had to have learned a lot." I insisted.

"I have." She expressed. "But I love working with Clair, she's a wonderful woman. We used to model together back in the days and she really taught me a lot about the business and the fashion world in general. Really she's like a mom to me; she's also Godmother to my son. I'm happy here, this magazine is my life away from my family; and like Clair, I will pour my heart into it to make it succeed."

"Wow." Was the only response that I could say, "I didn't know the two of you were that close. I've always admired her and would love to accomplish the things she has. Do you ever think about going back into modeling?" I asked.

"Oh no, have you seen these models out here? I'm good here. What about you Chloe? You can defiantly be a print model, have you ever considered it? Clair works with Slone Hill's Modeling Agency that's where we get a lot of our models; I could give her a call." Cassidy claimed.

"No, no, no. I like writing about fashion and lifestyle; I'll leave the modeling to the experts." I laughed.

"Ok," Cassidy breathed. "But if you ever change your mind, let me know. By the way the meeting tonight is for 'The Pit' so have your ideas ready. Clair doesn't call on newbies for ideas often, but when she does you better have them."

"Ok, thanks." I said as I walked back to my office. I did have a few ideas written down, but I had no idea tonight was a 'Pit' night! I have to text Jay to let him know that tonight was a no go.

Sending Jay a quick text, I decided to check Indulgence's Editorial Schedule to see what else Clair had is store for us; I should have checked it earlier, but I thought it only pertained to the editors; I had no idea the assistants had to be aware of it this soon.

This place had so many daily meetings; I wondered how everyone kept up with the comings and goings of new clients, models, photographers, etc. Seeking a little quiet time before my first 'Pit' meeting I snuck away to the ladies room. As I was about to walk in I heard the wild laughs of two women.

Not recognizing their voices I walked in and went straight into a stall. Catching a quick glance I saw it was Kellendra, and another girl giggling like two hyenas. Closing the door behind me, I heard the girl whispering to Kelly *'is that her?'* responding with a hushed *'Yes'* I wondered what the hell they were talking about! I know good and well this heffa wasn't in this bathroom talking about me! Stepping out the stall I looked at both women with an icy glare so cold they could have frozen in place. Washing my hands ever so slowly, as to see if one of them was going to approach me (they didn't); I dried them and left.

Returning to my work space; I was so heated. I mean, she couldn't have thought that she was going to get the better of me! First of all we started at the same time so whatever diabolical ideas she had, she better forget right away because I'm not letting anyone take this job from me, or make me look like some kind of fool; she don't know me!

I logged on to my computer and started to set up the meeting that Clair requested. First call was to Margaret Chapman's assistant Holly. Holly is sweet girl; she seemed a bit naïve, but cool all the same. Margret's designs were more ready-to-wear business attire. She did have a couture line, but that was going to premier in the next season. If you haven't noticed from being a shopper, fashion is always a season ahead. So, you'll notice that in the dead of winter you will start to see spring/summer clothes. I know you've done it and I'm guilty of it myself, but I've bought clothing in the Winter for the Spring and worn it in the Winter; freezing my tail off, we all do it in the name of fashion! I booked Margret for Friday morning.

Next is Faruka John, owner and designer of the Gemini Collection. I don't much about her besides she's new on the fashion scene, but word has it she's crazy obsessive with her fashion line. With hardly any help from an assistant; she insists on being hands on with every aspect, even down to the show productions, model choices, music, you name it; chances are Faruka is doing it. Faruka's designs are for both men and women and have a fun, funky, sort of eccentric vibe style. She dabbles in fun comfort pieces not really high, runway fashion; but more for the everyday person. I scheduled Faruka for Monday afternoon, I wouldn't want her to show up to an early morning meeting with fabric swatches all over and coffee stains on her clothes.

The last meeting I scheduled is with Hennison Black, and Isabella St. Scott of Rouge Magazine. With my mouth agape, I wondered why Clair would be in a meeting with them, Hennison I could understand; but why Isabella? She has nothing to do with Indulgence. Rouge Magazine is geared for straight sizes, and it's been noted for years that the two didn't get along. With Indulgence being for full figure men and women, Rouge was just the opposite. In fact the only thing they had in common was the fact that both were owned by Black Industries. With a quick call to both parties assistants, I scheduled them for

Monday morning, I thought it would be better to get the bad news, I mean if it is bad news; out of the way first, so that the rest of the work week would flow like normal.

Approaching the five o'clock hour, the office started to clear out, most of the interns had left, and the cleaning staff was ready to start their evening routine. Changing my shoes, I got my tablet, and notes together for the meeting. Not knowing what to expect, I assumed that it would be like any other meeting. Did I mention that I was wrong?

Dominique

The past few weeks with Chase have been a whirlwind. The sex with him was not what I expected. He was very attentive to me; which is something I'm not use to. In the past, the men I've dated only had one sexual level; aggressive. So, that became something I expected. Chase is different, like he's said to me before; he's not the other men I dated. For him, I came first; literally. It was about me, and if I wasn't sure about how he felt about me before; he certainly let me know in the bedroom.

Over time our relationship progressed, and we have been doing things that you would expect couples to do; which is also a strange new frontier. I guess you could say that's what we are… a couple. I haven't been in a steady relationship for so long, that I didn't recognize what one looked like. Being with Chase forced me to see what I've been missing all this time I was clubbing and bouncing from one man to the other.

We practically lived together; we spent mornings racing to the shower, talking throughout the day, made dinner plans, and occasionally we visited the club in the back ally where we had our first dance. I can't say that I was in love with him, but what I can say is that I really enjoyed the time we spent together. Once we became intimate, it became hard for us to concentrate on anything else. To tame the sexual cravings we both had, we exercised together as much as we could. Some mornings we went for runs in the park. I was never a girl about working out, I've always maintained a naturally slim figure; so it was no surprise that within ten minutes of running I was so winded that when Chase asked if I was alright, I couldn't answer him.

Slowly, running became easier, and I understood why so many New Yorkers did it. It helps clear the mind of whatever chaos is swimming in it. And on a good run, you can develop a 'runners high' and that just keeps the blood pumping. Afterwards you feel like you can conquer anything life throws at you. Sometimes I would get up earlier than Chase and just run alone to clear my head.

I thought a lot about my life, and foolish choices I've made. Mostly, I thought about Chloe and how in finding happiness in my new relationship with Chase, I sort of abandoned her. I haven't been at my apartment in weeks and I know she was missing me by how she sounded when we talked on the phone. I've invited her out with us a few times, but she would babble something about being a third wheel, and change the subject. Her job is going well, so she says; but I know it's a chick there that's giving her a hard time. I think tonight I will sleep in my own bed and catch up with my friend; I miss her tons.

Arriving at work, I thought it would be like any other. Still dressing to the nines, I wore my sleeveless green bodycon midi dress, with black shoes, and duffle skirt coat, paired with a green and tan Bumble and James structured bag.

Riding high from my run, I expected to see the sad faces of my co-workers dreading the end of the weekend; to my surprise the office was in an unusual uproar. I saw interns running with stacks of files, executives yelling at anyone who crossed their paths, and a chorus of different phones ringing in unison like some kind of damn symphony.

Rushing to my desk and throwing my belongings anywhere, I picked up my phone that rang with such urgency that Hershel ran out to see why it wasn't being answered. Finishing with the call, I saw Hershel glaring at me with a look I've never seen.

"Dominique, where the hell have you been? You were supposed to be here hours ago! Didn't you get the email that went out?" screamed Hershel.

"No, I didn't. When did this so called email go out? I checked all my messages before I left Friday night! What's going on Hershel?"

"Your dad is acquiring a new company and in doing so he needs to see every division's finances in three hours. Depending on what sort of deal they work out, some of our people might be out on their asses, and people from the other company might be taking their place. But don't you worry," he said with venom in his voice. "Daddy isn't going to fire his baby girl. Hell, you might get promoted!" he said and stormed off into his office.

Not knowing how to react, I went in Hershel's office right behind him. Not expecting to see me standing in front of his desk, he looked up in utter shock. As he began to speak, I shut him down with the quickness.

"First of all, don't you dare speak to me like you've lost your damn mind, ever again! You might be my boss, but that's not how you're going speak to me!" I hissed at him. "Second, this is just as much my worry as yours, so if you can pull your head out of your ass, and stop worrying about what's coming my way, maybe we can convince the board of directors that this department has people worth keeping... And by the way, last time I checked you have a rich daddy, and in-laws that will provide your stuck up, privileged ass with enough golden parachutes to last you the next ten lifetimes! Other people here aren't so damn lucky like you and me. So, man up and tell me what we need to do!" I said with as much disdain as he had given me.

With an apology for his actions, he explained how he loved what he did, and that there were good people who worked hard to get in their positions and it bothered him that they could be out on the street. Who knew Hershel had a soul? Offering my own apology for how I spoke, we started to get to work on proving the worth of our division. I didn't know exactly how that was going to happen, but I knew it needed to. In the middle of gathering all the info I could find on the revenue we brought into the company for the past few years, I got a call from Chase.

"Hi, sweetness how's your day so far?" he asked.

"Babe, it's so crazy here. The company is acquiring another one, and they might be eliminating departments. I'm trying to make sure that this one isn't one of them." I explained.

"I'm sorry to hear that. Something similar is going on here, but it's sort of the norm. I won't hold you up, I just wanted to know if you wanted to stay in, or go out for dinner tonight? He asked.

"Well, Chase I can't tonight. I thought that I would go home. I haven't spent much time with my bestie and I want her to know I'm still here for her. You're not mad are you?" I wondered.

"No, no, its fine, I know the two of you are attached at the hip. I'll just call later to check on you." He agreed.

"Ok." I said.

"I'm going to miss you tonight babe. It's going to be weird sleeping without you." He confessed.

"I'm going to miss you too. I'll talk to you later."

"Ok talk to you later… And Dominique, I love you." He said with no trace of hesitation in his voice.

His voice was steady and sure of what was being said. Blurting out a quick 'yeah, you too,' I quickly hung up the phone. My heart was pounding so hard, that for a while it was the only sound echoing in my ears. Did he say that he loved me? Maybe I misheard him. I couldn't think with the chaos of the office humming around me, so I got up to get some air.

Taking the elevator to the lobby, I stopped at the news stand near the exit; I grabbed a soda and honey bun. In times of stress I needed sugar ASAP! Sitting at one of the small bistro tables I noticed that someone pulled a chair out to join me. Thinking that it was the office pervert Rob, I quickly said without looking up 'now is not the time Rob, step off!' With a chuckle I heard a voice most unexpected.

"Who is Rob?" the voice said calm and collectively.

Looking up slowly, I knew exactly who it was at the table with me. It was Ramir. I didn't see him on Hershel's schedule when I came in. Then again, I didn't have any time to look at it due to the mess I walked into; I also doubt that Hershel had remembered. Wait, I book all his appointments. So If Ramir is here, either he made it through someone else, or he's just showing up. How presumptuous of him to think that everything would get dropped just because he walked in. I didn't know if that was the case or not, all I knew was that it gave me an excuse to get away from him.

"Do I get a hello?" Ramir insisted.

"Hello." I said as even as I could muster. "Do you have an appointment with Hershel; I didn't see you on his agenda?

"No, I actually came to see you. I've been thinking about you since I saw you last, and I wanted to know if you were available for drinks."

"Umm, I can't do that. Aren't you and Kasha still married? Would she be joining us?"

With a slight laugh, he answered "No, I just thought we could catch up, and maybe discuss how things were left." He encouraged.

"We have nothing to discuss. What happened; happened and I've moved on from that." I asserted, as I stood to leave.

Grabbing my arm, he clarified "we do have something to discuss, and if I'm going to continue to work with your father's company, I think that we should talk."

With contempt in my body language, it took everything in me not to smack the taste buds off of his tongue. "How dare you! How dare you threaten taking business away from this company to get me to have a drink with you! You sorry sack of shit, you waltz in here like I owe you something. I don't owe you shit! If you want to take your business elsewhere, then do it. But you will not manipulate me into doing whatever you want. Think again!!"

"I'm sorry. I didn't mean to cause an offense. You just make me so nervous that I thought I would take an assertive approach. Please have a drink with me tonight and we can clear up whatever misunderstandings between us. Please." He pleaded.

"I don't know how late I'm working tonight..." I started to say.

"No problem. I'll stop by later this evening. And hopefully you will be able to attend. Say around 7:00 p.m.?"

Feeling myself starting to relent, I agreed to meet with him. Returning to the office, it seemed calmer than it was when I left. Speaking briefly with Hershel, we planned a presentation and some key notes to bring up to the board during the meeting. There was nothing to do but wait at this point. Joining the other assistants in the break room, we talked about what was going on, and what they would do if ever they lost their jobs. Listening to what issues would be waiting for them made me feel worse about the situation, hopefully Hershel's Ivy League education and ability to talk circles around people would be put to good use.

Most of the office staff, I've really come to like over the past few months of me working here. It was a bit of a rough start with this being my first actual job, but eventually I warmed up to it. I had zero experience, and some of the veteran assistants showed me what had to be done, and how to do it; for that I will always be extremely grateful. In the beginning, everybody had assumptions about me because of my dad, but I know that those assumptions changed once they really got to know me.

Returning to my desk, I decided not to wait to hear the outcome of the meeting. Leaving a note for Hershel, I packed up to head home for the first time in weeks. Exiting the building, I was surprised to see Ramir waiting for me. Forgetting for a moment that I agreed to have drinks with him, I walked up to him. Embracing me with a kiss on the cheek, he gestured for me to get into the car that was waiting. He instructed the driver to the first destination. When I asked where the first destination was, he laughed as said it was a surprise.

We rode in silence the entire way. I didn't know what to say to him, nor did I ever think that I would be sharing a car with him. The last time I saw him, he was dating Kasha; then they were engaged. It probably would've been polite to ask about his family, but to honest I didn't want to be polite to him. He broke my heart with no regard for how I felt. He just moved on, and I had no choice but to except that he didn't want me as much as I wanted him. For him to step back into my life after all this time really threw me. Arriving at a restaurant near the Metropolitan Opera House we went inside and directly to a private dining room.

Once seated, we ordered drinks, when they arrived I waited for the shit show to begin. Taking slow, steady sips I tapped my nails on the glass repeatedly to annoy him. Perhaps tired of the silence between us and seemingly endless tapping, Ramir began to start the conversation.

"I'm happy you agreed to meet with me. I know it was short notice, I want to thank you."

"Sure, why not? I can make time for the guy that broke my heart and didn't even have the decency to tell me he was getting married. You are welcome." I spat sarcastically.

"I apologize at how quickly it happened. I did not mean to hurt you in any way. I did care a lot for you; it was just that it was my duty to marry the woman my parents chose for me. If it had been my choice, it would've been you. I can't change the past; all I can do now is attempt to make things right between us." He confessed.

"Make things right between us, why? Why now? You've had years to reach out to me, and you didn't. The only reason why I'm here with you right now is because we ran into each other in a place where we didn't expect to. The reason why I think I'm here is because you have some kind of guilt about what happened. I'm not here to make things easy for you, because they haven't been easy for me. You hurt me; I loved you and you abandoned me. And now you want my forgiveness. I just can't give it to you." I insisted.

"I do want your forgiveness. But I am willing to earn it from you." He said as he attempted to stroke my face.

Pulling back from him, I stood to walk out the door. Following behind me closely, he quickly reached for me. Anticipating that he would do that, I dodged him and went to open the door. Pushing me against it, he pinned me against the door and kissed me a kiss that good Persian boys don't do. I felt every emotion I ever had for him surface in that moment. And without thinking or knowing what I was doing, I kissed him back. His kisses were more aggressive than what I remembered, more grown up. He wasn't the sweet, shy, Ramir that I once knew, but a grown man that was sure of what he wanted. And at this moment what he wanted was me.

Kissing him brought back so many memories that I had of us being together when we were naïve kids. Removing the pin that held my hair, it fell past my shoulders. As he kissed me, he held my face in place with his hands. Unzipping the back of my dress, I felt him easing it past my shoulders. Laying me on the table he climbed on top of me and began to remove his tailored shirt. Pausing to make sure the door was locked, he returned with his pants removed.

I can't lie he is a better lover than I remembered. Back then I had to show him how to touch me, this time he knew. Raising my leg to kiss my foot, he led a trail all the way up. Pausing at my hip he grabbed the string of my thong with his teeth and pulled them down, there was no going back now; and I'm not sure if I wanted to.

Sitting up quickly, I stumbled out "I can't do this with you. I can't let you hurt me again. I've wanted this for a long time, I've even… it doesn't matter. I just can't."

Kissing my neck and stroking clit, he murmured in my ear "I'm sorry I hurt you

Dominique. But I promise if you let me I can make you feel better." He swore.

Easing my back against the table, he then dove face first into my va-jay-jay, something he had never done while we dated. Hell, I didn't even know that he was into that.

I was so fucking hot that I felt like I would melt the table. Stopping to wipe his face, he whipped out a condom, and in one swift motion it was on him, and his dick was in me. Pulling my hair, and groping my body, he made me feel all the things I wanted to feel.

Adjusting me to a seated position on the table, and holding me tightly against his body, he stroked, the table shook, and I tried desperately to stifle moans. Closing my eyes and leaning my head back; I allowed myself to forget that my heart was broken by him, that Chase had just confessed his love for me, and that Ramir... the sexy and exotic, love of my life wasn't mine to let him make me feel this way.

He was married to someone else, and for just a second I felt a twinge of remorse. But I convinced myself that this is what I needed to move on, and it wouldn't ever happen again. Well, at least it sounded good in my mind. It wasn't until we finished that the guilt came really rushing into my mind.

On the ride home, I sat quietly and stared at people as we passed them by. What did I just do? Could Ramir and I be starting a relationship, or was this something that just happened? Just as the thought passed through my mind he reached out to stroke my leg; looking at him, then looking away, I thought of Chase and suddenly became confused about what was happening. Ironically the DJ on the radio thought it was a good idea to play some throwback jams, all I could think was; really? I had loved Ramir so deeply for so long that every man I was ever involved with I compared to him, and if they didn't measure up, I found some way to push them away. Now, I had him. He is back in my life, and I don't know if this was a permanent stay, or was he just passing through. Chase on the other hand was exactly what I needed in a man, even if I didn't know what that was.

In front of my apartment, Ramir opened my door and told me repeatedly that he missed me, and how he could've been so stupid as to let me go. Embracing each other one more time, I entered my building. Unlocking the door, Chloe was surprised to see me walking in. Quickly telling her about the office, I excused myself to take a quick shower. After getting dressed, we talked about her job and some crazy power meeting she had. While talking, I got a text from Chase saying he missed me. Returning the comment, I said that I would call him in the morning.

While Chloe talked, my mind drifted to what I had done earlier that night. I thought seriously about telling Chloe about what happened, but decided against it. I know she loved me, but she wouldn't understand how difficult it was for me to let him go, then to have him make a re-appearance. It was a difficult thing to let go of, to have him give me what I've wanted for so many years. Realizing it was getting late, we went to bed. Climbing into my bed, it was like having a sleepover with her there with me. We continued to talk, mostly about the Gala coming up, until we were both overcome with tiredness.

Waking up early out of habit, I peaked at my friend still sleeping. A creature of a new habit, I started to get ready for a run. Snapping a quick selfie and sending it to Chase with the caption 'Good Morning Luv!' I made my way out of the apartment and began a slow jog. It was getting really cold outside, but luckily running built up heat, so after a few minutes I didn't feel it anymore.

On my run, I decided that what happened with Ramir wouldn't happen again, and that I wouldn't allow him to take me back to that place where I felt helpless. Perhaps thinking too hard, I didn't notice that someone was keeping pace with me. Turning my head, I realized it was Chase. Finding some momentum, I tried to run a little faster. Keeping up with me stride for stride I couldn't shake him. Finally tiring myself out, I decided to stop at a bagel stand. Grabbing two coffees and cinnamon buns, I waited for Chase to take a seat with me on a bench.

Smiling, he said "you've really taken to this running thing, haven't you?"

"I guess I've learned from the best." I assured, as I handed him his coffee and sweet bun.

"I was coming to your place to surprise you with a run, I thought that with girls night you would still be sleeping and I could make you ladies jog with me, but I saw you rounding the corner after your apartment and tried to catch up." He informed.

"Is that right? You should've known that you are no match for me!" as I laughed loudly.

Wiping cinnamon from my face, he leaned in to kiss me and instantly my thoughts of Ra were gone, and I knew that I wouldn't have sex with him again, like him I've grown to want other things that didn't include us laying naked together. Finishing up, he walked me home, and we made plans for him to pick me up for the Gala at my apartment. Being a few days away I would spend that time playing catch up with my friend and trying to forget my indiscretions.

When I got to work, there was a full bouquet of the most beautiful Lilies I've ever seen. Receiving cat calls from all the secretaries about the flowers; with some saying they wished that they had flowers waiting on them when they came into the office, I snatched the card hoping to see Chase's name scribbled across it.

My Dearest,

I remembered that you loved Lilies and wanted to send you something that you love to hold my place in your heart. Until next we meet.

R.G.

Realizing the note was from Ra; I ripped it up and tossed it in the trash before anyone could see me. I was happy he sent the flowers, but scared of what it meant. Was I an official side chick?

Chloe

I was pleasantly surprised to see Dee walking into the apartment last night. She looked different somehow. I don't know if it was the look of a working woman, or of a woman that was hiding something, either way I was worried for her. Removing her coat and shoes, she quickly told me about a merger at her office. Explaining that she wanted to wash off the stress of the day, she practically ran to the shower. She was in there so long, I was sure that the only reason she got out was because the water got cold.

Missing my friend, I updated her on all the madness at Indulgence, I even told her about Hennison. Giving me the side eye, she asked if I was going to take Hennison seriously; not really knowing how to answer, I shook it off telling her it was only harmless flirtations. Continuing my story I told her about my first 'Pit' meeting. While I was explaining, I could see that she was somewhere else. Dee had something else occupying her thoughts; I wondered if it was something about Chase.

The next morning I woke up with no Dee next to me. Assuming she got a head start on work, I did the same. Praying that Dee left me some hot water, I stepped into the shower. Hoping the heat didn't cause my curls to drop; I pulled the shower cap off my head and started towards the hall closet to find something sexy to wear to work. Selecting a tan pencil skirt, plum color top and similar colored Remy Dolton shoes, I was ready to show Hennison that a curvy girl can dress just as well, if not better than the slim girls he was used to. Not to say I had anything to prove, I just wanted to show that I was just as beautiful as any one of them… ok maybe I did have something to prove.

Taking hold of my tan trench coat, I snatched my bag, and headed for the door. Running into Dee on the stairs, she had a different look than the one I saw last night; she seemed happier.

"Hey love, I thought you left for work already." I assumed.

"No, I went for a run. Chase and I ran together and I feel great! Off to work?" she said.

"Yeah it's almost 8:10am, I have to catch the train or I'm going to be late. Will you be home later?" I asked.

"8:10? Shit I'm going to be late too. Ugh, yeah I'll be here. We have the Gala in a few days and we need to get ourselves together. Have you spoken to Jayshawn?" She asked.

"Yeah, yeah, were still on. I think he's going to pick me up here, and we'll go together. Look, I have to go; see ya later!" I assured.

"Ok, later." She responded.

Getting to work at almost 9:30, I prayed that no one noticed my tardiness. Getting to my cubical unnoticed, I sighed a sigh of relief. Taking out my files, I proceeded to finish up the work left over from yesterday. Typing the memos Cassidy asked for, I glanced to see Kellendra with her arms crossed and tapping her foot giving the resemblance of an upset parent.

"Late I see." Kellendra snorted.

"Minding my business I see." I retorted.

"Don't flatter yourself. You know, I hope you don't think that because Clair noticed you last night that somehow you're on her radar. She couldn't care less about your little idea. So, don't get your hopes up." She snarled at me.

"No Kellendra, I don't think she noticed me, I know she did. And if you didn't think so too, you wouldn't be standing in my space with a sour look on your face. Unlike you, I plan to be more than a mere assistant." I threw at her.

"More than an assistant, don't make me laugh, you're lucky to even walk these halls.

You're not cut out for anything around here but errand girl. What do you want to do? Write articles, I doubt you could do better than me. In fact, I bet I could be promoted to writer before you. And if you don't watch out, I might request you to be my assistant when I do. By the way, I take cream and three sugars in my coffee. I like it hot and steamy as soon as I get into the office." She spat at me.

"Kellendra, you couldn't write the obituaries. As far as a promotion, your work is half ass'd, unfinished, and has no basis in reality. I heard about the photo shoot incident. How could you mistake one designer for another, when clearly they have two totally different concepts? This is a fashion magazine, it requires that you know something about fashion; but then again, I see how you dress. And on top of that how could you insult a client? I heard Cassidy had to clean it up for you and you're not allowed to attend shoots for a while, well, at least until you learn that it's not what you want, but what the client wants. Looks as if it will be you that will be an errand girl until further notice," I snapped as I turned towards my computer.

With nothing further to say she stormed off on her broom perhaps to think of a snappy comeback. I wasn't expecting to pitch an idea that Clair liked, it just happened. Walking into the meeting, I was greeted with a cloud of cigarette smoke, a crowded conference room, and rows of stressed out eyes; that looked as if they hadn't slept in days. Cassidy leading the way, I took a seat at the middle of the table and waited for the meeting to begin.

Looking stunning, Clair walked in wearing a pair of light-colored stone-washed jeans that hugged every inch of her curvy body, a midnight blue sweater, and a pair of red stilettos. Styling her hair in loose waves, they bounced as she took her seat at the table's helm. With a strained look on the faces that surrounded the table, I knew the meeting started.

Wasting no time, she immediately attacked the Stylist Department about featuring the designers who make the biggest contributions to the magazine. Offering in unison murmurs of excuses, Clair simply waved her hand to give them pause; and immediately the mutters ceased. Taking one for the team, the stylist director offered a few suggestions to Clair and his staff as to not have future problems. Nodding slightly, she then moved on to the Beauty Department.

Receiving compliments for their artistic execution of bringing the concept to life, they were off the hook. Next, was advertising. The Ad Team's job was to secure the big advertisers we already had, and to acquire new ones. So far that task has not happened. Momentarily telling them about a meeting with the company head Hennison Black, she urged them to find new advertisers big or small to make their quota. In my mind, I concluded that this was the reason behind the meeting, but what about Isabella, how did she fit?

Continuing, she switched tones and viciously destroyed into the editorial staff. Rising from her seat she circled the table and bellowed to each of them that she wanted better material for the columns. With the precision of ninja, she sliced at them until there was nothing left but their cigarette ashes. Lastly, addressing the assistants, Clair required that we take our jobs seriously.

No one person is above the magazine, and improper decisions that cost the magazine clientele would be dealt with swiftly, relieving said person of his/her duties. Retaking her seat, she demanded ideas for the next issue. Immediately chaos ensued, everyone was talking at once and yelling across the table. By everyone's reaction to her demands they all thought long and hard about what they would pitch. Regardless to how long they've worked on finding new ideas, Clair shot them down one by one. All you could hear from her was, 'It's been done, not the right season, the concept is dull…' And so on, and so forth. Out of frustration she stood and pounded on the table.

"No, no, no, does anyone have something worth printing! These concepts are old, and repeats of other magazines, Indulgence represents a new age of full-figured women! You, would you read the trash they're pitching?" she said as she looked to me.

"No, like you said; I've read blogs similar to some of these concepts online." I answered.

"You see that! You're giving me ideas that can be found online and written by one daring to call themselves writers! We are not leaving this office tonight if no one here can come up with decent ideas for the next issue!" Clair ruled.

In an attempt at redemption, Kellendra stood and pitched her idea. Calling her idea, 'What's Hot Now,' she explained that it would involve visiting hot spots, fashion shows, designer trends, etc. it would be Indulgence Magazines finger on the pulse of the city. It wasn't a bad idea; the only issue with it was the fact that Indulgence had a similar running column called Trend Crave. Kellendrea should really pay attention to the inner workings of the magazine. It's like she did no research when she applied for the job.

A receipt of a blank stare from Clair, she slowly took her seat and didn't utter another word. Asking is that was all we had, she waited for the next victim to make themselves known. Taking my place on the guillotine, I stood and pitched.

"What is missing in the lives of Indulgence's readers? It's not fashion trends, great hangouts, or even up-and-coming designers; all those are a dime a dozen, and has been done to death by us, Rogue, and all the other publications in our market. What we need to do is set the bar so high that there is no longer a bar to reach. What if we did a piece about influential women of the plus world? We can feature women like you Clair, or Slone Hill who are self-made, and started this industry when there was nothing like it before. We could interview these women, while giving our readers something to aspire to. We have to inspire each other in order to have staying power. Who knows who could be reading these articles, and what they would be with the proper encouragement." I claimed.

The room quieted, and I didn't know if I should sit, or leave for making a fool of myself. The editors each nodded in agreement at each other, and Bruce the lead editor looked to Clair and said 'it's doable'. Agreeing with him, she concurred that we would go with that concept, and a few others she approved. Dismissing us, we all scurried out of the conference room before she could beckon us again.

Back in the safety of my cubical, I collapsed into my chair and breathed a sigh of relief. Startled by a knocking on my desk, I jumped to see Cassidy. Sitting on my desk, she told me that Clair was impressed with me. Although it was my idea, she thought I wasn't seasoned enough to write the piece alone; so she gave the task to more experienced writers, but she did want me to do one of the interviews. The one she assigned me was Slone Hill, former full figured model turned mogul; starting her model management company, and school. Legendary Plus Models Inc. is the premier modeling company in the Tri state area jump starting the careers of many well-known women.

10:00 p.m. came so fast, next thing I knew I was on the train home; I sent a text to Jay. Immediately replying, he said that he was in his office working on a project. When I asked if he wanted company, he jumped at the chance and insisted I come there. Luckily, the train I was on passed near his office. On the ride I wondered what was keeping him in the office so late, and if it would render me dateless for the Gala.

Jayshawn

I was in for yet another late night in the office fixing whatever mistakes Makayla made. I don't know what the hell was wrong with this girl! She's not the best assistant; she's constantly late to work, but she used to be dependable, now it's like I'm working for her. The past few weeks have been a nightmare, she's double booked appointments, had me on the wrong side of the city when I was supposed to be somewhere else with a client, and lately she's taken to not coming in at all. If this kept up, I was going to have to let her go. She's been with me since the beginning, but I don't think she believes in the dream anymore.

In the middle of me re-writing an email Makayla opted not to do, that has to be sent to James Vincent owner of Island Gem Art Gallery, where I'm creating an event for an upcoming artist, I got a text from Chloe. With the usual pleasantries, we exchanged hellos. Taking a new turn she asked if I wanted company, not one to turn down the company of a beautiful woman; I agreed. Trying feverishly to straighten my office, I tried to hide the fact that I had been partially living out of it. I opened up the windows to purge the office of the pungent smell of old Chinese food floating in stale air; then dimmed the lights, and lit few scented candles; I waited for her to arrive. While waiting my phone vibrated, expecting to see a text from Chloe, it was Tarin.

From Tarin J.:

> *Hey Babe, can I see you tonight? Missing U.*

To Tarin J.:

> *Hell No! Tarin, it's over between us. Remember you chose someone else over me, I've moved on.*

From Tarin J.:

> *Oh, baby don't be that way. I've always loved you; I just needed to breathe a bit. We were moving so fast.*

To Tarin J.:

> *Goodnight Tarin. Wish you the best.*

From Tarin J.:

> *Don't play like you don't miss me. Do you remember how we used to be together? The sex was never boring was it Jayshawn? I remember what you liked; do you remember what I did? We could still see each other without being messy, can't we?*

Putting my phone away, I did remember the wild things we used to do. But that was the past, after the dirty shit she did to me, I could never go there again. I don't care how good she was in bed; my sanity was worth more than good head. I can't believe I considered marrying her.

I remember when we went to Las Vegas; I was promoting Players a new night club by the Urban Squared Group out of the South. Taking her along, we had all expenses paid, spending accounts, and a smorgasbord of people at our beck and call. Our suite at the Wynn could hold twelve average size New York apartments, and we made love in every square inch of it.

She had a body that young boys could beat off to. Standing five foot seven, with a small curve figure, smooth complexion, short brown bob, c-cup breasts, and two dimples on her lower back leading to a full ass; she was a trophy for any man.

Recalling one of our many interludes, I remembered we were coming back from a party when we started kissing in the elevator on the way back to the suite. Removing a breast from her thin dress, I ran my thumb across her nipple. Alternating between her lips, and her neck, while continuing to stroke her breast; I could tell she was moist between her legs.

The quicker her pulse became the more aggressive my assault. Entering the room and pushing her over the couch face first; I lifted her dress. Stunned to see she had on nothing underneath; I dove into her wetness. Knowing how she loved for me to pull her hair as I repeatedly knocked against the walls of her pussy, I grabbed a fist full of it and rammed. Squeezing my dick tightly, her walls poured with the desire she felt. Moving from the couch to the bathroom, she ran a bath, and we continued the party. Chest to chest she rode me, the water splashed and clapped against our skin as if to cheer us on.

Just when I thought she had enough for the night, we lay in bed and had a little pillow talk before I could fight sleep no longer and finally dozed off. Not yet dawn; I was awakened by a familiar sensation. Lazily opening my eyes, I caught the sight of Tarin massaging the shaft of my dick. Expertly guiding her lips against my shaft from bottom to top, I could feel the warmth of her breath as she rose to greet the head of my dick.

Waking up from his slumber; my dick was ready for the treat he was about to be given. Putting her hands in an interlocking position around it, she moved them up and down while coiling her tongue underneath the base, then the top of the head. Back and forth she stroked to the point where my hips rose up off the bed, as I tried desperately not to allow myself to let the moment end quickly. Not being able to hold on any longer, I exploded, and she drank every last drop of me until there was nothing left, but heavy breaths and a feeling of euphoria. By the end of the night my energy and my balls were empty.

Two weeks later she went with her modeling agency to Miami for a job. Coming to surprise her, I went to her hotel room to find her sucking the dick of a high powered rich kid, while simultaneously getting head from another woman. I walked out of that room, caught the next flight home, and never spoke to Tarin again. She called, left messages, and even showed up at some of my events screaming and crying; none of it worked.

That little exchange is what sent me running to the bar where I met Chloe. As a last ditch effort, she told me she was pregnant. Like everything else, it was a lie; turns out she asked her pregnant sister to pee on a stick so she could pass it off as her own. She confessed to that bit of information when I forced her to go to the doctor so we could be sure. I was done with Tarin, but by the looks of her popping up lately she wasn't done with me.

Hearing a soft knock, I realized that Chloe had arrived. I watched a slow smile creep across her face when she saw me. Strolling pass me, into the waiting area. She began to speak, but I didn't hear a word she said. I watched her remove her coat, and I caught a glimpse of her ass in a tan skirt she was wearing, and wanted nothing more but to bury my dick in it. She wasn't Tarin, she was better.

Every move she made seemed purposely done to get a reaction out of me, and it did. She leaned against Makayla's desk still speaking; as she spoke I noticed her curls bouncing around her face. At that point I couldn't hold back my feelings anymore. I walked straight to her and leaped onto her lips. Placing my hands on the small of her back, I let them fall to their primary destination, THAT ASS!

This is the first time I kissed her since she ran from me. I held her tightly against me, so this time there was nowhere for her to run. I wanted her right then and there, not because of the memory of my interludes with Tarin, but because I've always wanted her since the night we first met; and by her reaction I could tell she wanted me too. Easing my hand to her hips, I kissed her as deep as I could, letting my tongue linger on her lips as we momentarily paused to take a breath. I attempted to pull her top loose from her skirt. Stopping me by holding my hands she said 'not like this Jay.' With that I tried to calm myself down.

Moving from my grip, Chloe walked towards the door, but stopped short. Turning on her heels, she dropped her arms as if to let go of a hefty load, and took off her shoes. Catching me by complete surprise, she came to me like I had wanted her too for so long. Allowing me to remove her shirt, then her bra; I released her breasts from their prison, feeling the weight of them in my hands, I gently rubbed them, and then eased my hands around her hips to her lower back. Unzipping her skirt, it fell to the floor; I led her into my office. Closing the door to offer some privacy, I led her to the desk. Making a meal of her, I kneeled in front of her to remove her panties and placed small kisses on her lower stomach, and inner thighs. Positioning her left leg on my shoulder, I went for the main course.

Caressing her softly with my tongue's tip, I worked my way from top to bottom. Licking, sucking, and nibbling on her clit. Using her elbows for support, she leaned on them and tossed her head back as I continue to devour every sweet drop of cum she offered. Feeling her legs start to tremble, I knew she was on the edge of letting go; but I couldn't let her do that just yet. Standing, I removed what little clothes I had on. Kissing her once more, I placed my hand between her shoulder blades to make her stand.

Arching her back she stood, and I pulled her down to the floor. Turning her around, as to make her back face me, I wrapped my arms around her torso and alternated my hands between rubbing her breasts and strumming at her honey pot, while licking her neck. Finally, bending her at the waist; I inserted the instrument of my passion. Rocking in perfect sync with each other, we moved as if we were one person. Bending lower to rest on her elbows once again, this caused her to arch her back more allowing for deeper penetration. Feeling her moisten more, I knew she couldn't hold back any longer. Letting herself go, I followed shortly after. Lying flat on her stomach, I laid my body atop hers.

Taking a few moments to compose ourselves, we tried to dress; but we ended up talking about things we should've talked about before having sex. Sleep slowly making its presence known, I decided to lock up the office and go home. I insisted she come with me to my place, but she declined. Sharing a taxi to her apartment, we held each other to keep the feeling of our body heat in the cold cab. Arriving at her place too quickly, I asked if I could come up; obliging my request I paid the driver and followed her in the building.

The apartment was empty, I didn't know when Dominique would be home; but I was glad she wasn't there. We showered together without the sex, which was different for me; but nice. Climbing on the couch, wrapped in a blanket, we watched whatever was on tv; until the tv watched us. Falling asleep in my arms, I felt a comfort with Chloe I hadn't felt before. Tring not to think too deep, I allowed sleep to take me.

Malik

Forget the subway, I'm taking a town car to
Midtown; I've got to start treating myself like a
mogul if I'm going run this town. First things first,
I have to meet Cyn to discuss our game plan for
tonight. I would wait until she gets home tonight,
but I want to surprise her and make sure she's
practicing those moves I showed her.

It's cool, Cyn staying with me; it's a great
way to protect my investment. I could tell she was
getting comfortable. But we have to maintain a
professional relationship outside of the bedroom
which is getting harder by the day. The other day,
I was scouting some talent, and she said
something along the lines of her being my only
female client. I stopped her with the quickness!
There is no way she was going to limit my money
flow, or dictate to me how to run my business; not
even Chloe could do that. Managing women in the
entertainment business was my meat and potatoes,
and Cyn isn't going to be taking food out of my
mouth! Either she was going to have to deal with
the fact that she's not the only female on my

roster, or she was going to have to step. Considering her options, I knew she wasn't going anywhere. I made her, and if she ever tried to leave me, I would destroy her. Hell, if Chloe could sing and dance I would have both of them making me money. I would've had them both all up on me too. I can see them now, making a sandwich out of me; one on the top and the other on the bottom.

Pulling up in front of a raunchy building, that housed not only a dance studio, but a slew of garment factories on each floor, I rode the elevator to the fifth floor of the building. Thinking for a second about Chloe, I considered sending her a text. Changing my mind, I thought I should pay her a little visit. I know she's staying with that friend of hers that didn't want to sleep with me, but I knew she was too bougie to be able to keep me interested, anyway. Still, I wondered how Chloe is doing.

Finding Cyn's studio by recognizing her songs, I opened the door to find her practicing her next stage performance in the mirrors. Pivoting in her high heels, she spun around with the microphone in her hand, stopping for a second when she saw me standing in the door. Continuing the show, she danced and sang as if she was really having a performance. I can't blame her for trying to get every step right, the criticism she received from her debut was harsh. One critic said...

"Cynsation, was everything but. Tackily dressed in what appeared to be a cross between a hooker and a Christmas tree, she arrived obviously intoxicated, and hours late to a stage performance that was less than expected from club owner Liam Cross, who is known for showcasing the talents of many known artists topping the Billboard charts. Sadly, with a name that evokes false advertisement, Cynsation will be of better use parking cars, than becoming one of the world's best performers. Cynsation, don't quit your day job; unless singing is your day job, in that case... QUIT!"

~Robert Graham

Reporter for the Underground Sound

Seeing that review made her practice harder for the next show; if another one of my ladies received a review like that, I would've had to comfort them by eating the box, or taking them on a long weekend to my hideaway and make them perform for me to re-build their confidence. Cyn, pushed herself; I guess she had something to prove. Finishing her imaginary set, she walked over to me as sweat left a trail from her face and neck, to her breasts; I loved to see women with that type of afterglow. Sitting on a folding chair, we discussed the logistics of the evening.

Getting into this Gala undetected would be difficult at best, as I attempted to keep Cyn in the dark about how we're getting in. Instructing her to arrive at the loading dock doors of the Guggenheim Museum at 9:00pm, I told her to wait for me there. When she asked why we didn't enter through the front, I told her this was the entrance where VIP guests entered. Taking extra care to build her confidence, I gave her the most passionate kiss that would keep her wet for hours.

Returning home to prep myself, I showered and put on my tuxedo. Knowing I would be meeting some movers and shakers, I rehearsed a few lines I could hook them with. Taking a cab part of the way, I walked the rest of the way to the loading dock. Meeting my man Chris at the doors, he threw me a chef's jacket and snuck me in through the kitchen.

Dumping my disguise, I slowly made my way through the crowd. All the who's who of the rich, societal, black and other elite were present. Snatching a glass of Champagne from a waiter, I engrossed myself with people I would've never met under any other circumstances. I don't know who they thought I was, maybe an up-and-coming athlete, possibly a rich kid, or maybe a new wiz kid from the Financial District. Whoever they thought I was, tonight I played my part.

Realizing the time, I walked slowly toward the doors where I told Cyn to meet me. Knowing all the servers would be on the floor of the party at this time, I would have no problem sneaking in

Cyn. Making my way through the kitchen, then down to the loading dock, I opened the doors to find Cyn talking to Chris. Walking up to them interrupting their conversation, I took her hand and led her into the building. Back on the main floor, the party was now in full swing. The Champagne was flowing and I see that everyone was having a good time.

Finding the first group of powerful looking individuals, we inserted ourselves in their circle and joined in. It was too easy to influence the flow of conversation and steer it to a more beneficial dialog. Introducing Cyn to them, expressing her passion for music, the men present in the group ate it up as if it was their last meal before execution. I reveled in how they fell over themselves to pass on good advice, and the right people to do business with.

A few hours or so into the party, I saw a few familiar faces. I stood astonished for a second to see Jayshawn and Chloe walking in together looking too cozy for comfort. Entering behind them was Dominique, with some white dude I had never seen her with before, I secretly wondered if he was the reason why she didn't give me any play.

Watching them closely as they spoke to other attendees, I wondered how Chloe knew some of them. She approached a few, and they seemed familiar with one another. I know I didn't introduce her to them, because I didn't know them myself. Then, one of the biggest players in the room, Hennison Black made his way to her circle. Reaching out his hand to Jayshawn, I could tell it was some tension between the two men. This was a different side of Chloe, one I've never seen before. She looked comfortable with the exchange and they all continued to talk longer until Hennison was called away by another woman.

Sensing, this was the time to approach them. I walked confidently to where they stood. Walking behind her, I lightly whispered in her ear. Turning to see me, she stammered while asking me what I was doing there. Avoiding her question, I began to question her. Noticing Jayshawn walking up to join the exchange, I welcomed him with a pat on the back. As we passed not so pleasant pleasantries, Cyn walked up and threw her arms around me not aware of whom I was speaking to. Chloe looked stunned by the person she saw embracing me. Expressing my need to show off my newest talent; I brought her into better view as I introduced her.

"Chloe, Jayshawn; met my newest client China 'Cynsation' Major. Chloe, I believe you two already know each other." I said, with a smug look.

The looks on both their faces were priceless! Chloe couldn't believe what she was seeing. Holding her purse as a shield, she backed up and began to curse loudly. Good thing that the music was louder than her shouts. With a sly smile; I introduced China as my client, and woman. China stood in shock as her sister had finally found out our little secret. I didn't know how long she thought we could keep our relationship a secret, Chloe was going to have to know sooner or later; why not now?

Realizing that her sister was who I was with all this time, and the reason we broke up, she smacked me across the face, turned on her heels and walked out of the main gallery. With Jayshawn following closely behind, they both disappeared.

Grabbing my face, I took Cyn to the closest waiter and got us some drinks. Cyn yelled and waved her hands and I just sat back and enjoyed demolishing whatever Chloe and Jayshawn had going on. Seizing China's arm as she was bringing it down to hit me as well, I squeezed it to make sure she knew that, that wouldn't be happening. Quickly putting her in her place, by letting her know that if she tried that shit, I would kill her and her career, China sat quietly, and then excused herself to the ladies room.

Peering out the corner of my eye, I saw Dominique skulking in a corner with some Indian dude. Watching her walk away quickly, I saw she approached the white guy she came with. I wondered what secrets she was hiding. As I walked to the ladies room to check on China, she was exiting. Soon after, the hosts announced that dinner would be served, finding the seats Chris added for us; we sat with the other guests, as if an altercation had never taken place just a few minutes prior.

During dinner China didn't say a word, just ate slowly. I on the other hand continued to thrive in the environment, getting all sorts of tips that would be instrumental to me taking on a more elite clientele, and really making power moves. Looking over to the other tables, it seemed as if other people were equally enjoying themselves. Allowing my eyes to rest on Chloe and Jayshawn, I could see some tension between them, but it wasn't much, because he still stroked her back as she ate. I also caught them glancing in each other's direction as if to show some kind of affection. I had to dead that as soon as possible.

As we left the party, China was strangely quiet. She usually talked my ear off asking about possible connections. Arriving at my place, she walked in, removed her shoes, and headed for the bathroom. Once there, I heard the bath water running. Taking this time to think up something quickly to get back in her good graces, I sent a text to Stewart Freedman who had a studio Uptown. He owed me a favor, and it was time for him to pay up. Waiting for his conformation text of the date and time I requested for studio time, I confidently walked into the bathroom to find China soaking.

"Hey bae, I have some good news for us." I announced.

"Good news?" She huffed. "What kind of news do you have for me? I mean, you just embarrassed me in front of a whole room of people and you decide that this is the right time to tell my sister about us? You have some nerve."

"Look I'm sorry, but we were there and so was she. At that point there's no sense in hiding it anymore. I didn't come in here to argue about what happened; I'm here to tell you about this amazing contact I made tonight. I met with this guy named Stewart, and I told him about our vision for your music career. He has a studio, and it just so happens he had a cancelation, so I booked some studio time. We can finally cut that record; all those songs you have in that notebook of yours could get some air play if you play your cards right." I proclaimed.

Shifting in the tub, she let what I said roll over in her mind. Her movements allowed the water to ripple across her curvy body, causing Mufasa to roar to life. I tried to appear patient as she thought about what I said. Agreeing, she rose to get out the tub. Watching her subtle movements caused the beast in me to take possession of her body right then and there, but the business man in me didn't want to seem too eager.

Once in the bedroom; without knowing what she was doing, she walked to the side of the bed where Chloe once occupied; and began to dry and lotion her skin. Similar in features they were, but their intellectual differences were so much more abundant.

China is a thick woman, whereas Chloe is more plus size. Chloe has worked more jobs than I can count trying to develop a so-called writing career; meanwhile, China concentrated on her music. Sure she danced in a club for a while, but she did that to make contacts out of the ballers that came through. That's when I too started to notice her as more than my girl's sister.

Walking into Ecstasy Gentlemen's Club, the last thing I expected was to see my girl's sister poppin' that coochie on a stage; but boy when she did, it was hypnotizing. China has ambition, where I thought Chloe had none. I always had to push Chloe to do things, I wanted her to be my trophy, but she ended up being a liability.

I would ask her to tighten up her body a bit and go to the gym, instead her waistline expanded more. I would say; babe focus on your career, next thing I knew she was jobless. But tonight I saw a different side to Chloe. I bet that our break up is what motivated her to finally make something of herself. So, really she owes me for helping her out; we will definitely be having a conversation, but as of now I have more pressing matters that need my attention, and right now she was putting on sexy negligee, and a fragrance that is making my mouth water. Time for me to have a midnight snack…

Dominique

I've been avoiding Ramir like crazy for the past few days. He's sent flowers, and has even called the office for Hershel, but I tried never to let the conversation go left. I have to admit, I'm weak for him. I really don't why; he didn't make me any promises, in the past, or now. But it's something about him that encourages me to hold on.

Leaving my office, I walked out the revolving doors to find Ramir's driver waiting for me. Walking in my direction, he told me that Ramir had asked for me to meet him in the Botanical Garden. My mind said no, but my lips said yes, and before I knew it I was in the car. Arriving at my destination, the driver handed me a note.

The note instructed me to meet him deep in the garden. Finding him near the Magnolia Trees, he instantaneously stood to great me. Taking my hands, and kissing me on both cheeks, we began strolling for a few minutes in silence.

We walked passed other visitors as they observed the beauty of the garden. The awkward silence started killing me and I had to speak.

"Ramir, why did you ask me to come here?" I blurted out.

"I tried calling, and I thought of sending more flowers, but I thought that might be suspicious. I want to talk about our last meeting. I didn't mean for that to happen, but when I thought of you leaving my life again, I acted on impulse." Ramir explained.

"I didn't leave your life Ra, I was dismissed. And as far as what happened, it can't happen again. I have someone in my life I care about, and you're married. This, whatever it is between us is done." I finalized.

"But, that's the problem Dominique. I don't think it's ever been over for us, it just stalled for a while. It's true, I'm married; but it's not a happy one. We have nothing in common anymore. I really want to find out if we still have something between us." He expressed.

Before I could open my mouth to retort what he was suggesting, his lips covered mine; losing myself in the ambiance, and his words stirring up emotions I thought long dead, I allowed him to take control. Hearing people approaching, we ducked behind a tree, and continued the assault on each other. Leaving the garden more confused than when I walked in, I actually considered continuing this affair.

I avoided Chase for fear he would see the guilt in my eyes. I cared a lot about him, and it just killed me inside that I was doing this, but Ra was the love of my life; how could I turn my back on what could be true love? Ramir and I started to spend more time together, and I made excuses as to why I couldn't be with Chase. He seemed to understand, when I told him about the pressure I was getting from work; but I knew that wasn't going to hold up too much longer.

Calling Chase, I wanted to make sure he was picking me up for the Gala. With strain in his voice he said he would; but then asked if work was going to be holding me up. Noticing the tension, I assured him that I would focus my attention on only him. Returning to my apartment, I noticed that Chloe was smiling a lot more. Being caught up in my own drama, I forgot to be a friend to her. After, I sort through this drama I have to make it up to my girl.

On the night of the Gala, I got a text from Chase saying that he was excited to be finally spending an evening with me. Honestly, I couldn't wait either. I missed how we were together. With Ra, we were always hidden. Either we would be in a hotel, or we would meet in some dive to have dinner. Everything was a secret, but of course it had to be for obvious reasons.

We almost got caught once leaving our usual hotel. As we were walking out, one of his colleagues, and his wife were entering a bistro across the street. Lingering in the lobby for a few minutes until they entered the restaurant, I considered ending it then. Even if this affair could lead to something serious, his family would never accept me. To them I would be every bit the trash they thought I was before, and carrying on this way, I'm not exactly proving them wrong.

Getting dressed for my mother's Gala, was like getting dressed for the prom; and waiting for our dates to arrive. My girl looked so good in her dress, that if I didn't love men, she would be my lady. I pinned her hair up in a bun and put makeup on her that highlighted her beautiful eyes. Getting myself together was a little harder. I spent a longer than usual in the shower trying to scrub off the scent of mine and Ramir's love making from earlier in the day. I took special care to make sure I was well put together, as to not alert anyone to what I had been up to.

Opting for loose waves in my hair, I curled my hair, dressed, and sprinkled Chase's favorite fragrance on me; in the prime spots. I felt like a nervous teen, that was about to have sex for the first time on prom night.

By 8:00 p.m. There was a knock at the door. Not sure who was there, I stepped out of my bedroom as Chloe opened the door. I couldn't see who it was until the door closed, and Chase walked in, looking and smelling wonderful. Complementing Chloe on her outfit, he handed her a single rose. Turning his attention to me, the look that spread across his face took my breath away. He walked up to me and kissed my hand. Telling me how good I looked, he also handed me a rose.

Minutes later Jayshawn arrived, and I noticed a similar exchange between him and Chloe. Something happened between them, and after the party; depending on how the night would end, I was going to find out. After we each took a shot of Tequila to start the night off, we were on our way.

Both guys had cars waiting, so each group got into their respective cars and planned to meet up in front of the Guggenheim Museum. The ride was awkward for the first five minutes, I was sure that I didn't scrub hard enough, and that he could smell my guilt. Perhaps feeling my tension, he reached out for me, and I slid closer to him and dropped my head on his shoulder, as I did he kissed me on my forehead. Of all the erotic things I've ever done, this by far is the most erotic, yet comforting. At this exact moment, my head was starting to spin from all the mixed emotions I was feeling.

Exiting the cars, I saw Chloe and Jay waiting for us. Presenting our invitations, we entered what was sure to be the dullest of evenings. I've been to parties like this before, and it's always full of people who praise themselves for their philanthropy and wipe their consciences clear for the rest of the year. There are some people who attend these functions with the intention of making a real difference; the problem is that there aren't enough of those types of people.

Taking the lead, Chloe and Jay walked in, and Chase and I followed. Immediately I knew that this was not going to be the same boring party I knew as a kid. There were a lot of young, powerful, movers and shakers here tonight. Breaking away from the group, I went to find my mother and congratulate her on her hard work; she had really out done herself this time. I knew my dad would be quite proud as well; these parties put his companies on the radar of many, which meant more money flow.

Marcellus Lawrence had chosen a prize wife in Olivia Pierre when they married more than twenty years prior. Their parents bred them to be a perfect match; one could say they were betrothed since birth. In those days it was important to keep money in the families, and what better way to do that then to have wealthy families marry into each other. I think my mother had always loved my father, even if he didn't show his love as much as she.

I remember as a kid, my mother was ever present, while my dad was sort of passing though. When I was younger, I asked for sisters, and brothers. My mom told me I had them, but they were in Heaven. She would tell me that I was special, and made for great things, and that's why God cloaked me with his protection, and allowed me to stay with her and dad. My mother was always a voice of reason for me; I know she meddles in my love life because she wanted me to be as happy as she is. But, my wish is for my husband to be as equally happy with me as I would be with him, not just when it was convenient.

Finding her surrounded by her friends, I cut through them and gave her the tightest hug my body would allow. Surprised by my action she chuckled a bit and hugged me back. Re-introducing me, she showed me off as much as she could to her friends who had single sons. Explaining that I came with a date I knew she would love, she told me that there was one more person that needed to make my acquaintance. Tapping a tall gentleman on his shoulder, he turned to greet us. Upon turning, I realized it was Ramir's Father.

"Excuse me Mr. Ganji, do you remember my daughter Dominique?" Olivia asked.

"Ah, yes. How are you young lady?" He said, as he extended his hand to me.

"Well, thank you. How is Mrs. Ganji?" I inquired.

"She's well, just stepped away to the powder room." He answered.

Just as I was about to walk off and find Chase to introduce to my mother; Mr. Ganji asked if I remembered his son, as he interrupted his son's exchange to invite him into another, I thought my breath would get caught in my throat. Turning around to acknowledge his father's request, Ramir and I stood face to face.

The look of shock engulfed his eyes, as we had to pretend we hadn't seen each other in years. Taking the initiative, I reached my hand out to him and asked how he's been. Returning the gesture, he asked the same. At that moment, Chase had walked up and handed me a glass of Champagne. Introducing Chase to my mother and the group as my boyfriend, I saw an enraged look in Ramir's eyes. Chase, unaware of our silent exchange, complimented my mother on the party, and shook the hands of Mr. Ganji and Ramir; Ramir hesitated then obliged Chase. Taking Chase's arm, I attempted to walk away only to come face to face with Kasha, and Mrs. Ganji returning from the ladies room.

If awkward silences could kill, I would've been dead on sight. Looking ravishing in her Alexa Queen gown, Kasha was a picturesque woman, with features most women would buy in order to have. Extending her hand to me, I shook it and Ramir's mother's hand as well. I now know the awkwardness Ramir felt shaking Chase's hand. Taking her place next to her husband, Kasha intertwined her arm with his and proceeded to force me to converse with her.

"The years have treated you well Dominique, what have you been doing?" Kasha asked with her prominent accent.

Fucking your husband I wanted to say, but I couldn't do that without causing a scene; so I answered, "Working with my father at the firm, and trying to find my career path." There, that seemed like a good enough answer.

"It's been a long time since college." She observed. "Haven't you found your path yet? I knew exactly what I wanted to do after school was over, besides marry Ramir." She chuckled as she turned to face Ra.

"Oh, Kasha; how brilliant of you to know exactly the man you wanted to trap… umm, wanted to marry. What have you been doing to keep your days busy?" I wondered.

"I've been very busy at the hospital and keeping up with our boys is a full-time job." She answered.

"Boys" I said surprised. "I didn't know you guys had children, how old are they?"

"Our boys are 7 and 5, and get into a lot of mischief as most boys do." She added proudly.

"Well, congratulations; if you would please excuse us." I spoke as Chase and I left.

Walking away, I had to force the tears that threatened to fall to stay back. Finding Chloe and Jay talking to Hennison Black and Clair Winters, I tried to keep up the conversation. No one seemed to notice that I had withdrawn, and no longer participated in whatever topic they were occupying. Whispering lightly into Chloe's ear, I excused myself to the ladies room to attempt to compose myself.

Once there, I took a few sips of water, and refreshed my face with fresh makeup. Giving myself a little pep talk, I strolled proudly back into the main gallery. Approaching the entrance, someone reached out and grabbed my arm. Swinging my hands wildly and cursing crazily, I slowed my rant long enough to see it was Ramir.

I wanted to slap him! How could he come to my mom's event with his wife and family; and not think to mention it to me. It's like; with him I'm always out of the loop and stumbling around blind. As much as I wanted to be with him; the chaos and drama that followed us was becoming too much to handle. Watching him peer around the corners, I didn't dare ask what he was watching out for; I already knew.

"Don't worry; your people won't catch you." I scoffed.

"Dominique," he said hurriedly, "I didn't think you would attend the party. We come every year, and every year you don't show up. Why would I not think that this time would be any different?"

"You're right; I don't make it my business to attend this event, but you still knew that you planned on attending and didn't bother to mention it. Oh and let's not forget that you have two children you also didn't bother to tell me about. I was under the impression that you didn't father any children." I barked.

"No, I did not tell you I didn't have children, you never asked, and I never volunteered. This doesn't change how I feel about you, or that my marriage is one of convenience. Please, can you meet me tonight?" Ramir asked.

"Are you fucking joking? Seriously, you can't actually expect me to leave my boyfriend to follow you to the nearest hotel room? No Ramir, I can't meet you tonight or any other night ever again." I professed.

I rushed off to put as much distance as possible between us. Running into Chase, I wondered if he had seen any part of that exchange. Noticing my heavy breathing, he asked if I was feeling well. Assuring him I was ok, it was just the Tequila and Champagne mix that was getting to me. Trying to shake off what happened we found our table and waited for Chloe and Jay.

Moments passed, then dinner was announced and everyone began to take their seats. I watched cautiously as Ramir and his family found their seats. I almost breathed a sigh of relief when I saw them sit three tables away from where I was. Chloe and Jay took their seats across the table from us, and I saw there was a look of strain on Chloe's face. When I asked what was wrong, she informed me that Malik and his new girlfriend were in attendance. When I look for them around the dining hall, I saw him in the distance, but he was alone. Walking up, I saw a woman that looked oddly familiar, when she turned I saw that she was more than familiar, she was my best friends sister!

I knew that bitch was not to be trusted! She's shifty and never reached out to Chloe when her and that bastard broke up and kicked her out; I know why now.

"That's so fucked up!" I said perhaps too loudly.

"Dee please," Chloe pleaded. "Don't say anything; I don't want to deal with this shit right now."

"No, fuck that! Who does he think he is? And her; NO EXCUSES!" I objected. Really, I just needed something to take my anger out on, and Malik's dumb ass just gave me the outlet I needed, without it appearing as if it came from somewhere else. As I attempted to rise from my seat Chloe jumped up and grabbed my hand before I could. The look in her eyes had so much pain in them, and at that moment I understood, and sat in my seat without another word being said.

Dinner was quiet. We ate and commented on the food. Occasionally, we spoke to the other party goers. By the end of the night, I believe both couples were mentally and physically drained. Leaving the museum as quickly as we could; I avoided Ramir, and Chloe avoided Malik and China. Entering our separate vehicles, we left the Guggenheim.

Opting to go to Chase's apartment instead of home, our ride was just as silent as dinner. As we entered his apartment, he removed his overcoat and mine and hung them up; as he did so I sat on the couch. Taking a seat next to me, he removed my shoes as he had done many times before and began to rub my feet. He knew there was something wrong with me; I could tell in his actions that he was being careful as to not provoke me.

"What's wrong Dominique? I know that scene between Chloe and her ex isn't the only thing on your mind. So tell me, what is it?" Chase asked.

I sat and wondered if I should tell him the truth, or at least some variation of it.

Chloe

Leaving home this morning, I couldn't wait for the work day to end before it had the chance to start. Arriving at The Black Building, I expected a day full of tedious tasks and uncomfortable silences between Kellendra and I. The only thing I actually looked forward to was seeing Hennison, and engaging in one of our flirtatious exchanges. I know it was stupid, he's a media/publishing God; and I am but a mere assistant. But I had my fantasies, and in them I was his every want and desire. Little did I know how much it was close to the truth.

I still harbored strong feelings for Jayshawn, but he worked such long hours that it was almost impossible for us to develop a relationship; or at the very least an understanding of where we stood. But Hennison gave me something that I haven't experienced in a long time… Desire. He gave me the attention that I wanted from a man, the only thing Hennison didn't do, is go beyond our innocent flirtations.

Indulgence hosted and attended so many events it was hard to keep track of Clair and Cassidy's schedule. Tomorrow, it was my team's job to iron out the details of Indulgence's All White Attire Affair. When I say team, I really mean Cassidy and myself. Mostly me, because Cassidy had enough on her hands managing Clair's affairs, and Kelly was useless. She spent more time whispering on the phone to some unknown person, than she did actually working.

To meet goals and deadlines, they scheduled everything, even personal time. To stay 20% ahead of last year's readership, Clair had to eat and breathe Indulgence. I wanted to be a force to be reckoned with in the publishing world, but I've seen none do it better than Clair. She was always first to arrive, and last to leave. She was very meticulous about Indulgence business. She looked at every aspect of Indulgence, down to the most mediocre of assignments; the interns would flee at the sight of her for fear that she would rip them another asshole if they screwed up. And even worse, she might fire them which would hurt more than the new asshole.

Though they worked for almost nothing, to add Indulgence on your resume as a body of work spoke volumes to your ability. Clair was tough, but fair, other publishers knew that about her. She didn't hire people who she felt was incapable of handling their business and making the impossible possible. For that reason, among many others; she is revered in publishing, modeling, and business worlds. She was never mean or rude (on purpose), she is just a focused woman.

She made it her business to attend every model casting, to make sure her vision is realized and portrayed in each model. If she couldn't find the right girls to fit a particular genre, she would have me contact Sloan Hill owner of Legendary Plus Model Inc. to send her the best girls to fill the quota. Sloan is a mogul in her own right and had a reputation for finding, and nurturing her models. More times than none, they went on to grace Parisian runways, build business, and have success beyond that of what straight size fashion thought should be occupied by curvy women. As a matter of fact, most of her pristine models would be in Femme Siueuse (Curvy Woman) Fashion Extravaganza in Paris around late February, where spring/summer collections would be showcased.

All the who's who of full figure fashion would be there to present their collections, buy for boutiques, scout talent, etc. Anyone who had a cent to their names; a passion to be in the full figured industry and wanted to make the right connections would be boarding a plane and flying across the Atlantic to be a part of Femme Siueuse celebration of events.

Wondering what transpired in the meeting of the minds with Hennison, Clair, and Isabella, I waited to see if the rumor mill had found out anything. I wasn't privileged enough to attend the meeting with Hennison Black and Isabella St. Scott, but I could tell it didn't end well. Upon exiting, Clair and Isabella had the look of scorned lovers on their faces, while Hennison grinned like a Cheshire cat.

Whatever it was, it was more to his benefit than both magazines. Walking towards the elevator with Isabella, Hennison quickly stopped at my cubical and drafted me into conversing with him. We spoke for the briefest of seconds before Isabella's voice was heard bellowing for him. Taking this moment to tease me, he lifted my hand to his lips and kissed it before he turned to meet her. I didn't want to read too deep into that, after all I know what kind of man he is. He was more than a playboy, he is what pimps aspire to imitate; so to be careful with him is the utmost priority.

Peeking at tonight's event list, I saw that Clair and Cassidy would be attending the same Gala at the Guggenheim. I didn't mention that I was attending; I thought I should keep this fact to myself. This might put me where I need to be with Indulgence, if they thought that I was important enough to attend such a prestigious event. They didn't need to know how I got the invite, just as long as I was there looking fabulous and talking to the right people. Clair and Cassidy left early, I assumed to get ready for the event. Stopping at my station, Cassidy reminded me to type and send the office memo before I left, we were going to have a last minute meeting tomorrow at 12 p.m. and Clair wanted everyone to prepare as much as they could for it. I suspected it had something to do with her meeting with Hennison.

Finishing my tasks, I took a quick break before getting ready to leave. As I walked to the elevator to go to the lunchroom on the 2nd floor, I saw Kellendra talking to Isabella St. Scott, and then they both got into the elevator. I wonder what the hell that was about, as far as I knew Isabella had no idea who Kellendra Bowden is at the magazine. We started with the magazine on the same day, there is no way she's high up enough on Isabella's radar to want to steal her from Indulgence. But when I thought about it, it wouldn't exactly be a bad thing if she left.

Heading home, I stopped to get me and Dee a bottle of Tequila to start the night off. We've both been working really hard the past few weeks and had hardly seen each other, so tonight we will drink, catch up, and get hella sexy for the party tonight. I was so full of nerves when I left for work, that I laid out everything I was going to wear this evening, down to the bra and underwear. Just in case I ended up at Jayshawn's tonight, I wasn't about to let him see my ugly girdle, but a sexy corset and panty set. A girl had to be prepared for anything, especially when it came to a man like Jayshawn.

When I got home, Dee was already in the shower, so while I was waiting for her I poured myself a few shots. Trying to get dressed with alcohol in your system was a humongous task, so Dee helped me with my hair and makeup. She did a remarkable job on my face, I barely recognized myself. I put on the radio and we listen to the latest hits as we took more shots waiting for the guys to arrive. About 8, Chase showed up first, and looking gorgeous in his tux, he handed me a rose before turning his attention to Dee.

Waiting for Jay; Dee, Chase, and I started dancing to the music from the radio. I didn't realize someone had walked into the apartment until I felt a cool touch to my shoulder. Turning around, Jay stood behind me looking handsome in his Black Label Tux. Placing his hands on my hips, we began to slow wind to the music. Before things could get too heated up between us, Chase walked over to shake Jay's hand passing him a shot glass as he did. We all joked and laughed for a few minutes longer, then decided to head out before we missed the party.

When we pulled in front of the museum I was shocked by the transformation Mrs. Lawrence made to its interior, she had really out done herself.

Holding Jayshawn's hand we worked the room, speaking to some people Jay knew. I had hoped to make some connections of my own, and just as the thought popped in my head, I saw Heidi from Indulgence's art department. Over the past few weeks, we have gotten really friendly. Introducing me around, through her I met Elias Moss, a hot new handbag and shoe designer, Jada Ray a plus size clothing designer and blogger, and then a most unexpected guest showed up... Hennison Black.

I knew Clair would be at the party, but I didn't think this would be Hennison's scene. But just as I thought it, I took it back. The room was full of heavy hitters, and there was no way in hell Hennison was going to pass up a party like this where he could secure more investors for Black Industries.

Trying to ignore the fact that my body began to vibrate uncontrollably at the sight of Hennison, I turned my attention to Jada Ray. We talked a lot about what inspired her writing. Telling her that I also was a writer, she asked where she could see samples of my work. My breath got caught in my throat as she asked me for my samples. Never did I think that an influential person like her would be interested in someone small time, like me. But unfortunately, I didn't prepare; how could I come to an event to network and not have a social media/internet footprint, a business card, or anything that could draw people to my work?

Truthfully, I hadn't written anything since the breakup with Malik. I just haven't been inspired, I've been trying to focus on working and being independent, in doing that I let my writing fall to the wayside. Explaining that I didn't have virtual samples, she suggested I began by starting a blog of my own. I took the thought seriously I mean, I loved to write. That was the whole reason I even worked at Indulgence, but I had no real evidence of my ability. My writing has been limited to office memos, setting up meetings, arranging dressing rooms, etc. After the Gala, I am definitely looking into starting my own blog, but what would it be about?

Just as I was turning the thought over in my mind, an unexpected guest made his presence known. I smelled him long before I saw him. The scent of Woodberry Heights cologne began invading the air that surrounded me. It pulled me further into the spell he was casting; wafting as he moved. Greeting Elias and Jada as if old friends, he then turned his attention to me and Jayshawn. Talking my hand, he kissed it once again. Never taking his eyes off me, he put his hand out to Jayshawn. Shaking it for the briefest of seconds Jay let it go.

"Ms. Major, I didn't know that you would be attending the event. How are you enjoying it?" He spoke with enough sensuality to get every woman in the room pregnant simultaneously.

"I… We are enjoying ourselves, thank you for asking. How has your night been so far?" I asked as I intertwined my arm with Jayshawn.

"It's promising, Ms. Major. I'm coming quite close to closing a major deal. My client is playing hard to get, but eventually I will get what I've wanted." He assured.

Before I could utter another word Jayshawn spoke for me. "Well, we sure hope that you're man enough to except the challenge from your client, and step up your game before some else out bids you." Jayshawn said as his words dripped with venom.

Having the most perfect timing ever, Clair walked up to join the conversation. Lightly touching Hennison on his arm, Clair introduced him to Sloan Genesis Hill. Not noticing me until after the introduction, Clair turned in my direction and smiled.

"Ms. Major, I didn't expect you to be here. It's not usual that assistants come to parties such as these. I hoped you remembered our meeting tomorrow? By the way, let me introduce you to Sloan Hill; I understand you've spoken to her assistant Tarin often for our model castings." Clair mentioned.

As I started to answer, I felt Jayshawn's body tense up. "Yes, I remembered and also I took the liberty of printing the mock up for the White party, so that we had a visual to refer to during the meeting." Clair gave a slow deep smile, and then I turned my attention to Sloan. "Ms. Hill, I am a huge fan of your work, your models are some of the most renowned in full figured fashion. I hoped to meet you and Tarin tonight, is she here?" I stated.

"Hello," Sloan answered. "No, I'm afraid Tarin isn't in attendance this evening. She had more pressing matters to attend to at the agency. I'll tell her that you asked for her."

She then turned to Jayshawn, and held her hand out to him and proceeded to say "Hello Jayshawn, it's nice to see you again, how's business?" she inquired.

"Business is fantastic Sloan; it has more than doubled in the past year. I also expect to add to my roster of prestigious clients. I have a meeting with the CEO of Elite Sounds Records. If all goes well, I'll be planning all their events; which include recording artists, industry parties' public/private, and listening events. The possibilities are limitless." Jayshawn sneered in the direction of Hennison.

Noticing the direction of Jayshawn's words, Clair ushered Hennison and Sloan off to a group of potential investors as to avoid any unsavory confrontation. Signaling a passing waiter, Jay placed a glass of Champagne in my hand and he guzzled two glasses before the guy could walk away. He acted like a man who just had the weight of the world lifted off of his shoulders. When I asked him about the exchange between him and Hennison, he opted not to explain himself; but he offered his apologies if their conversation had made me uncomfortable.

I had to take a break, all this power moving was making me hungry. Walking to the hors d'oeuvres table, I piled on crab cakes, shrimp, and whatever delectable things I could find. Returning to Jay, I saw that he was still self-medicating alternating between Wine and Champagne.

The band began to play the instrumental to Breathless, and Jay held his hand out to me. Taking it, we began to sway to the soothing sounds. For a moment I rested my head on his shoulders and let the melodic sounds take me. Lifting my head to meet his gaze, I found myself nose to chin with him. The music perhaps having the same effect on him, he bent his head down to reach my lips. And as the music played, we swayed and kissed as if there were no other people in the room. For a moment, I forgot about my meaningless flirting with Hennison, and the mistake of a relationship with Malik.

When the music stopped and the band began to play yet another instrumental rendition of another famous artist; feeling the effects of being high, it all came crashing down with an unanticipated tap on my shoulder. Turning to see who belonged to the tap, my breath got caught in my chest when I saw Malik standing behind me. He looked more handsome than I remembered, maybe it was because I hadn't seen him in in a few months, or maybe it was the rented suit he had on. Either way I found myself caught between a rock and a hard place.

With a grin as wide as the Hudson, he began to bombard me with question; some casual, others more spiteful. Explaining that he had been watching us all evening he noted the tension between Hennison and Jay. As he spoke, he held a drink in one hand, and the other hand he kept in his pant pocket. Just as another toxic word was about to spill out his mouth, a manicured hand with stiletto nails made their way around Malik's torso. His grin got wider as the hands traveled across his chest.

Taking the mystery woman by one of her hands, he pulled her into view. I swear I saw blood soaked fangs as he introduced my sister as his woman/client! If I wasn't knocked sideways by seeing him unexpectedly, I definitely fell flat on my ass seeing China with him. My first instinct was to slap the shit out of him and her, but I got him first. As I lifted my hand to give her a piece, Jayshawn grabbed it. Standing in the middle of a crowded room at the Guggenheim with my hand raised in the air, and my chest heaving heavily, tears began to emerge from my eyes despite my best efforts to hold them back. Easing the pressure

Jayshawn had on my wrist; I lowered my arm and ran out of the gallery.

On my heels, Jayshawn caught me around my waist and bear hugged me from behind. I wiggled as hard as I could to get him off of me, I even tried to elbow him in the ribs; but he just held me tighter. After a few seconds, I stopped fighting him. Really, it wasn't him I wanted to hurt. In a way, I wanted to not just hurt Malik, but myself for allowing him to take my heart for a ride for the last few years.

Whispering in my ear; Jayshawn said, "Don't let the dumb motherfucker chase you out of here like this. You're better than both of them. He's a clown; all he has is the show he puts on. He can only entertain the crowd for a short time until they figure out his tricks; then the show is over." He continued by saying, "We were having a good time tonight before he showed up, don't let him ruin tonight for us. If you want to go, we can leave; but don't let him be the reason you do. Do you want to go?"

Swallowing hard in a vain attempt to get my breathing and tears under control, I shook my head no. Turning me to face him, he cupped my face with his hands and wiped away my tears with his thumbs. Instead of calming the thumping in my chest, doing that caused to beat harder.

Allowing a few minutes to pass before returning to the party, we entered the gallery to the announcement of dinner being served. Once seated, I told Dee about the previous exchange and I saw rage in her like I've never seen; to prevent further embarrassment on my part, and not wanting to explain to Dee's parents, or my co-workers for that matter; why we all had to be escorted off the premises, I held her wrist before she could leave her seat.

Leaving the museum, I didn't want to go home. I wanted to hide from the world, in a safe place where I felt like nothing would hurt me, so with no insisting from Jayshawn, I told the driver that we would be making one stop. The ride was quiet; I didn't say anything; truthfully what the hell could I say. Oh, maybe something like; did you have a good time? How did you find the steak, I thought it was a bit dry? By the way, can you believe my ex is fucking my sister? No, silence seemed like a better choice.

Getting off the elevator to his apartment, I could barely raise me head. Before opening the door, he lifted my chin and kissed me lightly on the nose. Taking my coat and tossing it on a chair, we went to the kitchen. Turning on the radio, perhaps to offset the silence, he asked me if I wanted anything as he reached for a bottle of water. Gesturing to turn down his invitation, I just stood at the end of the island counter and watched him drink. At that moment, I knew that I wanted this man. What was holding me back from him, a silly loyalty I had to a man who shouldn't even be called one. I know what I want, and for once in my life I wasn't going to wait for him to chase me. He had chased me long enough, metaphorically and in reality. It was time I stopped running.

Walking over to where he stood, I took the bottle from his hands, and placed it on the counter. His lips were moist from the liquid, and all I wanted to do was drink it from his mouth. Wrapping my arms around his neck I raised myself up to meet the wetness of his lips.

Following my lead, he hoisted me up, cupping my ass in his hands; then resting me on the island counter. With his hands still under my dress, I felt them roaming all over my back, ass, and torso. I felt precious being touched by him, like every trace was to preserve the beauty he saw in me. Pausing, to be positive of my intentions; Jayshawn asked if I was sure this is what I wanted. Matching his intensity, I assured him that there was nothing else I wanted more than him inside me. With that I removed the pins from my hair and let it all down my back. With his hands he smoothed it out softly and twirled his fingers in it. It felt wonderful for him to play in my hair, it put me at ease.

Tilting my head slightly, I felt Jay licking my neck; while softly tugging at my mane. I don't know how long we were locked in our embrace, but we decided to continue our exploration in

Jay's bedroom; I was finally about to get my chance to test drive his bed.

Being in his bedroom at night with the city sounds as a soundtrack; made me feel as if all my inhibitions had melted away. Standing at the foot of his bed, he stood behind me; cupping my breasts and kissed my neck as he slowly unzipped my dress. Allowing it to fall to the floor, I could tell he appreciated what was underneath it by the gasp I heard. Turning so that he could get a frontal view, his face reflected that of a man that was about to tear the flesh from my body. Slowly and deliberately removing his own clothes, he opted to leave on his boxer briefs; Jay laid me on the softness of his plush comforter, the rising print of his manhood was enough to make me cum on sight.

Starting with one of my legs; he raised it in the air and rested it on his shoulder. Leaving a trail of kisses from the tips of my toes to my inner thighs, I shook with anticipation of what would happen next. Running his hands up my thighs to the front of my corset, he unhooked it slowly exposing bits of skin from bottom to top. Undoing the final hook, my breasts spilled out exposing the hardness of my nipples. With his tongue he made circles around my belly button; then made his way up to nipples that were so hard they could cut glass he engulfed them in the warmth of his mouth.

Arching my back and spreading my legs to allow Jay a better reach; I didn't know whether to moan loudly or pass out from the desire he was building. This exchange between us was nothing like the first time. This was more sensual, and passionate; whereas the first time we had sexed it was hurried and animalistic. Turning me on my stomach and positioning me on my knees; he removed my panties. Gliding them down slowly, I felt him put his lips to one of my butt cheeks and teasingly bit it.

Spreading them, he plunged face first into my slickness. Arching my back so hard I heard it crack, I bucked softly against his gentle strokes. Unable to hold the position, I dropped to my stomach as the first of many waves of orgasm passed.

Eager to return the favor I reciprocated the bliss he so graciously gave me. Laying him on his back, I took him in to my mouth and glided slowly up and down his shaft. Tasting the sweetness of him, his moans were like cheers to keep going. Changing my rhythm a bit, I alternated between fast and slow strokes; and took special care of the most sensitive area.

Letting him go before he climaxed too soon, I put my legs on his sides and directed him inside the wetness of my body. Riding slowly at first to get used to his size, I began to get more comfortable and sped up my strokes. With every grind of my hips, I felt my clit rub against him, trying desperately to hold back my orgasm; I held on to the wall and head board to steady myself. Sucking my breasts and thrusting below me, Jayshawn made it impossible to hold back any longer. Exploding, I lay atop him as he continued to stroke me from the bottom. Finally, letting himself go; we lay wrapped in each other's arms. We made sweet pillow talk for a few minutes before sleep crept up on us.

Waking up the next day in his arms with a feeling of satisfaction was a sensation I hadn't felt in a long time. I wanted to lie in bed with him all day, but I had to go home to get ready for work. I would've called out, but I had to submit all the information for the White Party Indulgence was having.

Gathering my clothing up quietly as to not wake Jay, I began to dress. Pulling me down on the bed unexpectedly Jay pulled me close to him. After some coaxing, he let me finish getting dressed. Calling a car service to get me, Jay wanted me to come back after work. Agreeing, I made him stay in bed as I left to catch my ride home.

Makayla

I think I'll stop at StarCoins Coffee &
Bistro before I go to work; what's a few extra
minutes, I thought as I was about to pass it by.
Walking into the coffee house, my senses became
heightened by the tantalizing smell of fresh coffee
and the anticipation of espresso. Momentarily
forgetting it was the morning rush, I stood in line
for what seemed like hours; as I did, my mind
began to drift. It was really horrible what I was
doing to Jayshawn, he was a decent guy; but hey, I
have to look out for number one.

When Malik approached me with a
proposition, I couldn't turn it down. Seriously,
where else was I going to get a management deal
for simply forgetting to a few things here and
there for Jayshawn. He's a good dude, but he
wasn't offering me anything. I don't want to be
just his assistant, I want to run the business or
marry into it; whichever came first. I used every
trick I knew to make him interested in me outside
of work, and when he broke up with that hoe of an
ex; I thought I had it in the bag. Now, he's
swimming in the piggy pond; and I don't do pork!

Arriving at work an hour late, I strolled in wearing my favorite black leather biker jacket, loose white top, leather leggings, and a pair of four inch, knee-high boots; yes, I had to show Jayshawn what he was missing out on at all times. You never know, he might come to his senses. Taking my seat behind my desk, I set out to start my daily tasks of answering phones and pretending to respond to emails. I did however; forward some of his emails to Malik. I don't know why he is so set on trying to take all of Jay's business, but whatever he had up his sleeve damn well better benefit what he can do for me. Not wanting to be too obvious, I made sure to book the appropriate meetings, called all the vendors, and approved all payment invoices to outside contractors; I can't totally leave him ass'd out.

I have more than bomb ass clerical skills, but modeling and lyrical skills as well. I've been writing rhythms since I was eleven years old. A female rapper with a Jamaican accent is a dime a dozen; I had to become a triple threat learning dance, getting a vocal coach, in addition to attending as many casting calls as possible. I have dreams too, and nothing and no one will stop my flow, but finding the money to fund my endeavors has increasingly become difficult.

So, to help fund my dreams and makes ends meet; I went out with a few ballers from time to time. I got what I wanted, and they got what they wanted; it was an even exchange of goods and services. But like everything else that got old, also I got tired of their low budget girlfriends calling me asking how I know their dudes. Then I realized, after we had our fun, they went home to them; and my money flow stopped. That's when I decided that I had to either marry into money, or climb my way up in the industry. With Jayshawn's company I got the best of both worlds. I became the assistant to the most high profile, professional, most sought after event planner/promoter in the business; and through him, I met some amazing, rich guys who didn't mind speaking, and setting up lunch meetings with his assistant when he was busy.

Emerging from his office, just as I finished a phone call with a client, Jay gave me a stare that could melt all the skin from my body. I had never seen him look that way before; I was sure he knew what was going on. As he approached my desk, I began to get nervous. Speaking in unison, we both said that we had to talk. Taking control, Jayshawn spoke first; and I stood to meet his gaze.

"Makayla, you've been working with me for a while, I appreciate the effort you have put in, in the past, but lately you've really slipped. You've been scheduling appointments on the opposite side of town from where you tell me they are, some of my clients have been complaining that they haven't been getting any responses to their emails, then opted to text me when they can't. Also, the lateness has to STOP! I don't know what's gotten into you, but this can't continue. I don't want to lose you, is there something that you want to talk to me about? Are you ok at home? Talk to me." He insisted.

Panicking for a moment, I gathered my composure and mixed a gumbo of truth and lies. Taking a deep breath, I began to weave a tale that would make Shonda Rhimes proud. Telling him that I had met a guy, and he was very demanding, jealous, and kept a watchful eye on every aspect of my life including emails and text messages. I also, told him that the stress of the job and a lack of a vacation slowed my normal pace to a crawl.

Lastly, I explained my lateness to being burned out. Taking a moment to inject a few sniffles as to stifle tears, I dropped my head so that my hair would block my face, as I forced phony tears from my eyes. I put on a performance Broadway worthy, and my former acting coach said I lacked depth; what the hell did that old bat know, anyway! She hadn't gotten any further than being a chorus girl, I was aiming for the headliner; and hooking up with Malik is a step in the right direction.

After my performance, I could swear I heard applause from a crowd. As I mentally began to take a bow, Jayshawn offered me some advice. I tried desperately not to roll my eyes at him. What did he know about relationships, anyway? Look who he's been keeping company with. He needed to understand that a powerful man needed an equally powerful woman at his side to continue the growth of his empire. What could Chloe bring to his business? '*Oh, I know; I bet she knew the best caterer in town. She can choose a menu like nobody's business*' I thought and a slight chuckle escaped my lips. It doesn't matter, anyway; soon I would be leaving this job and Jayshawn for good to peruse my own dreams.

The rest of the day flew by; I noticed Jay kept a closer eye on me. Perhaps it was out of concern for what I told him earlier or maybe it was that his trust in me is beginning to falter. Either way, I tried to stay mindful of what I did and the end goal I'm trying to accomplish. Usually I left before he did, but since our heart to heart, I decided it would be a better look if I made it seem like I was putting in some effort.

Leaving his office and locking the door behind him, he walked up to my desk and asked if I would be okay. Assuring him that I would be, he said for me to call if I needed anything; and as soon as I was done I could go. I really was beginning to feel like the ground would open up and swallow me. Closing up the office I had to run to my voice lesson across town.

While trying to urge my voice to reach an octave higher, Malik waltz's into my session, with swag that reached me before his hands could. Reaching out for my hands, he twirled me around the studio as I continued to sing a song I wrote called Rapture. As the song came to an end, he grabbed me by the waist and pressed me close to his body. As my pulse quickened from his strategic caressing of my lower back, my voice slightly wavered. Letting me go, he clapped as if I had put on a show worthy of Carnegie Hall.

Informing him briefly of what happened earlier, he instructed me to cool off for a while; he had all the info he needed for the time being. Taking this time to discuss my contract, I insisted on him shopping my talent to a few record companies and I had a few songs ready for a demo. As I spoke he gazed at me with intensity. Convincing me that he knew exactly what he had in mind for me, I wasn't entirely sure he was speaking about my career, or his bedroom. Inviting me to dinner to discuss the possibilities, I realized what type of guy Malik really is; He's an opportunist that will use any and every one he could to get to the top. He thought that because he was a very attractive man that he could manipulate me into being one of his flunkies, well two can play that game.

Chloe

Arriving at work just in time to walk into the meeting room, Cassidy gave me a dirty look mixed with relief. Having just enough time to pass out the schematic for the event floor plan, I placed the color copies in front of Clair's seat. Awaiting Clair's arrival, Cassidy inquired about last night's festivities then began to question my tardiness. Speaking briefly, I told her that for me it was a night to remember. Just as I was about to continue, Clair made her presence known as she brought with her an air of authoritative command; taking her seat the meeting began.

Starting this meeting the way she did any other, she went down the list of to do's. As I felt the meeting winding down, I knew I was up next to face the firing squad. I had no idea if she would approve of the ideas I had for the White Party's Majestic Winter Ball theme, but I was going to give it my best shot.

"Ms. Major," Clair said. "Are you ready to show us what you have for our White Party?"

Standing with papers in hand, I felt my heart pound in my chest with a trembling in my fingers. "Yes, can everyone please flip the packet to the first page marked floor plan." I instructed.

As I began to paint the picture of the vision for the party, I made sure to include all the specifications Clair required, such as winter white trees draped in icicle lights, flat screen monitors that will play videos of Indulgence's most successful issues, public appearances, and behind the scene inner workings. Moving through each section of the proposal, I suggested vendors that would be beneficial and would draw attention to our philanthropy in helping start up business, with advertisers that are high profile and would bring in other high profile clients. Next up was the catering menu, musical accompaniment, guest lists/appearances, as well as possible award presentations to give some staff and contributors a sense of accomplishment and productivity.

For the most part Clair agreed with the direction the proposal suggested. She decided to change one key feature that I hadn't anticipated. She suggested we shoot the video for the party at a ski lodge, and bring a few models from Legendary Models Inc. Quickly writing down everything she said, Clair insisted that I attend the trip with Cassidy, herself, Kelly, and a few others from the magazine to ensure that everything came out flawless. I hadn't expected to be onsite for something like this, but I was very excited to be on her list of people who received the privilege.

Walking back to my cubical, Cassidy crept up behind me then began to rip my ass apart then hand it to me on a stack of memos. We had become really close, and I understood why she's upset. If I had been just one minute later, she would have caught pure hell from Clair. Though, this was my assignment Cassidy is my superior, and whatever work I didn't accomplish would have reflected heavily on her abilities as well. I knew she had a close relationship with Clair, but this was business and business has no friends; in the publishing world, or any other for that matter.

"Chloe!" Cassidy yelped. "What the hell happened to you this morning? You knew we had an early meeting! Look we're cool, but if Clair told me to fire you; you're gone simple as that. I know you're still new, and you haven't quite got the hang of this lifestyle yet. But let me tell you, we attend parties all the time; until the wee hours of the morning and start work promptly the same day. It's not fair, sometimes I think management asks too much of us, but it's our job and this is what we have to do."

"I'm sorry Cass, I will be more mindful next time; I appreciate you being honest with me." I concluded.

"Look, just watch yourself. I have to leave early today, so you have to make the arrangements for the trip. Kellendra is making the travel plans, so you have to rally the troops. Here is a list of people from the office that you have to inform of the trip. Make sure they are packed for three days and ready to meet here tomorrow morning at 8 A.M. The cars will be here at 8:30 on the dot. Don't worry about the models; I've taken care of that." Cassidy instructed before walking to her office.

Observing the list of names, I thought is would be smarter to call each person rather than send an email. Given how the trip is last minute, everyone had to be informed right away; sending an email ran the risk of key people not attending, and I didn't need Clair or Cassidy holding that against me; it would make me seem incompetent.

At the top of the list is Hennison Black. Though, I reveled in the thought of being with Hennison in a secluded ski lodge for three days with a slew of people from the office; I don't know if I could handle it. Dialing his extension, I expected his secretary to pick up.

"Hello, this is Hennison Black." He said in a deep baritone voice.

"Hello Mr. Black, This is Chloe Major from Indulgence. I calling to inform you that your presence has been requested to attend The White Party photo shoot at Emmerson Lodge tomorrow. Please pack warmly for three days; the limo will be leaving promptly at 8:30am." I instructed in my most professional voice.

"Ms. Major, hello to you to. No need to be so formal, I know exactly who you are and where you work." He said with a smile in his voice. "Who approved this trip to Emmerson Lodge?" He inquired.

"The trip was approved by Ms. Winters. She thought it would be more authentic to shoot on site instead of a studio." I answered.

"Oh, I see. And are you attending this trip Ms. Major?" Hennison questioned.

"Yes. Ms. Winters, Ms. Martin, myself, and a few others from the office are required to attend." I notified.

"Consider me well informed Ms. Major. I'll see you tomorrow at 8." He sensually crooned.

Hanging up the phone before another word could be said, my legs began to shake uncontrollably; I had to place my hands on my knees to stop it from hitting the desk. Continuing down the list of names, everyone confirmed their attendance. Really, the only person who had the option of saying no to it was Hennison; everyone else had no choice but to show up, Clair basically gave them a command, they just had to recognize that they got it.

Feeling drained, I dragged myself out of the office and started home to pack for the shoot tomorrow. On the train ride home, I thought about Hennison. He was extremely attractive, but I'm with Jayshawn… Or was I? We sort of just fell into whatever we are. Yes, I cared about him, and I know he cares for me, but we didn't have a label on what we're doing. *This must be how Dominique feels when she's juggling multiple men,* I thought. But I'm not sleeping with Hennison, it's just harmless flirting. Or maybe the real question is, did I want to sleep with Hennison. Before I could entertain the thought further, I decided to text Jayshawn.

To Jayshawn Thomas:

Hi Jay, I can't see you tonight. I have to be onsite for a photo shoot for the next three days. Can we get together when I get back? Let me know.

I checked my phone every few seconds waiting for a response that never came. When I got home, I began to pack. Rummaging through my suitcases, I pulled a couple pairs of Lilly Ford jeans, a black sweater, a black and white wrap sweater I got on clearance at The Sweet Spot, a silver tone blouse, a screen printed high low top with embellishments, a pair of leather leggings, my Canadian Falcon jacket, a little black dress, some snow boots, and a couple pairs of heels in the event of a formal dinner; basically I didn't want to be caught off guard. This is the fashion business, plans change faster than a woman can change her mind; with that in mind, I threw a few more things inside of my carry-on bag.

Checking my phone one more time, I saw nothing on my phone's screen but my own face smiling back at me. Taking a deep breath while shaking my head, this is exactly what I'm talking about I said aloud. Jayshawn was only available for what he wanted to be available for. That's why we never hooked up all those years ago; he had no time for me. I really like Jayshawn, and against my better judgement I pictured us having a relationship; I see now that's not possible. Maybe we're better as friends, with benefits of course; but friends none the less.

Really, he was giving me what I needed; sex with no strings attached, on his part anyway. I promised myself that I wouldn't dive crotch first into another relationship, especially after what happened with Malik; and we all know how that turned out. Maybe, for real this time; I need to be alone. Switching off the light, I decided to go to bed for the night, though I did look one more time at my phone.

The next day, I was up and out early. Dee hadn't come home; surprise, surprise. I should just take over this apartment; I'm the only one who spends time here, anyway. Sending her a quick text before leaving, I double checked to make sure I had everything in my bag; I didn't want to leave anything essential behind.

Arriving at the Black Building, I saw sprinkles of fashionistas, and metrosexual men on the sidewalk all decked out in the latest ski wear. Donned in puff jackets, sunglasses, and jeans, the women are in full face makeup, and all of them on cell phones, you could hear the chatter from their rushed talking before you could reach the middle of the block.

Waiting for the rest of the team to arrive, the next to show up was Clair in her Road Rover. When her driver opened her door, she looked like The Goddess of the Alaskan Tundra, decked out from head to toe in white. Wearing a white fur coat, sunglasses, red lipstick, and Saint LaRue leather boots; she kept the all-white theme of the party going.

As she stepped out of the truck, I could see the team murmur to each other that they should've known to wear all white. At least they were dressed for the climate, I wore a pair of blue jeans, a royal blue blouse, and black ankle boots with my Heather grey wool dress coat, and I dressed for casually for the weekend with the girls; instead of the snowy wilderness.

Pulling up to the curb as if by clock work, was one limo and two passenger vans ready to make the trip upstate. Exiting the building, Hennison shooed away his assistant and walked up to me with a sly grin on his face. I hoped he wouldn't grin at me like that throughout the trip, if he did; I would be able to melt all the snow with how hot he was making me.

Passing by me briefly he whispered, "I look forward to working closely with you."

Those few words sent a shiver down my spine, that I scarcely heard Clair calling for me. Turning just in time to watch Hennison enter the limo, I slightly panicked knowing that we would be sharing the car together; I had half hoped to be in the passenger van with everyone else. Walking briskly to Clair, she gestured for me to enter the car with her and Hennison. As I entered, I prayed I would be able to keep my composure. Noticing that we were pulling off, I asked Clair if Cassidy and Kelly would be coming. She informed me that they would be joining us the next day. Great! I thought now who will distract me from all of Hennison's flirting? I chanted in my head that I wouldn't let him get to me, over and over again. And the more I chanted, the more I realized he was already in my head.

The ride was long and for the most part quiet. What I really mean is, I was quiet; Clair typed away on her laptop and periodically asked me a few questions or asked me to make a few calls. Hennison sat on the other side of the limo and talked on the phone. He had tons of paper; and files spread out around him. I was amazed at how diligent he is. One would've thought that because he was handed this business, that he didn't really care about managing it properly. But watching him right now, I can see that it was a misconception. Occasionally he would catch me looking at him, and he would shoot me a smile with a wink. Then he would quickly go to back to doing whatever it is that inhabited his time for that moment.

Being of no need to Clair at the moment, I decided to give thought to what I discussed with Jada Rae at the charity event. I needed to get back in the groove of writing again and the perfect way to do that was to establish a blog and create a following. Pulling out my tablet; I Google some blog sites to find out what my options were. After what seemed like an eternity, I settled on Blogtalk.com It's a free site, so I didn't have to pay to get it started; which was a plus for me since I'm broke , anyway

The next thing that I had to give serious thought to is the name of the blog. Every name I could think of was already taken by another blogger. Out of frustration I began to look at the things around me that could give me some inspiration. Taking into account what industry I worked in, and my ability of being a writer; I played around with a few words, and phrases that sounded good together. After a half hour, The Stylish Mind was born.

I felt accomplished with creating the blog and naming it, but I was at a loss for trying to come up content; can't do everything in one limo ride. Driving the narrow road to Emmerson Lodge, we were surrounded by the most picturesque scenery I had ever seen. Movies and music videos filmed here, didn't do the lodge justice, it was more magnificent in person.

Past the narrow roads end waited a lodge that more closely resembled a mansion. Entering a circular driveway, my vision became engulfed by the sheer beauty of the architecture. With a massive stone exterior lined with snow covered hedges, large windows, and two stone columns at its entrance; I had now discovered how the rich, famous, and privileged spent ski vacations.

Stopping in front of the main entrance, the driver of the limo rushed to open the door. Hennison first to exit played the part of the gentlemen assisting Clair, and I out, and through the snow covered walkway. Upon entering the lodge; I was in awe of how it looked as if the staff were expecting the royal family at any moment.

Maybe this is the Jersey girl coming out of me, but when you think of a ski lodge, you would picture in your mind something out of the 18th century. For example, it would be outdoorsy, dark colors, logs for walls, old style stoves, close quarter rooms, with little to no walking space and no closets to speak of, with enough plaid prints to last you ten lifetimes.

Emmerson Lodge didn't embody any of the stereotypes you would expect a nature based vacation resort to be. Walls Painted beige with gold trimmings, high ceilings, white marble floors, and beautifully crafted skylight above a large arched staircase in the buildings center; this hotel had no place in the mountains covered in snow and ice.

Watching everyone enter the hotel as if unfazed by their surroundings, I wondered if this was the kind of life I would soon become accustomed to. Walking towards the atrium, we were approached by Greer; our personal butler for the duration of our stay. Showing each of us to our rooms, most of the staff would be sharing; lucky for me my roommate wouldn't be arriving until the next day. Having just enough time to throw my bag in my room, I was summoned to Clair's suite.

Finding her in a very plush room which was arguably three times the size of Dee's apartment, she immediately put me to work on organizing the photo shoot. Not wasting a bit of daylight, I sent the photographer with a few of the models to take candid pictures of them doing regular things a vacationer would do around the hotel. The large windows provided great light and made everything look authentic, while the photographer took a couple shoots of them attempting to light one of the fireplaces; Greer was definitely on standby for that one, we didn't need one of the girls lighting their weaves on fire. If that happened, there would be no way we were going to be able to get good human hair all the way up here. Making sure that everything was executed to Clair's specifications, I didn't notice that I was being watched.

By sunset, my body hurt so badly that I couldn't move. I went to the main parlor and collapsed on the closest sofa I could find. The next thing I knew, I was waking up to find Hennison seated next to me with his legs crossed, and drinking brown liquid from a small glass. Trying to regain my composure I sat up quickly and struggled to smooth out my hair, I secretly hoped that I didn't let a snore slip while he was there.

Clearing my throat I blurted out, "how long have I been asleep?"

In a voice as smooth as the liquid that touched his lips, Hennison answered, "Not long, maybe twenty minutes or so. You looked so tired that I didn't want to disturb you. So, I took a seat, got a drink and made sure no one else could either."

I tried to keep the flush that was slowly rising in my cheeks to a minimum, when he said that. Inarticulately saying thank you; I shifted my body to get off the sofa. Catching me by the knee as I began to stand, Hennison urged me to rest a while longer. He assured me that Clair was otherwise occupied, and wouldn't be in need of my presence at the moment. Taken by surprise, I eased myself back down, and nestled into the spot I had broken in.

"Would you like a drink?" He asked.

"Uh, yes umm… Whatever you're having is fine." I requested.

With a slight laugh he asked, "are you sure you can handle this, it's very strong?"

As seductively as I could I told him, "I'm positive I can handle it."

Signaling a nearby waiter, Hennison asked him to bring another Crown Majestic. I didn't mean to play into his games the way I did, but I found myself unable to avoid it. Did I like his pursuit of me? Yes I did, especially since I haven't heard from Jayshawn since the night before last. Besides, I don't see the harm in playing this little game, at the end of the day I would go back to my life and he will go back to his.

With his life filled with models to bed, fancy parties, expensive drinks, with a publishing empire to conquer and all; he had his hands full. I was but a small blip on his radar; multiplying his family's legacy was at the top of his to do list, and if he just so happened to make sport out of flirting with a few office assistants; why not?

We talked for a while, surprisingly about regular things that had nothing to do with work, just common things people would talk about when they're trying to get to know each other. The problem is the conversation is one sided. I knew almost everything about him (that has been published that is), but he didn't know much about me. So I found myself telling him all about growing up in New Jersey, and how I majored in journalism and fashion. He thought that those two categories together made for an interesting match. I agreed they were unconventional together, but for me it was the most natural fit. Being a writer is in my blood and in every fiber of who I am. Fashion is something that affected me daily. Existing in a world that praised sizes zero to six and utterly loathed sizes eighteen to twenty eight; it became as much a part of me as my own limbs.

We talked until the rest of our party began to fill the parlor. Through the dim lighting, I could make out the perplexed faces of some of my coworkers as they entered. Continuing to converse until Greer called us for dinner, Hennison and I walked together to the dining hall. We were all seated together at a long table, and as everyone began to order drinks, Clair arrived; she always had to be the last person to enter a room to make a grand appearance.

During dinner, Clair informed every one of the jam packed schedule we had for the next day and advised we all eat up and got a good night's sleep. Other than that dinner was quiet, everyone ate and had their side bar conversations. Feeling slightly tipsy; I ate as much as I could so the food could soak up the liquor in my system; it's not a good look to get drunk in front of the bosses. Noticing a conversation brewing between Hennison and Clair, I sat back and listened to them take jabs at each other. The only thing they could agree on was the direction the business was going, which seemed to be promising. Quickly turning her attention from Hennison to one of the photographers on staff, Clair instructed her to get shots of Hennison the next day doing manly, outdoorsy things. Clair thought it would make him look more 'average Joe' and approachable to the critics.

Leaving dinner, I started up the stairs to my room. Holding tightly to the banister I walked slowly up. Catching me mid-way up, Hennison asked me if I wanted to take a walk with him around the grounds; he wanted to finish our earlier conversation. Agreeing to walk with him, we walked to our separate rooms and agreed to meet at the bottom of the staircase in ten minutes.

Entering my room, I dug through my bag to find my heavy coat. As I was about to walk out the door, I decided to check myself in the mirror to make sure I was presentable. Besides the tired look I was sporting, the face that looked back at me was good.

My natural curls held up nicely, my subtle makeup looked natural, and not overdone like some of the other girls; all in all I was good to go.

Changing my shoes to boots with a good grip on them, and putting on my blue parka, I was out the door.

Dominique

Things have been a little tense between Chase and I since the charity event. I know he can feel that something is off between us, but I'm not sure if he's figured out what that something is. When Chase asked me why I was so upset at the party once we got back to his house, I had to lie to him blaming my ill disposition on the possible job loss my department is facing. I wanted to tell him the truth, but I knew that if I did, he wouldn't ever look at me the same. Good thinking on my part right? Wrong!

He started to look at me different from that point on. I thought that if we made love that night to take his mind off of me being distracted, and my mind off of Ramir, his wife and kids, it would be a decent solution. Really, I think all it did is drive the wedge deeper between us. In the past I've been able to use sex to my advantage with men; hell, women too for that matter. With men, sex gave me a way to get validation, and control; being able to deal with things on my terms instead of his. With women, sex appeal was a conversation starter.

When two hot women are together in a club, it's easy to become the center of attention, and get whatever baller happened to be in the place to buy us whatever we wanted. Also, it didn't hurt to throw a woman at the door or at the bar a few complements to get better service or gain entrance into an exclusive club, or VIP lounge; a well-placed complement could melt any icy exterior.

The silence between us was deafening, and as the days passed it got louder and louder until I opted to go back to my own place. Expecting to see Chloe, I remembered she went on some job related trip and would be gone for the next few days. Taking a shower and putting on my favorite faded grey sweats I planted my ass in front of the tv. Occasionally, I would get a call or text from Chase, but it would be something like 'hi', 'what are you doing', or 'I miss you, come over.'

I waited for a call, but it wasn't Chase's I waited for. I waited for the same man that had occupied my thoughts for years. The same guy who could make me feel complete in one breath and completely make me crumble in the next. Truthfully, I don't know what I'm doing. I want to be with Chase, but there is still something unfinished between me and Ra. I've loved him for so long I don't know how to turn it off, no matter how bad I wanted to. I couldn't take not seeing him, so I picked up the phone and called. The phone rang a few times before he answered.

"Hello Dominique." Ramir whispered.

"Hi Ra, Can you talk?" I questioned.

"No, not at the moment; but I want to see you. Can I see you tonight?" He asked.

Hesitating for a second, I obliged his request. Telling him I was home, and if he wanted to see me, he would come here; he agreed. I waited for him to arrive, and waited, and waited until my eyes became so heavy that I was unable to continue fighting the sleep that was overtaking me.

When I woke up, it was 3:30 A.M. and there was a soft knock at the door. Rising to answer it, I opened it to find Chase standing in front of me. I panicked because I expected the knock to be from Ramir. The jolt from the shock of seeing Chase woke me up completely, inviting him in, he took a seat on the couch and I excused myself to the bathroom. With phone in hand, I sent a quick hate text to Ramir, telling him that I was pissed he stood me up and that I was going to bed, and don't bother coming by cause I am done with his bullshit. I don't know if he would see the text or not; but I hoped he did.

Going back in the living room, I saw that Chased had dozed off. Gently waking him up, I led him to the bedroom. We didn't have sex that night, we just slept together. With his head on my chest, it seemed like the most natural thing in the world. That's when I realized that he didn't come

233

over for a quick booty call; but because he missed me, and obviously couldn't get a good night's sleep without being in my arms. Now only if I could get this kind of response from Ramir, I would be a happy girl.

The next day I went to work like normal. The moment I entered the office, the entire department staff was called into the meeting room. Walking in all I could think was that this was it; we're all going to be given our walking papers. Normally, I wouldn't be bothered by losing a job; I always had my parents to fall back on. But what about the people in the office who had nobody for support, financial or otherwise? Most of them have families and children to take care of, how would they bounce back from something like this? Looking tragic, Hershel walked in with files in hand; I didn't know what to expect.

Placing his files on the table, Hershel stood, paced back and forth at the tables head; as if trying to form the right words. Opting to start his speech off with words of praise to the head bosses, he continued his speech now addressing the rest of us.

"Ladies and gentlemen, it has been my pleasure to have worked with you all for the past ten years. This department has seen its share of triumphs and periods of uncertainty. As we all are aware of the changes, the company is experiencing, this has been yet another test of our resolve through these uncertain times. Today, the uncertainty that has plagued us is now over. As many of you know, one of the changes the company is considering concerns the continuance or dismantling of our department. I have met with our Senior Advisor and a decision has been made." Hershel informed.

The room was so silent that you could hear the hum of the electricity through the fluorescent lights. I could tell everyone was holding their breaths when Hershel paused; I did too. The next word out of his mouth would determine whether some of us were going to be able to make the rent; we might have to moonlight as strippers or go over to Hunts Point and go on a few 'dates' in order to make ends meet.

Beginning again; Hershel continued, "The Senior Advisers have decided that we are much too valuable to disperse our department! We will remain a part of Lawrence and Associates!" He uttered excitedly. As the room roared with cries of happiness that we would maintain our jobs, no one noticed that after Hershel delivered that news, he immediately became somber once again.

Unbuttoning his suit jacket, and loosening his tie while taking a deep breath, he balled up his fists, and knocked on the table to get everyone's attention again. With the look of regret in his eyes, and with a slight tremble in his hands as he began to speak; then I realized that there would be a few casualties to keeping our department open… Some of us would have to go.

By the end of the meeting we were told that our staff would have to be reduced, and that some of our team would be randomly selected to be separated from the company.

The decision would be based on an array of factors that he would not be privileged to, Human Resources would have the task of evaluating everyone's performance and once that was finished they would give Hershel a list of the names of people who would be chosen. He also, informed us that there would be a severance package; as to make the adjustments more tolerable. He had given out cards HR had given him; on these cards is a number to an employee hotline if anyone should need to discuss the situation with someone to make the transition easier. Since at this point we didn't know who was staying or going, he gave the cards to everyone in the conference room.

Somberly walking to my desk, I plopped down in the swivel chair to give thought to everything that was going on. In doing so, I felt massive piles of weight bearing down on my shoulders. A few minutes after I sat down, Hershel rounded the corner and walked straight to my desk. Seeing my distraught state, he asked if I was ok, and told me to continue with business as if nothing had changed. He knew the tone of the day would now be amiss and instructed me to keep things flowing as much as possible. After agreeing with his request, Hershel walked into his office where he remained for the duration of the day.

By the end of the day, everyone was mentally and physically drained and ready to unload the stress that had been placed on them. Most of the staff decided to go to a bar close to the job, I opted to go home and have a pity party for one that I had a reservation for. When I left the office, it was deserted, and I felt a stillness that I had never experienced before. Hershel still in his office would probably work until the wee hours trying to keep his job relevant so that he's not on the list HR is constructing.

Leaving the building, I sent a text to Chloe, to briefly tell her about today's events, and I walked into someone who had been blocking my path. Apologizing profusely before realizing who it was, the breath got caught in my chest when I realized it was Ramir. Rolling my eyes as I passed him, I headed for the Subway. For a few moments he walked behind me quiet. The longer he followed the angrier I became.

Turning around with such ferocity that he stumbled backwards, I yelled at him with as much base in my voice as I could find; how could one man make me so angry and turn me on at the same time, is beyond me.

Yelling to the point of my voice echoing between the buildings I asked, "What do you want Ramir? What could you possibly want from me now? You've already humiliated me, broke my heart, and haven't given me as much as a sorry..."

Interrupting my tirade, Ramir began to explain. "I'm sorry for last night. One of the boys was ill and refused to go to sleep without being in my arms. I intended to be with you, but please understand that my child needed me."

"I understand." I said flatly. "I understand a lot of things, but I'll tell you what I don't understand! Why are you continuing this game with me? Do you enjoy hurting me; is this a sport for you? Cause I'll tell you something, I'm done playing it."

"No, this isn't sport, its love. I have deep feelings for you and I'm not ready to give them up. But I also love my family, my children. I want to leave Kasha, but now isn't the time to do it. I couldn't live every day not having my children in my home. I need for you to give me time." He bid.

"I've given you nothing but time. Now that time is up, I can't..." I said not having enough words to describe how awful I felt about loving and continuously fucking a married man with children.

As I began to walk away, I heard him utter 'I love you'. Pausing mid step, I turned to see him walk briskly in my direction. My voice refused to leave and echo from my mouth, I stood in the middle of the sidewalk stun by his words; and I began to feel the warm, salty tears trickle down my cheeks. Dropping everything I was holding, Ramir scooped me up in his arms and kissed me like a dying man that only had this moment left to live, and through our embrace I breathed life back into him.

The next thing I knew, I was in his apartment and in the bed he shared with Kasha. Lying on his sheets, I could feel the softness of a high thread count and soundless motion the bed made as we bucked wildly atop. Resting in between romps, Ramir dozed off. Taking the opportunity presented; I set out to tour what could be my new residence; I put on Ramir's button-down shirt and walked through the halls.

Going from room to room, I found the boys rooms first, since they were in proximity to the master bedroom. They were typical boys' rooms, messy with just enough funk that you wouldn't pass out upon entry. Venturing further into the apartment, I found the living room that was adorned in family memorabilia and knick knacks. Picking up one of the framed pictures from the console table, I looked into the happy faces of Ramir, Kasha, and their children. Studying each face individually, I felt the cold sting of jealousy and the bitterness of regret.

Attempting to wash those feelings away, I gravitated to the butlers table to pour anything that resembled vodka into a glass. I couldn't believe what I just saw, how could I have been so blind as to allow this man to not only take what is left of my dignity, but turn me into the side chick that waits for the man she loves to leave his wife in order for us to be happy together.

Taking the glass back to the master bedroom, I eased beside Ramir and watched as he slept with the look of satisfaction across his face. I think that I realized in that moment that I had to let him go. I know, I've said that before. My guilt weighed me down heavily, regardless of how I felt about him the simple truth of the matter is that this man… This handsome exotic man, is not my man. Maybe there was a time he could've been, but that time has long passed.

Nudging him slightly I whispered, "it feels strange to be in your apartment; where is Kasha and the boys?"

Sighing as he answered, "They are visiting family members in Boston. I don't expect them back for a few days. Kasha doesn't get to visit that side of the family often."

"What happens if they come back early?" I questioned with alarm in my voice..

"They won't come back early Dear. She is on a not so rare shopping excursion. I get notifications whenever she makes a purchase and according to today's trip she's still happily shopping in Boston's most exclusive boutiques." He countered.

"So that's why you brought me here?" I whispered to myself.

"What was that?" he asked.

"Nothing," I repeated. "Nothing at all."

As he rolled over and drifted back into a deep slumber; I quietly slithered out of bed and put on my clothes. Taking one last look at him before leaving, I actually considered if I was making the right choice. Satisfied that I had, I crept out of the apartment and made my way to the elevator. While waiting I put on my shoes; the carpet in the hallway would muffle the sound of me walking so that their neighbors wouldn't peek out the doors; seeing a strange, black woman leaving the apartment.

Getting to the lobby without anyone giving me so much as a forward glance I stepped out on to the street and asked the doorman to hail me a cab. Forgetting for a moment that I was still holding my panties in my hand, I quickly stuffed them inside my bag and leapt into the cab. Speeding quickly into the night, I thanked God that no one recognized me.

Riddled with guilt for standing up Chase, I called him while I was in route to my house. The phone rang a few times before going to voicemail, hanging up quickly I tried again; this time it went straight to voicemail. That wasn't like Chase, he normally answered quickly. Changing direction, I told the driver to drop me off at Chase's condo.

Scrambling out of the cab, I didn't give a second thought to my appearance; it hadn't dawned on me that I was going to see my boyfriend with the 'just fucked look'. With tussled hair, un-kept clothing, and the pungent smell of musk from sex permeating off of my body, I had seconds to get myself together. Getting on the elevator and only having enough time to smooth out my hair, douse myself with body spray, and apply some fresh lip gloss, I walked to his door and rang the bell; I waited for an answer. Ringing again, I still got no reply. I knew he was there, I heard music playing loudly coming from behind the door. Again I rang it, but this time I sent a text saying that I was outside the door; this time he answered.

Swinging the door back harshly, I saw a look in his face of an enraged man. Jostled by his appearance, I inquired if he was ok. He just stared at me with eyes filled with anger. Leaning on the door frame, he held the door ajar while lifting a bottle to his lips. When he began to speak, I could tell he had been drinking everything but rubbing alcohol for hours.

"Oh, there you are," He stammered out. "It's nice of you to show up."

"I know, I so sorry…" I began to say.

"Oh… Wait, let me guess. Work kept you late, huh? Again, right?" He slurred.

"Um, yes it did. Did something happen to you? You're not acting like yourself. Can I come in; I'll make you some coffee?" I offered.

"No! I'd rather have this conversation right here!" He barked loudly enough for his voice to echo up and down the small hallway.

"I have something to tell you." He informed. "After work tonight I was so excited to see you, so much so that I decided to make a reservation at Jupiter Restaurant and surprise you with dinner; being that you've been so stressed out! I took a cab to your job; I knew when you would be leaving. On my way, I saw you walking towards the subway. Rushing out the cab, I tried to catch up to you. I got about a block away when I saw you standing in the middle of the sidewalk in the arms of some Indian guy. And the kiss you gave him was not the kiss of a friend or stranger, but of someone who you knew intimately. And then you show up here hours later, smelling like funk, looking like a cheap whore and expect me to be waiting with open arms; bitch you must be crazy! I trusted you, I see now that you don't deserve my trust, and you are incapable of loyalty."

At that moment I stood at his front door stunned, feeling naked and raw. I attempted to explain what happened, he just yelled and ranted with such ferocity that some of his neighbors came to their doors.

Lowering his voice to keep our spectacle to a minimum; he uttered calmly, "I loved you, and looked for you after our first night together. I should've known better that a woman like you, who would sleep with a man she didn't know from a club would be nothing but a cheap lay. How stupid I've been to think that a whore would be anything else but a warm spot to rest my dick. I don't ever want to see you again! Good luck with your new relationship."

The last thing I saw was the hurt in his eyes as he slammed the door shut in my face. I had to take a step back so that in wouldn't hit me. The only thing that lingered after our exchange was the stench of the liquor on his breath that was so pungent it wafted into the hallway and lingered long after he closed the door.

Jayshawn

Damn! I really fucked up! I thought to myself as I sat on the edge of my bed. Chloe has been texting me for the past few days, and I haven't sent her so much as a 'hello' back. She must think I was in it for a quick bone; that's it. But, how could I call her when I had Tarin in my face for the past few days. I didn't mean to sleep with her, but when I saw her again after all this time a ton of old feelings I didn't know I had come rushing back.

She just showed up out of the blue. I left work and headed home, still riding high from the night I spent with Chloe, I was looking forward to spending another one of those nights with her. I had plans to make our relationship more solid between us. We were already making strides in that direction, but I wanted to express it verbally; sometimes a woman needs to hear the words, not just feel the actions.

Taking out the keys to my apartment, I noticed someone lingering close to my door. As I walked closer, I immediately recognized the figure. I had traced the outline of her body so many times with the tips of my fingers, how could I not know each curve by heart. She looked better than I remembered, and I could see she had some work done on her breasts; they were larger and had more perk.

Maintaining her slim/curvy frame nicely, she wore a black dress with a deep, plunging neckline that stopped just a touch above her navel. On her feet she wore stilettos sandals that showed perfectly manicured toes, and on her right foot an intricate vine tattoo; she got a few months after we started dating. Two vines becoming one; they were supposed to represent us joining together. To add some creativity to such a delicate piece, she added thorns, I didn't realize how accurate it was that I would be the one punctured repeatedly by them.

I tried to walk past her, but the scent of her perfume wafted as I passed; it made my senses become more alert to her sexuality and the power that still remained charged between us that's so passionate; you could almost reach out and touch it. Never one to be ungentlemanly, I opened the door and left it ajar; whatever she had to say I hoped she would say it quickly and leave before Chloe came over. Walking in, she stood in the middle of the living room as if calculating what she would say to me; meanwhile I poured myself a drink and sat down. The room was so silent I grew antsy and spoke more harshly than I intended.

"Will you just say what you have to say and leave?" I blurted aggressively.

"I've been trying to call you. You've been ignoring me and I don't like you treating me like some common chick in the street. I know I messed up, but you don't have to act like I didn't mean anything to you!" Tarin yelled.

Standing quickly, I began to charge at her as if I was gearing up for a fight that was years in the making; I confessed, "You did mean something to me, EVERYTHING! How do you think it made me feel to see you fuck anything with a dick, pussy, or some money to throw around? I WAS GOING TO ASK YOU TO MARRY ME DAMN IT! AND YOU MADE ME LOOK LIKE THE FOOL!"

Stunned by my outburst, she looked at me mouth agape and eyes threating tears. Regaining some composure the last thing I needed was for one of my neighbors to call the Homeowners Association on me; I tried desperately to calm down before I uttered another word.

"It hurt me to see the woman I love, fuck other people. I'm not going to ask you how long it's been going on, because I know it had been awhile. And I hope you're not here to apologize to me, cause I won't except it. What do you want from me Tarin?" I sighed.

"I want to say that I'm sorry for hurting you. I was in a bad place at the time and we were moving so fast, that's when I went to Miami, partied a little too hard trying to forget how confused I was. And you're right, that wasn't the first time something like that happened; but it was the last." She paused to take a breath and then continued.

"After the shoot, we all had decided to go out; we were in Miami, why wouldn't we party right? So, I went back to my room, had a few shoots and got ready for a night on the town. We hit up a few bars, some clubs, and partied at several celebrity bashes. We had been flirting all night, even though I told him it was over between us; I wanted to be with just you. I knew what I was doing was wrong, but being with him just let my inhibitions run wild, and once I was in free fall, it was hard to stop. We met the other girl at one of the parties and decided it was a good idea to bring her back to the hotel with us, sort of like a farewell fuck before I came home to you. I didn't know you would show up, I was too high and drunk to care if you watched us or joined in. When I got back, I called and texted you, I was ashamed to show my face; but I had to. When it became too much for me, I left you alone. I'm so sorry that I hurt you and I want you to know that I still love you. I wasn't ready for the intensity of your love then, but I am now." She declared.

As she told her story, I received a text from Chloe, but I was so wrapped up in the emotions Tarin was throwing my way, that I shoved my

248

phone back in my pocket; I could only deal with one thing at a time right now. I didn't know what to say, she had finally put everything on the table. She admitted that she had been fucking him before Miami, but she never said if it continued after. Did I really want to know if it did?

I told her that I appreciated getting the truth from her; she said her peace, and she had to leave. Nodding slightly, she grabbed her clutch bag and headed to the door. Just before opening It; she turned to kiss me on the cheek, then leaned in to kiss the other. As she took a step back, I saw tear stains running down her face with fresh ones immediately following. I couldn't watch her cry, so I reached out to wipe her tears away.

As I did, the softness of her skin gave me a flashback to happier times. Lightly stroking her bottom lip with my thumb, I didn't have time to think about what I was doing. She looked so vulnerable and desperately apologetic that I before I realized what I had done; she was already in my arms and we were locked in a deep embrace. Every ounce of emotion came out of me; the love I still had, the anger for what she had done, the need of her body, and the adrenaline pumping through veins that begged for me to discover if she still felt as good as I recalled. We spent that night and every night there after together never leaving my apartment.

There were a few times I attempted to call or text Chloe, but Tarin craved my attention. She lured me back to bed at every chance. It was like she was trying to make up for past indiscretions. The only time she let me out of her eyesight for more than ten minutes, I had to be in the bathroom; when I wasn't there, I was locked firmly between her thighs. Even retrieving food was somewhat of a chore. Some days I cooked for her; she wasn't much of a cook, or we would order take out. It was as if the years that passed between us had never happened, and we picked up from where we had left off. If I hadn't recalled thoughts of how I was treating Chloe, I would have continued with Tarin as if I didn't have some explaining to do when next I saw her.

The guilt I was beginning to feel started to weigh heavily on me. The calls and texts from Chloe had become less frequent, and I still hadn't reached out to her; I can only imagine what she was thinking. Then I was hit with the realization that I not only would have to tell Chloe what had been going on, but I would also have to make a choice between them; this was so fucked up!

I hadn't been to work, I worked mostly from home. Makayla had finally stepped up and took her job more seriously, so I was able to rely on her to take care of the office. The past few days have been the happiest being back with Tarin, I wondered if we could actually work on our relationship; but what about Chloe? I didn't want to hurt her, we were on our way to being something great; but Tarin is the love of my life and if God had given us a second chance, I would be a fool to turn it away. Some of my clients had begun to complain about not being able to reach me, that's when I knew it was time to go back to work. I had neglected the business I spent years building; now it is time I got a handle on things.

The next few days, I walked around in a haze, Chloe was back from her trip but I had not reached out to her yet. Every day I went into the office, I expected Makayla to hand me several messages from her, though she never did. I looked at my phone repetitively to see if she text me or in a vain attempt to text her; neither happened. The more time passed without speaking to her, the harder it became to pick up the phone. All I could do at this point is pray that when I did reach out to her hope that she receives me.

Creating a new work routine to suit the growing demands of my budding relationship with Tarin was beginning to get settled. Work was booming of course, and the lack luster work ethic Makayla had before had all but disappeared. I don't know what happened, maybe she got rid of that boyfriend of hers; but whatever it was, I was happy to have the old Makayla back. But I couldn't avoid Chloe any longer, some events were coming up that I would attend with Tarin and I knew we would run into each other. To avoid any drama, and to be a grown man about what's going on, I reached out to her. I called, when she sent me to voice mail, I left a message apologizing and asked if she could meet me at The Sky View Restaurant for an early dinner.

Unsure if she would arrive, I asked the waiter to seat me near the windows for a great view of the city. The Sky View is a large, plush, restaurant at the top of the most exclusive hotel in the city. Each reserved table came complemented with exclusive top shelf only bottle service, it boasted a five star menu, outstanding service, ambiance suited for only the most elite of guests, and the hotel staff catered to clients with the most secretive demands only afforded to the rich, and newly rich that are more than capable of paying for that type of attention. Put it this way to rent the cheapest room would be nearly five thousand dollars a night, and the things management could arrange only added to their exclusivity.

If this was the night, I was going to lose a lover, hopefully I would still be able to keep a good friend. So, to say I want to treat this meeting carefully would be an understatement. I didn't want to lose Chloe from my life, I had known since the night we met that she was special to me. At the same time I couldn't keep her as a lover; especially when that part of my life is being occupied by someone else. I had to give her the respect she deserved by telling her the truth in the most delicate way possible and minimize any potential reaction she would have.

Arriving on time, she looked stunning. Rising to greet her, she was escorted to our table by the maître d'. She sat down and waited for my explanation. As she stared at me, I began to feel the tension between us. Taking the liberty of pouring her wine, I sat to formulate what I would say. I found myself in the same position Tarin was in when she approached me.

"Why haven't you called me Jay? What happened to you, you just disappeared on me?" Chloe said through clinched teeth.

"Maybe we should order dinner, what would you like? They can make you anything you want." I avoided.

"Really, JayShawn... You're going to pretend that I didn't ask you a question?" She sneered.

"Ok," I breathed heavily. "I asked you here tonight to tell you why I haven't reached out to you. That night you texted me to say you couldn't come over, someone else showed up at my door unexpectedly." I paused.

"Someone showed up at your door unannounced and that gave you license to blow me off? I thought we were friends... No I thought we were more than that, at least that's what you led me to believe. Or were you just bullshitting me like Malik did? Was I part of your torrid revelry, a game the two of you could play whenever you want? Was I!" She began to yell.

"NO! It wasn't like that! I care a lot about you, but I didn't know how to tell you…" I tried to calm her.

"Tell me what JayShawn? Tell me what?" She snapped hostilely.

"That my ex is back in my life!" I professed. "I didn't mean for it to happen, but it did. That night, she showed up and explained what happened, and one thing led to another…" I tried to explain.

"And you fucked her." She interrupted. "She showed up, gave you a sob story; and you fucked her" she uttered slowly as if it caused her pain to say it aloud. "So, you asked me here tonight to tell me that whatever we had going on is done?"

"Not done," I insisted. "I still want to remain close with you, but…"

"You don't want to be with me, is that what you were going to say?" She asked.

"Yes. I want to see if I can work things out with her. We have so much history; I have to see if I can forgive her enough for us to move on." I expressed.

"Do you love her?" Chloe questioned.

"Yes, I do. I don't know if I ever stopped." I confessed.

When I said that, she stood up and walked out without saying another word.

Malik

The arrangement I had with Jayshawn's assistant Makayla was beginning to prove beneficial until that bitch grew a conscience on me. She was sending me valuable intel for weeks until she asked about why I hadn't been sending her on auditions. I tried to work my magic on her; but she eluded me at every turn. She insisted that she wouldn't give me any more info about his clients if I couldn't hold up my end of our agreement. So, I threw her a little something and set her up with a quick modeling gig to shut her up. I even threw in some extra cash to show her that I believed in her 'talent'. When the information started to pour back in again, I set my sights on infiltrating the next big event.

I attended every club opening, listening party, and low budget performance I could in order to find more artists and make connections. I wondered how the hell I was back to this after having a taste of what the good life could offer. I started to remember the advice I got from the contacts I made at the charity event. If I couldn't find a prestigious event to frequent, I would create one by producing my own showcase featuring my own talent of course, but I had to figure out how to get the right people in the room at once.

Placing a quick call to Makayla, I had her send invites to all the heavy hitters in Jayshawn's contact lists; from me of course. Then I had to reach out to the contacts I made at the Gala and offer them a sponsorship package in order to finance this showcase. I had everything in my head planned out to the letter, I just had to get my acts in order and scout for some new ones to fill the space. Getting the acts I already managed was nothing; I had to bring in talent that was creating a buzz in the streets in order to get money at the box office, and asses in the seats.

In my travels, I came across a new up-and-coming designer Reagan Marshall, she owned a clothing line known as Curvy Couture Fashion & Costume Designs. I met her through Chloe, it seems like all the big bitches know each other; anyway, Chloe would order outfits from her from time to time. As far as I saw, the outfits were flattering to the plump girls and having someone like her would be sure to attract the plus size crowd; which didn't bat an eyelash at the prices of anything; because they always expect it to be expensive.

To my understanding, due to their massive sizes sewing acres of fabric together to make one mumu cost a pretty penny, In addition, they always had good jobs to pay for it; and the ones who didn't had excellent credit; that's the same as cash to me. All money is good money and big woman spent more money than more slender, attractive women did. From observing their spending habits, they spent dough on anything, especially if it presented the promise of being in a room with eligible bachelors, who would be drunk on their asses and had no idea or even cared who they brought home from the club; beer goggles like a motherfucker!

In any event, I knew she wouldn't turn down an opportunity to show clothes that had enough lycra in it to wrap around the Fashion District twice, so I had China call her and book her for the showcase. I also had China reach out to Lena Cassidy, an indie designer with a flair for the theatrics; she would bring some bang to the fashion portion of the show.

Besides Cynsation, and Makayla, I invited my veteran performers Terrod 'TNT' Nelson, and Sienna 'Sin' Pride to round out the roster; what's a party without a little sin to make it interesting. With everything coming together well, all I had to do was make sure my team was ready for any possible outcome. One of my artists could very well be offered a recording contract, and with me managing their careers I would be making money hand over fist; and possibly be able to broker myself a little something extra in the sign-on bonus to secure my continued service and interests. Also, if they had gotten any idea that they wanted me to walk; they would have to pay dearly for the pleasure. After I've groomed and nurtured their talents, I'm entitled to a healthy severance package if necessary. Satisfied with my arrangements, I decided it was time to reach out to the old flame.

I knew that if I called she wouldn't answer, so I opted to stop by her friend's apartment. Knocking at the door, I was surprised to see how quickly she answered it; she knew not to ever keep the king waiting, at least I taught her that much. Pushing my way through the narrow slit in the door, I glanced around the apartment and shook my head at what I saw. I mean; it was decent and all, but I expected better accommodations from the daughter of Marcellus Lawrence.

Letting Chloe take in my presence, I asked her if she was going to ask me if I wanted something to drink. With anger in her face she proceeded to throw profanities as if her words had any barring effect on me. Grinning at the emotion I evoked in her, I invited her to my showcase. Tossing a few tickets to the ground as I walked out, I insisted she bring her little boyfriend Jayshawn to the party so that he could see what a real business man could do.

The days leading up to the showcase were the most exhausting I've experienced, more exhausting than holding up Chloe's legs during sex. I managed to get a few sponsors to help me out, but most of the money to put on the production came from my own pocket. I needed people to show up and spend money ASAP! I had anyone who ever owed me a favor either selling or buying tickets, and after a slow start they had finally begun to sell. With all the stress of ticket sales and promotion, rehearsals hadn't panned out too well either.

Booking studio time, I had my newest money makers make an appointment with me for a two-hour session, so that we could get a good recording for playback during the event; and to attempt to develop a stage presence. The easiest of the three to mold to my specifications is China. She's the hungriest and already had a bad performance under her belt, she was anxious to redeem herself. Her voice was a little horsed, and she had convinced herself she was a soprano when she really possessed the range of an alto; but that's nothing a little auto tune can't fix.

As China finished up, Sienna showed up, in a dress so tight I could see the imprint of her ovaries; and damn did I appreciate the view of that ass. As she sauntered in, China walked past her, it was clear that they would eventually come to blows. The air was so filled with attitude, if anyone else had walked into the room they would freeze instantly from all the shade that they were throwing. Taking a seat next to me, her already short dress rose up another three inches. Crossing her long legs, the only thing I could imagine was putting them over her head. After discussing a few details, she took her fine ass in the booth, and laid down tracks that would make seasoned R&B singers croon; damn that girl knew how to seduce the crowd.

She had complete control of her audience and made them feel whatever she was feeling through the music; that's star quality. After having my own private session with Sienna, she got dressed as it was getting close to time for Makayla to show up. Only spending half the time with her, I ended her session early; I simply didn't have enough energy after Sin left.

In a week's time, the night had finally arrived; I cut it pretty close too. There were so many private events happening due to the rush of the holiday season and the uncertainty of weather conditions; it was any man's game. Arriving at the venue hours ahead of schedule, I threw myself into mogul mode. Refusing to let Jayshawn out maneuver me, I turned the venue into the most lavish event money could buy; impressions were everything.

Making sure my sound and lighting were on point, I checked on my ladies to ensure they were ready for each of their knock out performances. I'm not sure if making them share a dressing room was the smartest choice, but I had to use the other rooms for VIP Suites, and my own private suit to entertain prospective investors. If I was going to change the game, I needed money to do it, and the most powerful men and women attending tonight had just that.

I watched people enter the club from the balcony, immersing myself in this moment; I poured a glass of Cognac, then texted my stage manager to start the show. The drinks flowed, the waiters passed the Hors d'oeuvres, and my special guests were seated in the balcony apart from the general crowd. The lights softly dimmed setting the tone for an intimate illuminated feel to the room as the intro music began to play, and the MC came to center stage to introduce both Curvy Couture Fashions and the live performer Cynsation.

The recording we made started to play and Cynsation began to belt out her pop ballad as the full figure models strutted down the catwalk. They didn't look half bad either, I expected different variations of cellulite to dance its way across the stage; I was stunned to see that the models made an effort to look presentable. I'm not a total jerk, I knew some plus size were good looking; Chloe was one of them, but I didn't expect to see models this caliber. The first collection Reagan showed was club themed, so the pop sound from Cynsation fit perfectly with the presentation. The full figured models moved seamlessly across the stage hitting their marks exactly.

Aside from the unmistakable curves, one would think they were professional high fashion models; it appears that I've made the right choice after all. Cynsation had also held her own; she performed better when she was sober. Lip syncing to a pre recoded track, she didn't have the same issues from her previous show. The next collection Reagan showed was a mix of casual and street style, and to say I was impressed would be an understatement. I found myself excited to see the next model hit the stage.

Taking a moment to observe the attendees, all their eyes were glued to the stage as they clapped, whistled, and cheered at the models as they passed. At the end of the set, the models and the designer took their final walk; when that was, done Cynsation was re-introduced, and the crowd presented her with a standing ovation. I could tell by the look on her face that the remarks of the critic from her first showcase were long gone from her memory.

Waiting for my queue, I walked out on the stage and made a few remarks, introduced the heavy hitters in the VIP section, and spoke a bit about the previous performances. As I did, I glanced through the crowd and spotted Jayshawn. At that moment a switch flipped on in my head; I reveled in the thought of showing him up. He had come to my event to see if it would be a success, and he was met with that and much more. I was ecstatic that he saw I am the better man and ran a business worthy of competition; my only hope was that he could keep up. I am coming for his so-called crown and I'll do whatever I have to in order to get it.

I introduced the next performer Sienna Pride and designer Lena Cassidy. Taking the stage in her skin tight, backless, black pleather jumpsuit with plunging neckline, which clung to every inch of her hourglass frame, the high heels she wore made her appear to be an Amazon queen towering over her subjects. There was a hush among the crowd as if taking in her beauty at once rendered them soundless. The soft spotlight rested on her delicate body giving her creamy complexion the perfect glow under the lights.

The music began to play a cool, melodic tune, and then her body swayed to the rhythm it created. As she started her first verse, the models appeared wearing Lena Cassidy's Lingerie Collection. Sienna's soft, sexy ballad fit to perfection with the exotic, sensuous feel of Lena's collection. Each model embodying different ancient Gods and Goddesses, the pieces gave more of a small theatrical performance than fashions for sexual pleasure and enticement. The collection started off with more of a playful theme, with whimsical, feminine panty and bra sets, adorned with floral, tulle, lace, and most things that one would expect from a lingerie show; then slowly transformed into a more sexually ravenous peepshow.

Lena showed her dark side with leather pieces that included peekaboo cut outs, nipple pasties, studded collars, a few bondage outfits, and accessories that encompassed wild head pieces and masks, with large statement jewelry that brought drama and glamour to the outfits.

Utilizing whips, and spiked shoes, added more visual effects to the use of each garment. One outfit Lena designed, I found completely erogenous. It involved a model that sported large, feathered, red and black wings, and dripped with chains that led a trail from her choker to her wrists, and more chains that were attached to her nipple rings from the cutouts in her bra that attached to the small hoop ring hanging from her belly button; that would be the outfit I left here with tonight for Sienna to wear for me.

With the musical accompaniment of Sienna each slow moan bellowed from her lips added to the depth of the collection's purpose. Toward the end of the set, the audience was so sexually charged that I was sure a couple of people snuck off to the bathroom for a quickie. Ending the show, Lena wore a racy outfit of her own; then strutted down the runway for her last walk with the model that was last to be shown.

Taking her bow and with cheers of satisfied, crowd Sienna exited the stage.

The MC retaking the stage for the last time, made his remarks, told a few jokes before presenting the next artist. While the MC did his thing, I sent a text to my stage manager to instruct the staff to start removing the seating; with the next artist about to take the stage, there would be no need for seats. TNT walked out and didn't need to utter a word to hype up the crowd; his presence alone was enough to get everyone on their feet. Being a local, high profile artist, the audience was familiar with him; he was what we call a 'hood celebrity'.

He didn't need any accompaniment; he held his own on stage and his presence dominated, but I had to include someone to sing the chorus; that job went to Makayla. She had the right attitude that fit well with the song, really all she had to do was stand in the background and look cute. The part she had to play in me taking over Jayshawn's empire was almost done, when I got all that I needed, she's out! TNT's music was so powerful, that it made people get out of their seats and start grinding. Closing the event with a banger like TNT is a great way to end the night and show investors the caliber of talent that I commanded.

By the end of the event, the audience members were tired, drunk, broke, and horny; which was just the way I liked them. While the crowd cleared out downstairs, the party continued in the VIP Suite upstairs. All the artists were in attendance and I found myself at the center of praise and admiration; which I enjoyed immensely. As I was engulfed by the success of the evening, I saw Jayshawn walking in my direction. Greeting Makayla with a nod, he then turned his attention in my direction. Taking my hand and bumping shoulders, he gripped my hand tightly and whispered.

"So, you the man now? You use Makayla to get access to my contacts, huh? This is only temporary for you. You're still that same low budget ass dude that was scrapping at my door looking for a job, with no style, jealousy eating at you, and no clout to pull off real work. You ain't shit bruh! You'll nerver have what I have, cause you aren't willing to put in real work to get it. You're worse than a bitch willing to fuck anything and everybody for five minutes of the limelight. And if ever fuck with Chloe again, I'll fucking kill you, you got me?" Jayshawn threatened.

Releasing my hand he smiled and gave me a heavy pat on my shoulder. As he turned to walk away, he gave China a dirty look, and told Makayla not to bother coming into work; I was her new boss. But I couldn't let him punk me at my own party so I grabbed his arm before he turned and whispered over the music with as much intensity as I could without making a scene.

"Don't be mad because the better man won. If you took care of business as much as you ran your mouth, you might be able to reach my status in ten years. And as for your bitch, I could fuck her whenever and wherever I choose, and I have. How does it feel to fuck my ex? Did she do that trick on you that I showed her? Remember, I fucked her first; Matter fact, I could fuck her tonight; her and her sister. The mighty Jayshawn Thomas; you're not even man enough to keep my ex; I bet being with you makes her crave to have daddy's dick back in her mouth. I ruined her for you anyway, she will always love me. Too bad for her, I have a weight limit; but I see you like the fatties. How about I offer you a job? You can dispose of the condom after I fuck Chloe, oh and that other bitch Tarin. I heard she was back on the scene." I blasted.

With that Jayshawn hauled off and punched me. As we began to scuffle, a few of the bouncers came and broke us up; then escorted him out. China and Sienna both ran to me and gave each other dirty looks. Scanning the room to see who had witnessed the brawl, I was relieved to see my investors were all but gone and hadn't seen what happened. Signaling the music to continue, we kept the party going. Jayshawn's days in this business were numbered.

Dominique

I left Chase's house broken. I didn't know how, or what to feel, so I walked the streets to clear my mind. On the one hand, I felt relieved that I didn't have to lie to him anymore. But on the other, I felt awful for hurting him; that wasn't the way I wanted him to find out about my affair. In any case, I was free to pursue a relationship with Ramir, the only problem was that the only relationship he wanted with me involved me on my back. Truthfully, I don't know if Ramir is who I wanted to be with anymore. Feeling defeated; I went home to wash off the day, and maybe things would look better in the morning.

Days went by before I got back into the grove of a regular routine. I went to work, came home, occasionally Chloe and I would talk, but I couldn't get up enough nerve to tell her about Ramir. She didn't say anything about Jay either, but if she wasn't talking about him and they weren't going out, I knew she had to be upset with him; the question is why?

There were days I missed Chase so much that I would be hyped to meet him and then realize that he wasn't speaking to me; correction, he loathed the ground that allowed me to walk on it. I was beginning to realize that I had made a mistake. Not only had I allowed Ramir to come back into my life, without giving me any assurances, I had hurt the only man that had taken the time to get to know me and appreciated me regardless of my short comings. Honestly, I felt lost and empty without Chase. That's when I realized something that I had been denying for so long, I loved him.

Coming to that realization was startling for me. The only person that I had loved; or so I thought, was Ramir. I was beginning to realize that what I felt the moment he walked back into my life wasn't love, it was the shock of seeing him again; and the yearning I had to finish something that had long finished before it started. The only answer I had left to search for is, can I get Chase back in my life and get Ramir out of it?

Leaving for work that morning, I was beginning to start feel normal again. I walked into the office and noticed that three more people were gone. When they said that some of our people were going to be let go, I didn't realize it would be so many; so quickly. Re-organizing the office structure is a daunting task, many responsibilities would fall on me that I was frankly unprepared for; but I would have to learn how to handle them just the same. Just as I got my bearings, Hershel sent me out of the office to meet clients. Because we were so short of staff, field work evaluations were now a part of my job description; I'm seriously asking for a raise when I get back to work, if he didn't give me one… well there are perks to your dad owning the company.

Taking the company car, I had the driver take me to Figure Eight Restaurant to meet a prospective client. Figure Eight is one of the city's newest restaurants that pop up out of nowhere, and create a new buzz with the bloggers, foodies, photographers, and whoever else deems themselves worthy of the 'The In Crowd'. When Hershel set up the meeting, of course he didn't know idea how expensive the place is, and I didn't volunteer to tell him; I took his corporate card and headed out the door. We have to do everything necessary to make sure the client is comfortable at all times; is what I said to myself as I dashed to the elevator.

Ms. Deltangam, who was eager to purchase real estate in the city, to meet with her request to have the meeting at a specific time, I had to tailor my schedule to make sure her needs were my highest priority. Going above and beyond for a client looked well on my resume. Maybe if I brought her into the company, I could move up in the company; maybe make Hershel my secretary, I thought as I entered the restaurant.

As I arrived, the hostess who knew who I was immediately approached me. Maybe it was because Hershel made the reservation, or maybe Ms. Deltangam alerted her to whom she was meeting, or maybe, just maybe it was because I had been there so many times with Chase that to see me again really wasn't a shock to her.

"Good afternoon, Ms. Lawrence, Ms. Deltangam is waiting for you in the corner booth; please follow me." The hostess said as she led the way through the partially crowded dining area.

Approaching the booth from behind, all I could see about my dining companion is that she had a beautiful head of brown, wavy hair. Upon closer inspection, I realized that I knew my new client well, perhaps too well. As I stood at the opening of the booth, someone knocked the air out of my lungs by who I saw sitting; it was Kasha.

"Don't be alarmed Dominique, please take a seat." Kasha said boldly.

As I stood in an utter shock of seeing her, I realized why she was here. She had somehow found out about Ramir and me, or maybe she just wanted to know more about his business with Hershel; or so I tried to convince myself. After taking our drink orders, the hostess disappeared, leaving me to face the dragon alone. I tried to prepare myself for every potential outcome of this exchange with her, even down to a smacking and hair pulling; but I hoped it wouldn't come to that.

"Why am I here, Kasha?" I uttered with an air of annoyance.

"You know why you are here. I must honestly say, I had expected this to have happened years ago. I never expected to be having this conversation with you after so many years." She proclaimed.

"What conversation?" I said, trying to play stupid. "Is this about the property Ramir is acquiring? If so, your meeting would have been more informative with Hershel Elliot, he's Ramir's agent."

"No, I don't think so; besides Mr. Elliot isn't fucking my husband, well at least not that I know of." She announced.

Kasha stating the words 'fucking my husband' at me, rendered me momentarily paralyzed. I sat across from her with my mouth agape and finding myself suddenly short of breath. As she sat waiting for my response, I felt a chill slowly rising from my feet to my head in 2.5 seconds. I trembled, in my ears a low ringing had started, and every hair stood up on ends as I stammered attempting to brush off her comment.

"Kasha, I… You've got it all wrong." I began to say.

"Do I? Well, let me see. I've seen text messages, and have seen your number repeatedly dialed on his phone, and his driver has also admitted to chauffeuring you both around the city; have I left anything out? I know what's been going on, but; I want to tell you a story."

Just as she was about to continue her assault on me, the server arrived with our drinks, and I had never been so grateful in my life to see a cocktail. Grabbing it quickly and ordering another, Kasha picked up where she left off.

She began with, "I noticed something off at the Gala, both of you were not at all shocked to see each other. However, you were shocked to see me, and to hear that we had children; it was written all over your face as guilt flooded into your eyes. I also noticed that the two of you had disappeared during the party, and when you made reappearance, the mood had changed drastically. Ramir seemed quieter, and you were acting hostilely at your table. I also noticed our car being gone more frequently and for long stretches of time. Ramir has also become lackadaisical in his duties to this profession and to our home life, which cause worry to me and our children. But the final straw; when I knew he was cheating with you, I saw you leaving our apartment building. Yes, I saw you!" She fumed.

If it was possible to be shocked by my lunch companion, I was even more shocked by her stunning confession. At first I wanted to deny it. Our families knew almost every socialite, business executive, and their families in the greater metro area; I could have told her I was visiting friends. But I sat there and listened to her continue to tell me the story I had written, as if I had no part to play in it, but more like I had been a spectator watching a movie.

"I returned early with the children from our trip. They missed their father since they saw so little of him as of late. I knew you were not visiting anyone," She noted. "No one of any proper standing lived in the building besides my family. When I saw you, you had the look of a tired woman; like you had been worked over. Your hair was out of place, clothing disheveled, and in your hands you stuffed something small into your bag. As quickly as you came out of the building, you were gone; so I had no chance to approach you."

As she continued with her story, I tried not to make a scene. The restaurant was filling with patrons, and quite a few of them I recognized, including Jayshawn who was with a tall, statuesque woman with dark hair, and fake boobs; maybe she was a new client. So I sat back and continued to listen. She seemed to be more hurt than angry with me. Like she said, she expected to have had this conversation years ago; I guess we were past due. If it had been when she and Ramir had first gotten married, I imagine we wouldn't have been so calm. We would've really had some cursing, chair throwing, and hair pulling going on. I guess with age came calmness, and the ability to speak as adults, on some real grown women shit; at least that's what I hoped for.

"Going into my apartment, I smelled musk in the air. Ushering the children to their rooms, I found Ramir in our bed where the stench of musk was the strongest. He was naked, drunk, and fast asleep. He didn't know I stood over him, contemplating if I should smother him with a pillow, or scream; I did neither. I walked out and put away our things, and cook for my children. Upon waking, I saw the surprise in his face to see us back early. He didn't mention what I had seen; he didn't ask if I had something on my mind; just continued his normal speech with me." She ended.

"What do you want from me, Kasha? To deny what happened, I won't. You've got most of it right, I knew you were still married, and I didn't know you had children; he never told me. I'm sorry, what I did was beyond wrong and I have no way of justifying it. What I can say is; I thought it was love. I had no closure for how things went with us. I thought if we could pick up where we left off, we could be happy together; but that was a girl's fantasy, and I'm a woman that should've known better. All I can offer you is the solace of knowing that it's over between us. I haven't spoken to him in weeks; also because of my stupidity, I lost someone that I truly loved, because I thought I was in love with the wrong man. I'm sorry, Kasha, I am truly sorry." I finished.

"I don't want your sorry!" she snapped. "I want you to know that you were not the only woman Ramir has had an indiscretion with over the years, you're just the one I thought would take him away. The others were toys; he played with them and threw them away like any other child. During that time he never neglected his duties as a husband or father; he always returned home. You, his newest toy, stayed around the longest and that caused me worry; you could have been the toy he wanted to keep. Do you know what Deltangam means in the Persian language? It means my heart is tight; and that's what his adulterous relationship with you did to me. I already know you are no longer involved with him, but I need to issue you a warning just the same. If you come near my husband ever again, I will ruin you and your family business. Many of your father's clients and business dealings are through the Persian communities. Our money lines your pockets. If I ever see you with my husband outside of your father's business relationships, I'll destroy you, understand? I have brought you a gift to show I harbor no more ill will toward you and please pick up the check; I expect Lawrence & Associates has plenty of money on hand to cater to the needs of their clients… For now." She said as she stood to walk away, leaving me in awe.

On the table she left a small box. Inside were the earrings I thought I lost; turns out I left them on her dresser before Ramir and I had sex that last time. I couldn't believe I showed up here and got verbally spanked by Ramir's wife. Though I know I deserved more than that from her, I appreciated that she came to me like a woman; I had to at least respect that about her. Paying the bill, I decided not to go back to work. Telling Hershel the client would get back to me, I explained that I had not felt well. I told him it could have been from what I ate at lunch; which was Vodka rocks, two Cosmos, and some fruity concoction, so being sick wasn't entirely a lie; he let me off for the rest of the day.

Every step I took to walk up the stairs to my apartment felt as if I was wearing cement boots; each step weighed me down. Walking in, I felt negative energy slap me right in the face, without even the courtesy of buying me another drink first. Seeing Chloe sitting by the window with a wineglass in one hand and an empty bottle next to her foot, I could only roll my eyes and silently ask myself 'what now?'

Taking the glass from her hand, I downed the last few drops in it. Judging from the look on her face, she had just as rough as a night as I had, but I'm not ready to tell my bestie what I've been up to. So I sat on her lap and asked her to tell me what's on her mind. I don't know what I was expecting her to say, but what she told me blew my mind; and I thought I was in a love triangle.

I've been so absent, that I hadn't known that Chloe had been in a semi relationship with Jayshawn that just ended due to the fact that his ex-girlfriend popped back in to the picture, now I know who he was with at Figure Eight today. She had also confessed to being mind fucked by Malik, who had stopped by; and rubbed her face in the fact that he's doing well in his business and still fucking her sister. Last, she admitted to playing tag with her boss; not just any boss, but publishing God Hennison Black; who I would fuck in a heartbeat if it meant never working again. In the past few months, my girl has been on an emotional roller coaster; I couldn't believe all this could happen to one person, and then I remembered my situation.

I couldn't stand another minute of being in that apartment and taking up residence in depression city, so I grabbed my girl; and went out on the town like old times. It had been so long since we've hung out and had a good time, we both needed a night off from the chaos that found its way into our lives. Leaving the house with no particular destination, we found ourselves in front of Avenue 6 Lounge. This was the first time we had to stand in a line and wait to get in; I guess that's what happens when you trade in your stilettos for work pumps.

Entering the club, it was packed to the brim with people, most of whom we knew well. Removing my jacket, I wore dark blue deconstructed jeans, black corset top, with knee high, six-inch heel boots. Chloe wore a cap sleeve, form fitting, little black dress with a sweetheart neckline, with black & gold platform pumps; that was the first time I noticed that she looked smaller. Maybe she stressed harder than I thought. We dressed with a purpose. I don't know what Chloe's purpose was, but mine is to forget about Chase, Ramir and his wife. It was time I move on from all of them. I knew I would have to tell Chloe about what was going on, but not tonight. Tonight, we are going to party it up like we have no troubles what so ever!

Taking my girl by the hand, I led her to the middle of the floor, and we danced with each other until pools of sweat threatened to make our edges frizz. Taking a seat at the bar, we ordered drinks and took in the ambiance of being in the club again. Sipping drink after drink, I swore I must have been drunk because I saw Jayshawn on the dance floor with the woman from earlier. I tapped Chloe on the arm and she turned toward where I pointed. Moving too quickly to stop her, she walked straight to the dance floor and slapped Jayshawn with all her might. Rushing behind her, I grabbed her by her arms and pulled her towards the bathroom.

"What the hell is the matter with you?" I asked.

"I'm sick of this shit! I'm sick of men like Malik, and Jayshawn running in and out of my life! Did you know that after I slept with him before going upstate, he never bothered to even text me? And when I got back, he still hadn't reached out. So, I entertained the thought of fucking Hennison; and I had the chance at the ski lodge." She revealed through slurred words. "But I couldn't... I couldn't leave things unfinished between us. So when he called me for dinner, I half expected him to tell me some bullshit excuse; but I hoped he didn't. At the dinner he told me about getting back with his ex... HER! I'm just sick and tired of being dogged by these men who claim they love me. And what hurts the most is that I trusted Jayshawn, not only as my lover; but my friend. We were so good together... We always had a spark of chemistry, and I thought this is it; we're finally going to make that move to be something more. As soon as I find happiness, Hennison comes along to change my mind; then make me think I have a real shot at a guy like him, but I don't pursue because of Jay; Malik is FUCKING MY ONLY SISTER WHILE WE WERE STILL TOGETHER! AND JAY'S EX IS BACK IN THE PICTURE! I MEAN WHAT THE FUCK?" she shouted at the top of her lungs as the makeup created new contouring lines from her tears.

Standing in the bathroom of a club, listening to the music pound repeatedly on the walls made me feel like we had no place being there suddenly. The party was over; back to reality.

Chloe

I woke up the next day in the club clothes from last night, with a pounding in my head, and the stench of liquor permeating from my body. Hearing someone clear their throat above me, I looked up to see Dee standing in front of me with a mug in one hand, and a painkiller in the other. Sitting up slowly, I took both from her. Swallowing the small white pill, following it up by hot, steamy, brown liquid, I instantly felt my senses coming back to me. I wouldn't dare play the 'I was drunk game on her', pretending like I remembered nothing that happened last night; I remembered it all. I wasn't sorry for slapping the shit out of Jayshawn; he deserved it. However, sorry about breaking a promise to myself.

Before I got into a romantic entanglement with Jayshawn and Hennison, I promised not to get involved with anyone until I got my shit together first. I allowed myself to reminisce about the day I saw Jayshawn in the café; I should've turned down his advances then. But the romantic in me wanted to see how far I could take it, and it turned around and blew up in my face. Deep down I knew that whatever we had wouldn't last, but I hoped it would. I also question if I did it foolishly to get back at Malik.

I think I knew it was China, Malik was with in the club that night; there were too many familiar things about the woman whose face I couldn't see. Her body type, profile, and clothing that she wore, that once were mine; were all telltale signs that I ignored. Well, I'm done with that shit; I have to break out of this mental prison I put myself into. The first thing I'll do is talk to my best friend about everything, while I'm in a sober mind to do so. After we have that conversation, I'll start looking for my own place.

While I sipped on coffee, Dee sat next to me in the bed; we sat in silence for a while until she broke it. I thought she was going to go in on me about last night; instead, she clued me in on what I've been missing. After about an hour, I discovered that my best friend had been sleeping with her ex from college, her current boyfriend; is no longer her boyfriend, her job had been on the chopping block, and she had an intense encounter with her ex's wife; talk about out of the fucking loop!

After our conversation, I opted not to go to work; Indulgence would have to function without me, because I am taking a sick day; I need time to sort out the madness in my life, before I could tackle the insanity of being a part of Indulgence. I cannot deal with the pressures of working, while my personal life is threatening to send me to the psych ward of the closest hospital. Dee wasn't so lucky, after our chat she left for work. She is no closer to a solution for her love life than I am; she confessed that she cared for Chase more than she thought she ever could, it's sad that it took cheating with a married man; and losing the man that could've been 'the one' for her to realize that. I don't think she knew how to get Chase back, but if I know Dee; (and I do!) it wouldn't be long until she came up with some way to get him to forgive her.

As I lay in bed, I listened to the hum of the heat come up through the radiator, and tried not to think about Jayshawn who led me on, Malik who uses everybody to get somewhere, and Hennison who is the epitome of a millionaire playboy.

In my efforts to forget about them altogether, their images continued to dance across in my mind. Unable to take the self-torture anymore, I let all my emotions melt away with a hot shower. As I stood in the scalding water, I closed my eyes and let my body relax as I soaped my skin. Somewhere in the trenches of my mind, I remembered that I had a blank blog page to work on. Is it possible that I could take all my frustrations out on the blog?

Dressed in a graphic tee and leggings, I sat down at Dee's scruffy looking, secondhand desk with a glass of wine and my laptop staring at a blank screen wondering; where the hell I was going to start! As I pondered, I realized that I didn't want to be the same type of blogger as the others. Most of the bloggers I've encountered say the same things such as 'What to wear? How to style this! And the all too familiar, Outfit of the Day. I'm experiencing an emotional hangover, and although I want my blog to be solely about fashion; I would be untrue to myself if I isolated my blog to just that. Using the blogging as self-medication, I want it to appeal to every aspect of what women encounter in their lives; whether it is fashion, love, sex, or relationships

In my blog, I want to speak about real-life situations that women go through, and through that appeal to their sense of humanity; of course I would interject fashion, as it is as much a part of me as being a writer is; I just had to find a clever way to get the message across. The idea entered my mind like a speeding bullet in search of its intended target. As soon as I got the idea of how to combine both fashion and Life, the words flooded my mind as my fingers tried desperately to keep up with the thoughts in my head.

The Stylish Mind

Presents

Plus sized relationships with a dash of
fashion

What does sex, relationships, and fashion all have in common? Each one of these subjects are fickle, dangerous entities that can change without notice. Bonding a relationship is hard enough, but add being plus size, and it's a completely new outfit entirely.

Sex is an immediate high, and like finding the perfect hip hugging, ass plumping jeans, it feels good from start to finish (with the right pair). Afterwards, the relationship aspect comes into play. The connection between sex, relationships, and fashion is a lot like the interactions between lovers. In the beginning it can render you breathless, and create anxiety around the need to have it exactly when you want it, and how you want it. Also, like a magnificent high, it can cause you to come crashing to earth, without the courtesy of a textured nylon and silk lined parachute to slow your decent.

Plus size women in particular have the hardest time finding the perfect fit (with both aspects that is). Finding a man (or woman if that's what you're into) is like walking into a designer sample sale, and expecting to find your size, NEVER GOING TO HAPPEN! Everything is too small or... No, it's just too small. Yet, we squeeze into it anyway; wiggling and sucking in your tummy. And don't forget the all too familiar shake, shake, shimmy, jump, pull combination in order to try desperately to make the thing you want the most fit you, the way you make yourself fit it. But if you're not careful; they can both leave in a state of utter disbelief, disappointment, and emptiness…

The words poured out of me, as if I would spontaneously combust if they didn't exit my body through the tips of my fingers. I typed furiously, trying to disguise that fact that my love life was in shambles. By the end of my rant, I felt like I was 10 pounds lighter. I had unloaded so much of the hurt and anger I was feeling, that once I was done, I felt light; the feeling could have possibly been the wine, either way I felt AMAZING!

The only thing left for me to do is to push the publish button. When I did my post, my life would be out in the world for the reading. Writing a blog isn't like writing a freelance article. When you're freelancing, you have to adhere to the person who's paying you to write. There is no insertion of personality, no connection, just cold hard facts. Blogging is so much more freeing; I wonder why it's taken me this long to do it. I'm lying, I know why it's taken me so long to do this; it was fear of someone finding out that I could be more than I was ever told I could be.

This is not an industry that is quick to embrace the different. Isn't that a contradiction? The Fashion industry thrives on being different. Re-invention is the name of the game. Of course, it repeats itself time and time again; but with a slightly different spin each time. What the experts don't tell you are; yes, to be daring and different is what they are looking for. But only within a comfort level built from their own standards. How else can someone explain not seeing full figure women in major mainstream fashion events around the world?

Don't get it twisted, full figure women are gracing runways, but in shows and productions of our own making; not in mainstream fashion arenas. In that aspect, the fashion industry has particular standards that they are unwilling to bend; even if it's a market for it. The business rule of thumb is; if there is a need or want, and then you must find a clever way to fill it. Well, as a full figure woman; I see plenty of needs and wants in wearing your personality on your body, without the fear and/or shame of someone laughing behind your back about an outfit choice.

To fill that need, many designers curvy and straight size alike have designed collections that showcase the beauty of a thicker woman. The problem with that is the lack of support from outside movers, and hit makers, amongst even each other, the support factor is nonexistent. The competition for achieving success is gargantuan, with little to no margin for error. Because of that reality, and the odds stacked against the artist/designer; it creates a concoction of jealousy and mistrustfulness.

Leaving for work the next day, I felt the same air of calm I felt when I walked into the café for the first time. I woke up with a purpose, instead of continuing to sulk; I took a different route. Entering Indulgence wearing a deep emerald tailored shirt, with black tailored pants, and six-inch pumps; I'm determined and focused on my job. Arriving at my cubical, I stole a glance in Kelly's direction, thus starting out our day like we would any other; by us shooting icy daggers at each other with our eyes.

Because of the success of the photo/video shoot at Emmerson Lodge, I had a growing list of demands for the upcoming All White Party the magazine is throwing to butter up the board members and stockholders, while masquerading it as an office Christmas party. I thought the ideas I presented were good enough. As it turns out, all my designs did were catapult Clair into making continuous additions in order to make the party more grand; tripling the original budget.

Instead of Clair turning her attentions to the next Issue of Indulgence, she continued to fuel a kind of inner rage that drove her; making her more and more driven as the event approached. Clair usually delegated the tasks she wanted done, either in a meeting or through Cassidy; she's now coming to Kelly and I directly. The way she's micro managing us, it seems like she has something to prove.

Personally, I think throwing an All White attire party a few days before Christmas is obsessive; but no one would tell her that. Clair had a vision, and nothing messed with that vision. To her credit, the ideas and ambitions she posed were made into reality when the company first started. She nurtured Paul Black's ambitions to bring style, awareness, and notoriety to the full figure fashion industry; first with Indulgence, and again with becoming a silent partner with Sloan Hill creating Legendary Models Inc.

Walking down the aisle as if once again back on the catwalk, Cassidy greeted me with the usual 'hey girl' and dropped a manila folder on my desk, as she let out a deep sigh. Following up with one of my own, I didn't need to ask what was in it. This had been happening every day since we've been back in the office. Clair would have some grand vision in her sleep (not that vampires really slept) and wanted her minions to make the impossible possible as soon as dawn approached.

Besides my interlude with Hennison, something else went down on the ski trip. I remember when Hennison and I had returned from our walk; I saw Clair arguing with Isabella St. Scott Editor & Chief of Rouge Magazine, Indulgence Magazine's sister Mag and closest competitor. The night air had chilled us to the bone, so we made our long walk along the grounds, to a short skip around the paved driveway, and around motor house where the staff stowed the cars; to prevent having to clean them off in the event of a snowstorm. Upon entering, we saw the two arguing on the staircase; judging by their wild hand movements, I thought for sure Clair was going to push Isabella down the stairs. The squeaking of Hennison and my boots alerted them to our presence, and they halted their conversation; Isabella walked towards the rear parlor, Clair marched up the stairs. The rest of the trip they kept their distance from each other, and I never got the chance to have that walk again with Hennison.

Meanwhile, Indulgence erupted with life to prepare for the Holiday Issue called A Curvy Couture Christmas that featured the collection from full figure couture Celebrity Designer Vincent Kincaid. As former runway coach, stylist, and art director of STYLED Magazine; Vincent Kincaid, with a slew of many others, pioneered full figured fashion into an unstoppable mega force. Debuting his couture collection for the first time, he reached out to Clair to give Indulgence the exclusive. I know you're wondering why he didn't reach out to his former home STYLED Magazine, right? Well, it's been said that he resigned not only to pursue a career in fashion design but also to avoid a nasty scandal that may have killed everything he accomplished. With the urgency to make the Holiday Issue a success, and the exclusivity of The White Party, I've never heard heels click so hard on granite floors as everyone scurried from one place to another.

By the time lunch came around, I didn't have enough energy to drag my ass to the cafeteria to replenish what I lost; but my stomach was threating to swallow my back, so I had no choice. The dinging of the elevator signaling my stop, I walked towards the salad bar to see what they offered today. As soon as my feet moved, I felt a burning sensation as I shifted from foot to foot that felt like it radiated from tip to heel. Not seeing anything worth eating; I opted for a yogurt with a fruit salad. As I stood in line, I heard a voice whisper to me, 'Is that all you're eating?'

Answering before I could see who it was, I answered "It's not much here I want to eat." I turned to see Margo, Hennison's gatekeeper, or better known as his assistant, standing behind me. Margo is a short, middle-aged woman, with flowing red hair, that she maintains in a bob style, and stunningly crystal blue eyes; that gives you the feeling of her piercing though you to the truth you may try to hide. Dressed appropriately for her age, she styles herself in vintage pieces, giving her the nickname 'The old school diva.'

"A shame," she said. "You won't even get to eat that. You're needed ASAP, follow me." She ordered.

Walking onto the elevator, assuming back to my dungeon; I wondered what the hell else they wanted me to do, that I couldn't even take an hour to eat! Asking Margo what this was about, that I couldn't eat lunch; she ignored me and continued to watch the elevator countdown to our stop, which just so happened to be the corporate floors.

Following her down a long hallway lined with office doors, we came to a door that looked as if they had fashioned it out of black, stainless steel. Taking a seat behind her desk, she instructed me to go inside; he was waiting for me. I knew that the entire building had been in an uproar, but I didn't think it was so much so that the 'Big Boss' Hennison Black had to be notified of every arrangement.

Pushing the door open, I found Hennison standing in front of his large, modern, chrome, glass desk with a single yellow rose in his hands. Shocked by his surprise, I strolled towards him, as he did the same; closing the gap between us, he handed me the flower. Taking me by the hand, he led me to a small seating area to the left of his desk, facing large, floor to ceiling windows. Set up on the table were a couple of sandwiches, a fruit platter, and sparkling water; I couldn't believe he did this for me, I half expected for someone else to walk in and our meeting turning into some kind of power lunch meeting; that didn't happen. I took a seat on the leather sofa, Hennison walked over to his desk to get a call; his only response to it was 'Yes, that would be all. Enjoy the rest of the day off.'

Realizing he was speaking to Margo, he walked back over to where I was and sat on the floor; I did the same.

"Are you surprised?" He asked. "We didn't get to spend time to get to know each other before, so I thought I would pull you away for a moment so we could now." He informed as he loosened his Ellie knotted tie.

"Uh, yeah, I am. I didn't expect to be ordered to leave the café by Margo. Did you tell her not to tell me where I was going?" I inquired.

"Yes. I wanted to surprise you. Anyway, I didn't want to risk anyone overhearing Margo telling you anything. People around here could get the wrong idea." He answered.

"We wouldn't want them to think you were interested in me, now would we? It's better to keep it cordial." I insisted.

"No, I want them to know I'm interested in you." He retorted. "I just want to handle my interest on my own terms, if you don't mind Ms. Major."

Taken back by his words, I nodded in agreement; he then insisted we eat before the models downstairs smelled the food and clawed at the door to get it; so he's a funny guy. We ate and talked; it came so naturally, who would've thought we could hold a conversation with each other as if we were equals in the business. He joked and was actually funny; I didn't expect that from a suit. I thought the only thing interesting about him was his status as a mogul; I'm quickly finding out that what I thought, and what is true, are two totally different things. I felt so at ease that I almost forgot that I had to go back to work. Taking my yellow rose, Hennison walked me to the elevator.

Returning to Indulgence, I watched everyone finish out the day in slow motion. I could no longer concentrate on my tasks, but reflect on every part of the conversation I had with Hennison during our lunch date. *Holy shit, did we really just have a lunch date?* Working through the day after a lunch date with Hennison was increasingly becoming difficult. Kelly was still attempting to beat me to a promotion. She took on more work than she could handle, and when Cassidy saw that she had difficulty completing her tasks on time; she passed them to me, as if I had nothing else to do.

The workload I was bringing home was steadily becoming heavier than the load I had at the job. Thank God it was almost over; only a few days stood between now and The White Party. As I packed up, I heard the alarm for emails go off. For a moment I considered not checking it, I had enough work to take home with me; I seriously didn't want to add to it. My curiosity got the best of me and I opened my messages to see what it was; I hoped it was a notification for 50% off at the Sweet Spot Boutique.

So much for sale notifications; the email I received is from Hennison. He asked for my personal phone number because all the emails/correspondence at Black Industries is monitored. Obliging him, I wondered what he had to say to me, that he couldn't say through the company server.

I sat for a minute, expecting to get an alert. When none came, I continued to pack up and leave the building; files in hand. Walking through the lobby with multiple tote bags, security stopped me. Instructing me to follow him, the guard took two of the bags from my shoulders, and led me to the front entrance. Once outside, he told me I would have access to the company's town car if ever I needed it. When I asked him who approved this, he answered Mr. Black.

I didn't need to give the driver my address; he had already known where I lived. Perhaps he had his own set of to do's given to him by Mr. Black. As I enjoyed the ride, I heard my text alert go off on my phone. Checking it hurriedly, it said.

Unknown:

Did you enjoy your surprise?

Reply to Unknown:

Who is this? Is this Hennison? Why don't you allow your # to show?

Unknown:

Yes, it's me. It's out of habit not to have it show. I'll give to you in time.

Reply to Unknown:

In time, huh, whatever. Thank you for the car. It is becoming difficult to get on the train with all my bags.

Unknown:

Anything you need, and I mean ANYTHING, please don't hesitate to reach out to me. Understood.

Reply to Unknown:

Understood, Mr. Black

Unknown:

Call me Hennison outside of the office. Is it okay if I call you Chloe?

Reply to Unknown:

Yes. I believe that would be satisfactory.

Unknown:

Chloe, it is. Goodnight, Chloe. The car will be in front of your building at 8:00 sharp, don't be late; or else I'll have the driver carry you into the car with only your bathrobe as clothing. Wait, please be late then ;)

Reply to Unknown:

*Goodnight Hennison. I'll be on
time and if you wanted to see me wearing
only my bathrobe, all you had to do was
ask ;}*

Unknown:

@@ lol

Laughing to myself, I put my phone away
and then quickly realized that it was happening
again. I was getting mixed up with yet another
man, who not only had the power to hurt me; but
fire me. 'GREAT CHLOE, YOU SURE KNOW
HOW TO PICK EM'! I said aloud to myself, with
a gentle slap to my forehead.

The days passed, and the workload became
more bearable as the event approached. Everyone
knew what is expected so to have a slip up would
cost you more than your job; but your future. The
days grew colder, and the night blisteringly bitter;
I'm beyond grateful for a warm car ride home.
The Holiday Issue is due to debut on the night of
The White/Christmas Party, and Clair's appetite
for adding additional elements to the party seemed
to be sated for the moment. So the staff became
free to plan where they would spend the holidays.
I thought about going home to Jersey, but I
immediately changed my mind. The thought of
China bringing Malik to Christmas Dinner made
me throw up a little in my mouth. No, I think I'll
sit this one out and stay in the city.

My mom called occasionally and asked how city life treated me. I gave her an overview; I left out a few details that she needn't be concerned about. If China brought Malik over, she would know all that had really been going on; and I really can't handle reliving that situation over again. Dee and her parents always made me feel welcome at their home, but it wasn't my home; and my family. Being with them, although comforting, it's not the same; they couldn't fill the empty space of my family.

Daydreaming about the upcoming holiday, I didn't notice that Cassidy had been calling my name repeatedly. She told me she is taking a trip to 'The Closet' to see if they had anything she could borrow for The White Party and wanted to know if I wanted to come. Taking her up on her offer, I locked my computer and followed. As we walked, I realized that I had nothing to wear; I wonder if they had anything left for me to borrow.

Working at a fashion magazine had its perks, but working at a Full Figure Fashion Magazine was even better! Not only is everything in your size, but in the sample sizes. Every item in 'The Closet' had been photographed exclusively for Indulgence Magazine readers. Designers never expected their items returned to them; they expected the executives to wear them to events to get them more notoriety, instead they landed in The Closet with a reference number. Only on rare occasions would Clair wear something a designer sent to her, and it had to be stunning for her to do so; she's a very particular woman.

The stylists at Indulgence were some of the most sought after in the industry, and no, they aren't all plus size; we don't discriminate, we have "average" size people here too. My favorite stylist in The Closet is Ingrid, she could put an outfit together out of string and paper cups, and every photographer within seeing distance would fall over themselves to get your photo; and she's just one of the many that Clair mentored throughout her career.

When we entered The Closet to describe it as a crime scene is an understatement. The racks were practically bare, and they tossed accessories around as if they were dime store trinkets, instead of costly, exquisite, high fashion garments.

Stepping over gowns, shoes, jewelry, etc, Cassidy walked up to stylists Heidi and Ingrid and sarcastically asked, "So do you have anything in the back?"

"No, love; They cleaned us out of everything." She answered in her British accent. "Do you think you could find something here that would help you? I can make miracles with a needle and thread." She stated.

"No, that's ok. I should have got here sooner; I know what it's like around here when we're having parties. I'll just have to pull something out of my closet." Cassidy concluded.

"How about you," Heidi asked. "Do you see something you could wear?"

Holding up a torn Joda Link Fit & Flare Midi Dress; I nodded my head. As we turned to leave, Ingrid waited for Cassidy to put some distance between us before she hurriedly told me to come back before I left for the day; agreeing, I left to catch up with Cassidy.

Returning to The Closet hours later, I found Ingrid attempting to put whatever was left back in order. Seeing me, she stood up and gestured for me to wait while she went into the back storage room. Walking back, she held a large white box with a gold ribbon around it and handed to me.

"What's this?" I asked, confused.

"It's a gift for you love, the boss asked me to order this special for ya. Don't just stand there, open it up and try it on!" she insisted.

Placing the box on her desk, I unraveled the ribbon and opened the box to find a single Orange Rose; beneath it was a white Vincent Kincaid, fitted off the shoulder, Cocktail Dress with quarter length sleeves, and deep V sweetheart neckline. Unraveling as I lifted it, I couldn't believe that Hennison had her special order this dress for me! Ushering me into the fitting room, Ingrid waited for me to come out so she could see if it needed any adjustments. Stepping out of the fitting room, I felt sexy as the dress molded itself to my curves perfectly.

"Well there, I don't have any adjustments to make; only bring up the hem line a little to show off those gorgeous legs, and that's it. Take it off now love, I'll have it ready for ya tonight; I'll have the driver bring it to ya." Ingrid announced.

Stunned, I thanked her a dozen times before I left. On the way to the car, I received a text from Hennison. How did he always know where I was? Temporarily losing my mind, I rolled my eyes at my question. This is his building; of course he knew my comings and goings.

Unknown:

Did you like it?

Reply to Unknown:

Of course I did! Thank you for the Gift. Can I ask you something?

Unknown:

Anything Doll.

Reply to Unknown:

Why have you given me different color Roses?

Unknown:

I would tell you anything you want to know, except that. If you truly want the answer, find it on your own.

Reply to Unknown:

Is that a fact? Ok, I'll find out what it means on my own. What do I get when I find the answer?

Unknown:

Whatever you desire.

Turning off my messages, I smiled slyly to myself, and wondered what the hell game he is playing with me. I know one thing; I won't get caught up like I did before. If this is a game, I am going to come out the victor. The snow beginning to accumulate on the ground made walking from the car to the building a daunting task. If it wasn't for the driver gripping my arm, I don't think I would have made it; high heels are not made to grip snow and ice.

Coming home to a warm apartment, a cold wine cooler, and my best friend, I'm finally beginning to feel like I have a handle on this thing called life; at least for the time being. Attempting to eat the concoction Dee called Spaghetti and Meatballs, I thought it would be… let's just say, not to appetizing; It was amazing; I guess she learned a thing or two from when she and Chase were still dating. I could tell she missed him. Instead of bouncing back the way she normally did (in the arms of another dude), she became reclusive. If we didn't go out together; she worked, that was her life now. I asked her if she would try to get him back; she changed the subject on me.

After trying over and over, I let it go. Maybe her losing him was the wakeup call she needed to realize that men weren't as disposable as she thought they were; every once in a while one would come along that will knock you sideways and love you more than you can handle. You could either go with it, or do what she did and sabotage it. I love my friend, more than if she were my blood sister; but this was a lesson she had to learn on her own, and no amount of talking I could do would help her. She had to look in her heart of hearts, take a chance, step out on faith, and go get her man back. But that decision was hers alone. In the meantime, I was dragging her ass to The White Party with me; hopefully that would cheer her up.

About an hour after I got home, there was a knock at the door. Answering it, I found the driver Mr. Bassett with the white box Ingrid had presented me earlier. Thanking him, I took the box inside and showed it to Dee. Whistling when I modeled it for her; she insisted I be careful with Hennison; a man like that wouldn't be spending money on a woman and not expect anything in return. Taking the dress off, I let her words turn over in my mind. I knew he wanted to get with me; he made that perfectly clear. What I wanted to know was, what did he plan on doing with me; if he ever got me?

On the day of the party, everyone was on edge; trying to make everything turn out exactly as Clair had instructed. The in house event planners had to have nerves of steel; they didn't give an inch as vendors, staff, and everyone else bombarded them that made their jobs more difficult. Instead of renting a space, The Black Building boasted its own event venue that could hold over one thousand people; that's just about the number expected to show up this evening, including the building's own staff.

Hennison allowed the employees to work a half day, so they could all be present at the party. In a fit of rage, Clair came shooting out of her office yelling for Cassidy. Finding me instead, she told me to find her, and bring her to her office immediately! Scurrying as the interns do, I looked for her in every place I could think she would be. Giving up, I started towards Clair's office to become the next target of her rage for not finding Cassidy; when I heard giggling and boxes shifting behind the supply room door. Walking to it stealthily, I put my hand on the knob and turned it quickly. I thought maybe Cass didn't hear me shouting for her, and that I would scare her a little by sneaking up on her. Instead, I was the one who yelled at what I saw!

Opening the door, I found Cassidy and Kelly in the room clutching each other and their makeup smeared across their faces. Being startled at what I saw, I yelped, slammed the door shut, and walked away. Standing in the path between the cubicles and Clair's office, I leaned on the wall to catch my breath and think of something to tell Clair; I damn sure couldn't tell her that her assistants were getting freaky in the supply room. As I was taking deep breaths to calm down, Cassidy hastily came around the corner and breathed a sigh of relief. Finding me before I got back to Clair's office. Maybe she thought I would blow up her spot.

"There you are! Look what you saw back there it..." She tried to explain.

"What are you talking about, I saw nothing. Clair just sent me to look for you, and I've found you. That's it." I insisted.

"I get what you're trying to do; and I appreciate it. It's ok really, I love who I am. Few people know about it, and I want to keep it that way; it's none of their business. Clair knows that I'm a lesbian, but she doesn't know about Kelly. I want to tell her myself, I just haven't found the right time. Please don't mention it to her, please." She pleaded with me.

"I won't, it's not my business to tell." I assured her.

Asking me if her face looked ok, she smoothed out her clothes and went to meet Clair. Standing in the hall, I realized I was holding my breath; I let it go when Cassidy walked away. Sitting at my desk, I watched as Kelly sauntered pass me and smirking as if to say that she's winning. I can't believe her, I hope she's not using Cass to get a leg up! I have to keep my eye on that bitch.

Trying to put everything to bed before I went home to get ready, I wrapped whatever loose ends I had before the office started in on a long holiday vacation; luckily for us, the holidays fell on Monday, which gave us a long weekend. Closing the windows on my computer screen, I received a call from Margo expressing that I make myself available to Hennison right away; I guess I wasn't the only one trying to put things to bed.

When I got to his office, without looking up, Margo told me to go right in; nobody ever got to Hennison without Margo's say so, and I mean nobody. They had a close relationship beyond boss and employee; I think she is the only person within the company that truly has his best interests at heart. I found him on the phone, while simultaneously looking at something on his computer. Seeing me, he immediately ceased what he was doing to give me his undivided attention.

Rising to greet me, he walked over to me, and without warning planted a kiss on my lips.

Stunned, I tried to hide my facial expressions by tilting my head down and half smiling.

"Are you ready for tonight?" Hennison asked.

"Yes, I'm bringing my friend to the party; she's been down, I hope the festivities will cheer her up." I answered. "Are you ready?"

"These events happen so often I keep extra tuxedos in my office. But this is your first event with us, forgive me, I forgot. Well, you will be quite pleased with how we suit party. I know you will enjoy it. I asked to see you because I want to ask; if you would be my date this evening? I know going public is a big step, especially because we work together. But I really want you to say yes. Do you want to go with me?" He probed.

I thought about it for a second and then agreed to be his date. Not because I wanted everyone to know that we were interested in each other, but because I'm beginning to like him as a person. He was peeling back the layers, and the guy that is peaking out seems like he's worth getting to know. And it also doesn't hurt to show Kelly that even when I'm not trying, I can one up her!

Getting ready for the party is much like getting ready for the Gala we previously attended; without being tipsy, that is. Dee and I did the same womanly rituals that we all do; shower, shave, moisturize, lift, tuck, and suck in our tummies into control undergarments so that our outfits looked amazing, and so our breasts could sit up so high they become chin rests; and Dee of course is on hair and makeup duty.

For this event I wore my hair down; Dee straightened then curled it into loose body waves. Dee wore her hair up in a high ponytail style, with hair extensions to lengthen it to tailbone length. She dressed in a white, sleeveless, belted jumpsuit and black pumps. Putting on the Vincent Kincaid dress, it blew me away by how much control undergarments made it look better than it did when I first tried it on; pairing the dress with accessories and royal blue pumps for a pop of color, we were out the door and ready for the car to take us to the venue. After we clipped, and clopped our way down the stairs, what waited for us was not the company town car; but a limo, with Mr. Bassett waiting with the door open. We didn't have time to hesitate; the snow was sticking to the ground (remember what I said about snow, ice, and heels?), and the cold air hit my legs like a ton of sharp knives when the wind blew. The warm limo is a welcome friend against winters in the city.

Arriving at the venue, you would think you were at the premier of a major motion picture. Complete with red carpet, step and repeat, and paparazzi; Clair made sure that this party would be the party that other parties envied. Walking arm in arm, trying not to slip; Dee and I hurried to pass the photographers before the next icy wind could attack us. Greeted by coat check girls, we got our tickets; Dee walking ahead of me as I walked in slowly taking in the venue's ambiance; it looked exactly like we designed it.

The cathedral like high ceiling that added drama and depth to the event. The long hall at the entrance of the building is lit with a bluish/white hue, making the hall appear to bathe in the moonlight, with two large ancient twisted columns on each side. On the columns are thin, white, needless trees mid-way the length of the column, and stretch out to the sides creating an archway affect; appearing to wrap you in wintery scene, each branch is adorned in crystal icicles that twinkled as they moved. The base of each column are also small spotlights that give the treed columns a glowing effect. The floor plan, perfectly executed by the event planners, looked like something out of a winter themed, fairytale, wonderland.

Walking down a grand staircase where the actual party is starting, the theme continues. As I looked down from the top of the staircase, I see high boy cocktail tables made of etched glass, and are lit with the same bluish/white hue. The wooden floor is polished to perfection, already had partygoers on the dance floor in the middle of the room, and the strategically placed flat screens tv's played videos and still pictures from the ski lodge; giving the watchers the feeling of a tight-knit company dynamic, with a splash of magazine covers, and media mentions.

Walking down the stairs, we were approached by one of the many servers that were floating from one side of the room to the other. Getting two glasses, Dee and I worked the room. I introduced her to some people I'm cool with and pointed out the few I'm not. Towards the bar, I found Cassidy and introduced the two. Grabbing a woman's arm to her right, Cassidy introduced her date to us; it was Kelly! *I guess they're out of the closet; I wonder what Clair had to say?* Continuing to mingle, I spotted Clair on the far side of the room, near the stage, surrounded by her adoring public. Approaching her group, we became caught in the path of a very handsome, tall, muscular man with a red rose.

Taking the rose from him, I introduced Dee to Hennison. Shaking hands briefly, he complemented both of us, and then asked if he could steal me away. Whisking me to the dance floor, he held me tightly as we danced. As we swayed, I felt all eyes on us. As if his presence wasn't enough to make a room full of women claw their way to him, he had to have me tucked firmly in his arms; which made the claws and daggers come out, I do not understand what he's trying to prove by this display; but like I said before, if this is a game; I'm going to come out the victor.

Dancing to three or four more songs; people really took notice. Normally, Hennison never spent so much time not bouncing from woman to woman; maybe they turned from being angry to intrigued. One of the many faces I saw as we danced was Jayshawn. He walked in with a thick, tall woman with long dark hair. Observing the way she held on tightly to his arm; this was the ex-girlfriend. I saw her more clearly this time; I wasn't in a drunken haze, and able to examine her features. She was tanned (obviously from a salon, since its winter), beautiful, and huge tits that would threaten to give her a black eye if she danced to freely, I could see why he would've asked her to marry him; she's the fantasy.

Behind them, making her way slowly down the stairs, is Sloan Hill being escorted by a man I had never seen before; *I wonder if he's of the fashion/media world?* Finally letting me go, Hennison had to greet his guests. I sat quietly at a nearby table when Dee came to join me. I could see she was having a good time. Finally, her demons were letting go of her. Motioning to the staircase, I alerted her to who had just walked in. Nearly letting a piece of shrimp fall out of her mouth, Dee was just as surprised as I was to see Jayshawn. With nowhere to run, I saw him walk over to where we sat; I prayed that he would pass us by, but I don't have that kind of luck.

Rolling my eyes as he approached, Dee put down her glass and immediately stood over me;

acting as my shield. Patting her on the hip, I told her I got this. Whatever he was going to say, I wouldn't let it bother me. This is my company's event, and if anyone wouldn't be welcome; it's him.

Arm in arm with his unfamiliar girl, Jayshawn greeted us, "Good evening ladies Happy Holidays, I hope you're enjoying yourselves. Chloe, you're looking especially beautiful tonight. Please let me introduce you to Tarin James, I believe you already know Sloan and this is her date Jorrie Kingsley. How are you both enjoying the festivities?" He spoke as if we are all strangers. Just a few weeks ago, Sloan had seen that he was my date at the Charity Gala; I could only imagine what she thinks about this situation. This is so embarrassing!

As Dee was on the cusp of erupting, I interrupted. "We're enjoying ourselves just fine, Sloan, it's always good to see you again; Happy Holidays to you and Mr. Kingsley. Tarin, I believe we haven't met officially, I'm Chloe Major; and this is my best friend, Dominique Lawrence."

Extending her hand, she proclaimed, "It's so nice to meet you. We've talked a lot these past few months, I feel like I know you. I'm sorry, I didn't make it to the Gala; but Sloan passed on your greetings. How do you know Jayshawn?"

Trying to move the conversation along, I replied, "We know each other through mutual friends."

"That's not the only way they know each other!" Dee remarked through clinched teeth.

Just as I was giving Dee a shady look, Hennison re-made an appearance. Approaching the group from behind, he patted Jayshawn heavily on the back, before he stood next to me like he had always belonged there. Smiling a predatory like smile in Jay's direction, Hennison rubbed my back, just at my shoulder blades. The strain showed on Jay's face, as too many emotions to count danced briefly across his face. Acknowledging Hennison, he then turned to leave; but before he could, Hennison opened his mouth to say, 'It's good seeing you all again, Jayshawn and Tarin. Oh Jayshawn, I guess I was man enough.' He uttered as his voice dripped with malice and venom. Taking a step back towards us, Jayshawn then stopping in his tracks; as if considering what would happen and then walked away. I couldn't take the pissing contest anymore and jumped out of my seat to get away, I don't know where I was going; I just know I had to get there quick!

Following close behind, Hennison yelled, "What's the matter?"

"What's the matter?" I repeated. "You just stood there and made a fool of me in front of people I have to work with! WHAT THE HELL IS WRONG WITH YOU! You knew we dated and you have to dig the knife in a little deeper by your comment! Why?" I snapped.

"I'm sorry. We have history, Jayshawn and I, you unwittingly walked into." He tried to explain, as he ushered me off into a corner where no one would hear.

"So, this is a game between you two? Play with the assistant; let's see who can make her cum first, or some shit like that?" I offered.

"NO," he insisted. "I'm not interested in you because he is. I'm interested in you, because you're not like any other woman who walks through the doors of The Black Building. I want to know more about you. We just have an issue from the past that comes up every time we're in the same vicinity. I can't help that we both have great taste in women. I don't want to upset you, I promise I won't make any comments like that in front of you ever again, I promise. Please forgive me."

I glanced around the room and everyone including Dee is watching us; I'm on the spot. Still standing in front of him, unable to answer his question; he turned away from me, then climbed the few steps to the stage where he made the band stop playing. Grabbing the mic, he announced to a room full of our coworkers, board members, and media; that he had unintentionally hurt the feelings of someone close to him, and he would like to offer his apologies.

Gesturing to me to join him on stage *(because this too wasn't embarrassing; I thought sarcastically.)*, I reluctantly stood next to him. Kissing my hand, he apologized once again, and asked me if I accepted. Quickly nodding, so I could get off of this damn stage; he then called out to his assistant Margo to bring him something. She emerged with a bouquet of long stem red Roses and handed them to me. I couldn't be mad anymore; That he had the flowers ready told me he had planned to give them to me. Also, that he was making a fool of himself is just icing on the cake; if I'm going to be embarrassed by the attention when we're together, he is going to be embarrassed by making a public display of affection; and all his flings could read about it in the gossip magazines/blogs before the night is over. That put a smile on my face.

The room erupted in applause when we left the stage; him guiding me down; as the band began again. Dee came towards me with the 'WTF' look; I shook my head and kept walking. Clair witness to the scene shot both Hennison and I a scolding look. *SHIT!* I thought. I know I'm going to be in the hot seat when we all come back from Holiday break.

ABOUT THE AUTHOR

Dominique has been a writer for many years, and fashion blogging for the past three years. It has featured her writing in publications such as Full Blossom Magazine, Curvy Connect Magazine, and Real Size Magazine. It has also presented Dominique with THE WOEM (Women Of Empowerment) Award by Mr. Elijah Harmon of Harlemvetz Entertainment & Management, LLC for outstanding and positive efforts made in the full figured community. Also, she was recently interviewed by Celebrity Publicist Ms. Lawrence for their May 2015 Issue of Exposure Magazine: Game Changers in Media Edition.

With her dedication to giving life and voice to women of various shapes, sizes, and backgrounds, we will see more from her!

Fashion Plus Blog: Plus Size Fashion & Lifestyle

 I created fashion Plus Blog out of obstruction in the lack of care shown to full-figured women. Before Fashion Plus Blog, I searched for a blogger/writer that spoke candidly about inner and aesthetic beauty. A person that pursued strength in awareness; and be the force of encouragement for full figured, curvy, plus size women in the fashion industry. Unable to find the traits I searched for, I created it.

In its beginning, Fashion Plus Blog sought to use fashion as a catalyst for women like myself that had concerns with finding clothing to fit my body type properly. As it grew and I with it, I searched to explore different ways of getting the message across. By introducing unique elements of importance that concerned the full figured community Fashion Plus Blog carved out its own genre unmatched by any other blog.

Introducing topics such as relationships, health, hair care, opinions, full figure related events, and a myriad of fashion advice were developed all to give readers a blog that understands the relationship between how you feel about yourself, and how you focus that feeling by how you dress. To explore that relationship further, segments within the blog focus on the emotional element of being a full figure, an area where a majority of bloggers never venture.

I love the confidence women exude on the outside by expressing their individual style. Though outer beauty is just the tip of the iceberg. I intend to pursue possibilities no other blogger dared to tackle, such as the emotional side of being a full figured woman in an industry that doesn't except you for being who you are but for what you look like. Segments such as The Diary of a Fat Fashionista, Confessions of a Plus Size Blogger, and related topics all to bring full circle the candor, complexity, beauty, and an unwillingness to accept anything less than we deserve, that's what makes Fashion Plus Blog a driving force in the full figure industry.

Sincerely Yours,

Dominique Ali

Dominique Ali

Creator of Fashion Plus Blog: Plus Size Fashion & Lifestyle

www.Fabulouslyp.blogspot.com

COMING SOON!

THE LIFE & TIMES OF A FULL
FIGURED FASHIONISTA PART 2: I'M
NO ANGEL!

By Dominique Ali

www.ingramcontent.com/pod-product-compliance
Lightning Source LLC
Chambersburg PA
CBHW051238260626
47162CB00002B/488